STORIES

Second Edition

C. L. Paur

Cover designed by Cover Designer

This book is a work of fiction. Names, characters, places, and incidents either are products of the author's imagination or are used fictitiously. Any resemblance to actual persons, living or dead, events, or locales is entirely coincidental.

C. Paur
Follow me on Twitter https://twitter.com/ArmorCate
Facebook https://www.facebook.com/carol.lpaur

Printed in the United States of America

First Printing: February 2013
Second Printing: August 2018

ISBN- 978-0-692-17554-5

For my parents, who always knew I had a story to tell.

He had become so completely absorbed in himself, and isolated from his fellows that he dreaded meeting, not only his landlady, but any one at all.

— *CRIME AND PUNISHMENT*, FYODOR DOSTOEVSKY

CHAPTER 1

I was dead. This I knew, but where I was, *that* I didn't know. The garments of age evanesced as youth materialized. My old body had ruled with tyranny for so long that at first I didn't recognize the signs of youth. Was it me? I wondered.

My thoughts were too clear and so was my hearing. The drone of silence which had blunted the use of my eardrums seemed gone, though there were no obvious sounds to test this theory. My chin felt smooth. I remembered my great niece yanking at the tiny bristles below the jaw.

"Ouch!"

"Hold on, Aunt Catharine. There's only three more." Carrie yanked. It was a never winning battle.

"My hair, my beautiful red hair," I said as I touched the soft ends. Where had the aged, brittle wire fled to? Along with the chin stubble, my hair had lost the battle against age. I tried to dye it, but each application took away the yielding locks. The few strands that remained had stood erect in brick-colored patches between the bald spots.

I blinked. The brume of cataracts succumbed to clarity though I was looking at vast, empty space. No glasses, just my eyes.

My feet stood motionless, yet I glissaded along an empty corridor. A twenty-foot high white door anticipated my arrival. I entered its domain, but nothingness still enveloped me.

"Hello!" I shouted. My voice sounded strong, not crackly and weak like it had just moments ago.

"No need to yell." A large man with a booming voice appeared. "We hear well enough up here." He eyed me up and down. "Hmm."

"What?" He had me puzzled.

"Oh, nothing. Just follow me."

The man stood more than seven feet tall. I had only seen people that tall in the Guinness World record book I had read as a child. My favorite entries were the bearded woman and the man with the long fingernails.

"Yes, I am tall." His sonorous voice permeated the empty space. "But I have never been featured in Guinness World."

Is he reading my mind? Inside my thoughts I tried to mirror the blankness that surrounded me, but more thoughts kept shattering the emptiness.

1

"I can only read what you're thinking about when it is necessary," his voice answered. "No, I'm not St. Peter. No need to worry about who I am. We are only interested in you."

My heart began to pound. Me? They are only interested in me? I gulped hard, my mouth drying up as suddenly as a parched desert after a rain. What secrets will they discover? Will it seal my fate?

I lived a good life, I reasoned, trying to calm my nerves. I never hurt anyone, at least not consciously. I prayed, went to church, and when I thought about it I helped others. What more was I to do?

A desk appeared. Everything up here was bigger than life. Suddenly I felt like Alice in Wonderland. I looked up. My neck is not stiff! Up, up, up my head traveled without arthritis's constraints. What joy! Suddenly I remembered I was going to be judged, and anxiety replaced my fleeting happiness.

From my vantage point, I saw the giant man open a golden book, about two feet wide and long and perhaps a foot thick.

"Why don't you sit down?" he asked.

Where would I sit in this oblivion? In answer, I was plunked abruptly into a towering, gilded wingback. My legs dangled, the diminutive sensation returning.

"Tell me about yourself," he said in a kinder voice. His curly hair and beard were white with rays of sunlight streaming out of them. It was as if I was looking at the sun shining through a window. The blue of his eyes took me back to the Caribbean. Golden eyebrows drooped like old awnings over his eyes.

"My name is Catharine Zimmer. I was born in...."

"I know all that!" he growled. "Tell me about you." He leaned forward, tilting his head so his right ear was close to me.

"There is not much to tell. I grew up in a large family. My parents loved each other and us very much. I only have happy memories of my childhood."

The man nodded and smiled contentedly.

"After high school, I took a job at a department store and worked there until retirement. I loved to travel and saw most of the world," I boasted.

"Never married?"

"Isn't that on my record?" My heart fluttered.

"I just wanted to hear it from your voice. I also see no college."

"Is that a problem here? Look, I lived a good, moral life. What more is there?"

"It says here that when your father died, he left you money to go to college."

They don't miss anything here.

"Yes, that is true."

"But you didn't go. Why?"

"I, I, I..."

"Because anything that required a challenge, you avoided," he answered for me.

"Maybe." I shrugged my shoulders. "I had a good job with the department store. I had benefits, four weeks of vacation, and weekends off. What more did I need?"

He bent down behind the desk. When his head reappeared, he held some worn journals in his hand.

"Do you recognize these?"

"My journals! I haven't seen them since I was very young. I thought they were gone."

"We keep everything here," he said wryly. "Good thing we have enough room to store it all! Look at the brown one, please."

The book flipped open. My childish handwriting appeared   like a ghost from the past.

"Read it please," he softly commanded.

"'Dear Diary,'" I faltered. I remembered what I had written so many years ago. I suddenly felt ashamed.

"Keep going," he prodded.

"'Today Mrs. Sweet had a guest speaker. His name was William, and he was a writer. He writes children's books. William was wonderful. He told about how he got his ideas and why he wrote. After class, I went up to him and told him I wanted to be a writer, too. He gave me his address so we could write to each other. He said it was a writer who had helped him when he was young, so he wanted to help other young writers. Wow! He wants to help me write! Good night for now.'"

I looked up. The giant was staring hard at me.

"Keep reading!"

"'Dear Diary, it has been five weeks since I've written to you or to anyone, period. Since talking to William, I feel pressure! Mom says I should send him some of my stories, but they're so terrible. Mom says they're beautiful, but she says anything her kids do is beautiful. When Tommy sang at the Christmas pageant last year, he was so flat. Mom said he sang beautifully. When Chrissy made her ceramic sculpture, it was hideous. Mom told Chrissy it was beautiful. I am sure William will just laugh at my stories and tell me to forget about writing, forever!'"

"He waited several months for your stories," the giant whispered. "After about a year, he figured you weren't really serious about writing, yet when he met you that day he thought you were different." The giant pulled out some paper from a torn folder. "Here are the stories. For a ten-year-old girl they're pretty good. Even I liked them."

Who are you to judge? You're just some Heavenly being who probably doesn't know good literature when it's in your face.

"We're not here to discuss me." The bearded man bored into my mind again. "If you were honest with yourself, you wanted to write at your earliest recollection, probably since you were five. At six, you wrote your first-grade play, which your

3

classmates performed. Each year afterward, your teachers requested your plays for the year-end productions. By high school, you were writing for the newspaper and won several writing contests. You even had a scholarship for college."

"It wasn't enough for school. It would have barely paid for my books," I blushed, remembering the phone call.

"'Thank you for the scholarship, but I am not attending college at this time,'" I forlornly hung up the phone.

"Your uncle offered to pay the rest."

"We were already beholden to him for so much."

"It was no problem for him. He was a very generous man who also saw your talent. Later, your father left you money, but you failed to pick up on that opportunity as well."

I shifted uncomfortably. Guilt scurried over me like a centipede as I recalled my last words with Dad.

"I want you to go to college," he rasped. "There will be money for you to go. I know you're twenty-nine, but I want you to pursue your writing."

"Dad, I haven't written anything since high school. I have a good job. I'm happy."

"Are you? Go to college. Maybe you'll find something besides that department store job."

"I'm a manager. I make good money."

"Life is more than money."

"Not according to Uncle Germain."

"Do you think he's happy, really?"

"He thinks he is."

"While the rest of us have to put up with him. His poor wife and kids. Promise me you'll go to college, please?"

I gave him a feeble nod, yet that was all I could muster, for I knew I was lying.

"So you lied to your father and took the money for a cruise."

I said nothing. He was right. My friend Mary met her husband on a cruise. I thought maybe I'd find Mr. Right. The only man I met was Fred, a forlorn taxi driver.

My head hung down in shame. I had wanted Dad to die in peace. He was so adamant about my writing. Twenty-nine, and I wasn't about to shift gears. I didn't want to start my life all over again. I had packed that childish dream away along with my toys and books, never to be opened again. Today, the day I died, it returned accusingly.

"After high school, it seemed like I could no longer write. My ideas all dried up."

"They were there, just neglected."

"What does some young girl's dream have to do with going to Heaven or Hell?" I demanded. I shifted uncomfortably, and then turned away as tears stung my eyes.

The giant returned his gaze to the journal, his eyes scanning from left to right "Where did this desire to write come from?"

I shrugged.

"It was instilled in your DNA. You were created to write the stories of life – to inspire, to bring hope, and to compel others to love.

"Today you will be the writer you were meant to be. You cannot run from it anymore." The giant leaned so close, his warm breath kissed my face.

"It's too late," I faltered.

"Never too late."

CHAPTER 2

"Bring them in," the giant's voice shattered my reverie.

As if a magician had waved his wand, two men and a woman appeared.

"Meet Aleric, Adrien, and Ursula."

We shook hands. When Adrien and I touched, electrical shocks coursed through me. My face smoldered. I was dead! What was this sensation? He must have felt the same for he clung to my hand and smiled warmly.

"Let's get started," the giant commanded. "Everyone take your seats, except for Aleric. You will tell us your story." He handed me a pen. "Catharine, you will transcribe their stories."

"What? Isn't there some kind of recording device up here?" I flexed my now non-arthritic hands.

He glared at me.

Aleric began, "*Mi nombre es* Aleric Sampino Regallito."

Aleric's voice was thick like buttermilk, yet as dry as dead, fallen leaves. Before me stood a young man, with a voice older than time itself, ready to unfold many tales within his tragic life.

"Could you speak English?" Adrien piped up.

Adrien was right. How would I understand this man's Spanish? "Leetle" for little, "ees" for is. I had always loved listening to the Spanish language. Its lilting words seemed to flow freely like a waterfall. To interpret it? That was another situation altogether. I clasped onto the quill, bewildered.

"Catharine, might I tell you that your eternal existence depends upon these stories and your response. I suggest you make an effort." The giant turned toward Aleric who twisted a green canvas cap in his hand. I hadn't noticed it before. How did that get here?

"Before my life in prison, I ruled my country, some say, with an iron fist. Looking back, I knew they were right. Many people died at my hands, some from my commands, and many from..." His tormented eyes confronted his own two hands.

"Start at the beginning, please. We need to hear it all," the giant said impassively.

Aleric's chocolate colored eyes transfixed themselves for a moment on each of us. Beautiful, black curls ringed an angelic face. How could he have killed anyone?

My father was a military man. President Alverez trusted him like a brother. He sent my father to Western Germany after the tyranny of Hitler. There, he met my mama. They fell in love, returned to San Xavier, and had me and my brother Antonio. Life was always happy, until General Gutierrez took over.

A mixture of sorrow and hate washed over Aleric's face.

Gutierrez's first job want to kill Alverez's men. They decided the best time for that was right before my fifth birthday party. Antonio and I were outside watching the piñata dangle in the wind. Soon the other children would come. I would eat cake, get presents, and play games.

The doorbell chimed, and Antonio and I rushed to the door. Standing there was a man with a red splotch smeared down the right side of his face. He wore his hat low trying to cover the birthmark. Behind him, were men in uniforms - soldiers.

Antonio ran away, screaming. I stared but did not let them in.

"*Niño*," he said. "Go get your papa."

"We're having a birthday party," I said. "You were not invited." I slammed the door and screamed like Antonio.

"Aleric," my father whispered from the library. I hugged him and mama. "You must be very quiet. Mama and I are going in our special hiding place. Say nothing."

Then the front door burst opened, and the soldiers swarmed in like fire ants shooting their guns. Antonio and I were hiding behind the divan when Antonio began to cry.

"Hah, the babies!" Gutierrez pointed his gun at us. "We will kill them first!"

"Mama!" Antonio cried. My parents rushed out of the false closet.

"You call yourself a leader?" papa shouted. "Killing innocent children. God have mercy on your soul."

Bang! Bang! They slumped to the ground. Antonio crawled onto Mama. "Wake up, Mama. There's a party."

The party guests must have known what had happened because no one except *mi tía* arrived."

"What's me tee-a?" Adrien asked.

"Aunt," I answered for him.

"Why can't he just say aunt, then?" Adrien sighed. The giant stared at us.

7

"Are you two finished?"

Aleric smiled. "That is okay. It gives me comfort to go back to my mother tongue, especially when I remember *mi tía*."

She was Mama's older sister and just as beautiful and kind. She had been crying when she had arrived with a priest. He blessed the bodies, and our men servants carried them up to their bedroom. We had to keep Antonio from crawling into their beds.

In a few days, boxes were made, and there was a funeral. People feared Gutierrez so stayed away.

"*Tía! Tía!* I will kill him for Mama and Papa," I said as I stared at the pile of dirt covering their bodies.

"No, no, *niño*. That is not the way," she said.

Gutierrez gave my parents' home to one of his filthy generals. When we moved to mi tía..."

"What is her name? Mi tía this, mi tía that is grating on my nerves," Adrien said as he pushed back his hair.

"You may leave if you don't wish to listen to the story," the giant said. "We're all here for Catharine's sake."

They turned to face me. Heat radiated to my face. My benefit?

"Yes, your benefit, Catharine. Heaven or Hell - it's your choice."

"I choose Heaven, of course," I laughed uneasily. What was he driving at?

"Now is not the time for your answer. Aleric, please."

Her name was Adoraciones Aquino. Captain Paredes, the swine living in our home, was gracious enough to allow us to take a few of our personal items.

Rancor dripped from Aleric's words.

When we arrived at mi tía's home, Gutierrez greeted us at the door. He pulled her into the house and slammed the door.

"Mi tía!" we cried as we pounded our fists onto the wood.

For days, we scrounged and searched for shelter and food. Survival was on our own because Adoraciones was gone. I thought Gutierrez had killed her. We wandered near the mountains and hid inside one of its many caverns, but we could not find anything to eat. One night mi tía appeared at the cave.

She wore a strange expression but she carried with her food and other supplies.

"I can't stay," she said as we munched. "I will come back."

Antonio pulled on her, refusing to let go. "You stay!" he shouted.

Tears fell down her face as she pulled herself away.

After she left, Antonio continued crying. I could not console him.

When she returned several days later, purple and blue replaced her beautiful pale skin, but she was happy.

"I will stay with you, mi niños," she said as she pulled out chicken, vegetables, and fruit. She reached out to hug us, but I was more interested in the food than her love.

We celebrated that night. She sang songs and danced for us. Antonio and I laughed for the first time in a long time. Things were going to be okay I thought to myself.

As the days wore on, I noticed mi tía sleeping more. She also moved like an old woman yet she was no more than thirty-years-old. I hadn't noticed that she wasn't eating.

I found her dead one morning. As I got older, I had realized that she had stopped eating so we could eat. *Mi tía* was the first person who died at my hands.

"You are Aleric Regallito!" I shouted. The realization filled me with terror and revulsion.

Standing in front of me was one of the most iniquitous men in history. The name Regallito scorched the history pages along with the likes of Lenin, Hitler, and Mao Zedong. What was I, Catharine Zimmer, doing listening to his confession?

"Catharine, we are concerned with your judgment, only. Aleric, please continue." The giant glowered.

Aleric caught his face in his hands and sobbed for what seemed a very long time. Adrien coughed like someone fearful of encountering anguish. Ursula, who hid in the back, moved forward and hugged him. Aleric began speaking again.

A sort of orphanage was put together to house all the children left without parents. Why Gutierrez even cared, I wondered. I found out later it was only to appease the outside world.

Inside, however, soldiers ran it like a prison. We were forced to wash and iron their uniforms, polish their boots, cook, as well as keep the building clean. Once, while washing clothes, blood dripped from my cracked hands onto one of the uniforms. The soldier, whose uniform I marred, whipped me. Antonio screamed, and the soldier lashed at him. I threw myself at him and tried to strangle him. For my punishment, they stripped me naked. Antonio, not understanding, took his clothes off too.

"I will kill you all!" I shouted.

They laughed and kicked me.

At night, the soldiers would get so drunk that many of the children ran away. I wasn't so brave until about a year later.

"Antonio, you must be very quiet. We are going to go outside to play tonight."

"Play? I like to play."

"Shhh! It's our little secret."

"Will we see Mama?" He asked that every day.

"Mama is gone to heaven," I said once again.

"I want to go to heaven."

I would hug him, tight. "No, Antonio, I don't want you to go to heaven, at least not now. I need you."

Once we fled no one bothered to search for us. They probably figured we'd die on the streets so they wouldn't have to feed us anymore.

Aleric stared at us again, sorrow swimming in his eyes.

Freedom had its price, he continued.

The food at the prison-orphanage was terrible, but at least we had food. After we left, many days would pass before I would be lucky enough to find anything to stuff in our bellies. That hunger that I had felt living in the cave grew like some horrible monster in my stomach.

After a few weeks, I think the baker and butcher both knew we were runaways because we would find *panecillo* and cooked meat behind their shops. One day while the butcher's wife was inside the store, she caught us. She berated her poor *esposo* for wasting good food. That horrible fat woman wouldn't even spare a few ounces of meat to two starving children.

Occasionally we'd pass by the market and grab a few pieces of fruit.

Platanos, my favorite. Before my parents were killed, I had fruit all the time. After, it became as rare as finding gold on the streets.

I tried to find work, but when you're a *niño*, no one wants to hire you. Then our salvation came. A mission arrived in town, Santa Maria del Eucharistic Jesus. There was one priest and three brothers. Every day Antonio and I would line up for food. Finally, Brother Jime noticed us coming every day.

He said, "Where's your mama and papa little *niños*?"

Antonio blurted out, "They were murdered. We're orphans."

"Shut up," I said to him. "No one needs to know that!"

Brother Jime told the others about us. Father wanted to take us back to the orphanage. I told them about that orphan. They decided to let us stay with them at the mission. Antonio and I had a place to stay, finally, and food every day, three times a day, with fruit at every meal!

Antonio and I helped the brothers during the summer. It was easy work compared to the orphanage. When the months cooled, the brothers sent me to school. It was a two-mile walk. Some days they let me take Señor Sombrero, their donkey. Most days I walked.

I began to hate school. The other students could read, but the words on the pages were like some strange mosaic I couldn't decipher. My mama taught me a little when I was three, but I had forgotten all of that. When I stood up to read in class I would stutter. One time I made up the words.

"The donkey eats plátanos," I pretended to read.

All the kids, especially the boys, laughed.

"Niños!" Señora Bustamente shouted. "That is not how niños agradables behave!"

They stopped laughing in the classroom, but decided to attack me after school.

I usually stayed after for tutoring with Señora Bustamente. When we finished I would wash the blackboard and sweep the classroom. I begged for more work because I knew the boys were waiting for me outside.

Señora Bustamente would often say, "Aleric, why don't you go home? I will clean up."

One afternoon, Señora Bustamente had to leave early. I pleaded with her to let me stay and lock up.

"You are reading very well, Aleric," she said. "Go home and have some fun."

I followed her from the back door. She walked and I walked next to her.

"Aleric, the mission is the other way."

"I just feel it's my duty to walk a lady home."

"You will not get back to your home until dark."

"Will you walk with me?"

"Aleric, you are very silly."

The schoolyard appeared empty. I started running only to see a bunch of boys carrying sticks racing behind me.

"We'll get you!" they chanted. Once they caught up, they threw me on the ground I soiled my pants.

"Hah, hah! Look at him pee his pants!" Julio, the ringleader, shouted. The boys jeered.

Señora Bustamente appeared from out of nowhere. She grabbed Julio by his ears and dragged him toward the school. The rest of the boys were terrified and stared as if frozen. She dragged each boy, one by one, back into the school. They were to wait until their papas arrived. I went back to the mission. I tried to act normal, but Brother Jime knew something was wrong.

"Tomorrow I will go to school with you," he said.

When class began, I noticed some of the boys were missing. Those at school had bruises and avoided me. Philip had a black eye. He told everyone that Julio's papa broke his ribs.

At first, I felt justified, yet for some reason, I felt sad too. I wanted them to stop tormenting me, but I didn't want their papas beating on them. After a few days passed, all the boys returned back to class. At three o'clock, when the school bell rang, the boys' fathers showed up. They fell to their knees.

"*Los sentimos*," Señor Quinones said. "Please pray to Jesus and ask him to forgive us." Señor Quinones' bowed his head.

"I am not sure Jesus would want you to torture your sons," I said. "I just want to go to school without the teasing. Don't beat your sons. Instead, teach them to be good men."

Everyone was surprised at my grown-up speech. They said it was because I lived in the mission. I was going to be a priest, they thought.

Aleric laughed.

"Why is that so funny?" the giant asked.

"I'll tell you why that's so funny," Adrien piped in. "This heinous excuse for a man..."

"Continue your story, Aleric!" The giant exploded.

After that, the families would come to the mission to bring Antonio and me special treats. I started expecting them. Once, when a family came to the door of the mission, I grabbed the plate of sweet alfajores the woman held in her hands. "No, no, these are for Brother Jime," the mother corrected me. I sulked in my room all day.

At school, I became king! Everything I said they listened to. Even Julio looked up to me. After my tutoring sessions with Señora Bustamente, I no longer cleaned the classroom.

One day Señora Bustamente said, "Aleric, I miss our little talks. Why don't you stay any longer?"

I tried to come up with some lie, something to make her happy.

"They need us at the mission to work," I tried to sound important.

"Really? Brother Jime said you play football all afternoon." Señora Bustamente smiled. "That is okay. You need to play too."

I felt bad for lying. I wanted to make it up to her; she was so kind and understanding. I didn't know what to say. She was truly like a mother to us.

Aleric paused, my quill stopped. Where would his story take us next?

CHAPTER 3

"Wow, that's quite a story, little man," Adrien stood up. "How much of this drivel are you going to subject us to?"

"Sit down!" the giant bellowed. "You'll have your opportunity!"

"I don't need a chance. I made my decision a long time ago." Adrien stood, defiant. "Beam me down, Scottie." Adrien pointed his finger downward. "Eternity with this dictator boy would be Hell."

"Okay," the giant acquiesced. "Send him down!"

Flames licked up around Adrien, as if he were a log in a campfire. He vanished. A wailing of pain and anguish arose to take his place.

"Help me! Get me out of here! Aghhhhhhh!"

The giant folded his arms.

"Aren't you going to bring him back?" Ursula implored.

"There's no coming back!"

The wailing continued. I shifted uncomfortably in my seat.

"Hey, Señor. Please, let him out," Aleric twisted his cap. Adrien's shrieks grew louder, more deafening.

The giant turned to me. "What do you think?"

He's getting what he deserved. Adrien Inveres had circuited all the talk shows and flaunted his atheism.

One night insomnia attacked, sleep evading me like a fly escaping from a fly swatter. I flicked through the television stations.

"Adrien Inveres," the announcer called. Slouching slightly, but with long strides, he sauntered out to the waiting chair. There he was, raising his left eyebrow as he spoke in earnest. The host and he joked for a while.

"So, Adrien, you're pretty vocal in your atheism. Wouldn't it be better just to keep your ideas to yourself?"

"I'm trying to save people from themselves and this silly notion of God. What god? Zeus? Jupiter?" The audience tittered. He turned and smiled to the camera. "Whose god is Thee God? What religion is right?"

For ten minutes, Adrien Inveres ranted about the insanity of religion. This is what he wanted. This was his life's mantra. He chose, and yet his screaming chilled my bones in a paroxysm of horror. Never in my eighty-nine years of life had such torment mired with despair assaulted my senses.

"Let him out!" I shouted.

Adrien stood before us as if he had never left. Terror replaced his insolence. Charred marks ran up and down his clothing.

"Are you okay?" Aleric asked; his dark skin pale.

Adrien said nothing, just plunked down onto his chair. His eyes beheld nothing.

"Why, Mr. Inveres, I believe you're quite a charlatan!" guffawed the giant. "You managed to convince the world of your magnificent atheism, but just now, at this very moment, you became a believer."

"So what? Maybe this is all our destiny - to burn in Hell. Why do we need to prolong our misery?"

"You're free to go to Hell; it is your choice, but I distinctly heard your screams, Mr. Inveres, to save you."

We shifted in our seats. Who would choose such a tormented fate if they understood, if they really knew? Ursula, Aleric, and I hadn't escaped the torridity. Ursula and my gossamer gowns, Aleric's uniform, the hair on our arms, even our toes were singed.

"Continue your story. Where were we now? Oh, yes. The teacher asked you to stay after school to help her."

Aleric hesitated. His eyes fell hard onto Adrien. After a few moments, Aleric shrugged his shoulders, twisted his cap again, and began.

"Yes, she did. I think she took a fancy to me. Actually, most girls did," Aleric smiled in remembrance.

He was indeed handsome. Compared to Adrien's blond, fair good looks, Aleric was darkly handsome. Even though he was shorter than I was, I could see how the opposite sex was drawn to him.

For my thirteenth birthday the brothers had a big party for me. Cake! I nev er got cake like that before or after. It was huge, and all the villagers came. There was this girl named Lupita. She was more woman, than girl. She was almost eighteen. Lupita stared at me all night. I was only thirteen, but I knew what that stare meant.

I couldn't sleep that night, thinking only of Lupita. I knew my thoughts were not holy. The brothers had given me the talk about how a real man should be, not a machismo. At that moment I could only think of being with Lupita in the way forbidden. I had never been with any woman or girl, but my body told me.

I left the mission and started walking the streets. I knew where Lupita lived. A light was on in her casa. It was late; the rest of her family were probably asleep. Her face suddenly appeared in the window as if she knew I would come. She was by my side in an instant, and pulled me toward the bushes, since there was no way we could go into the house.

It was my turn to interrupt. "Do we have to listen to this part?"

"What do you mean? It's finally getting interesting," Adrien interjected. His eyes roved up and down my body. I mustered up as much bravado and stared back defiantly.

The giant looked at Aleric. "We don't need all the sordid details."

Aleric laughed and turned toward me. His leer was so lascivious, that I blushed.

"You no like love stories?" he asked.

"That's not love, it's lust," the giant boomed. "Just keep it clean!"

When we were finished, Lupita begged me for some money. Since it was my first time with a woman, I didn't know you had to pay for this stuff. Lupita said her family needed money and food. After that, I started to steal from the mission. Lupita got what she wanted, and I got what I wanted.

Eventually I got bored with Lupita. Oh, she was fine, but there was so much ripe fruit out there, all willing to fall into my hands. Before I knew it, they were saying Aleric was unfit to be a priest.

One day, Brother Jime took me to his office. "Aleric," he said. "I heard you're having your way with the ladies. Don't you remember the talk we had?"

I said nothing. Had he talked to me a month or two earlier, I might have been ashamed, but at that moment I was so full of lust and dirty thoughts I didn't care. I craved being with women, any woman. I tried to have one every day, and for the most part I was successful. Married women, single women, old, young, it didn't matter. It was like a drug, and I was addicted. I stopped going to Communion because I knew I was wrong, but I wanted women more than Communion.

Aleric returned his lewd attention toward me, and then leered at Ursula.

I was sick for so long, I almost forgot how much I loved women.

A shudder of revulsion coursed through me. Ursula looked down, embarrassed as if she were the cause of this man's indecent behavior.

I promised to go to the priest and tell my sins. I said it to make Brother Jime happy. I lied. I told the priest I only had a few women. He knew I was lying so refused to give me absolution.

"Aleric, your soul is so corroded you can't even tell the truth in confession," he said. "There have been at least twenty different ladies in here telling me about their dalliances with Aleric Regallito. You're not only putting your soul in mortal danger, but your life, too."

What did he know? I told myself. He was just some celibate priest who never felt the warm caress of a woman.

Then I got in trouble. Lupita's father found out. One night, we were on the road playing fùtbol. It wasn't much of a road, more like trampled down rocks and grass.

We were finished playing, so Antonio went inside. I was throwing and kicking the ball, when it bounced off my head. "Ouch!" I said, not seeing Señor Sanchos standing next to me.

Señor Sanchos pushed his face into mine. It must have been days or weeks since he had washed in the river. I plugged my nose. La pistola appeared in my face.

"What's la pistola?" Adrien asked.

"Gun, you know, pistol," Aleric replied.

Anyhow, Señor Sanchos began screaming at me. "You cur!" he spat, my face getting wet. "You get my daughter pregnant. I'm going to kill you, so you stop slutting around with all the girls in town. You don't deserve to live!" He raised the black pistol.

Brother Jime limped out of the mission. Señor Sanchos turned to watch him while he pointed the gun at me

"Señor Sanchos!" Brother Jime shouted. "Put the gun down! Let us talk."

They talked for a few minutes. Then the gun went back up, toward me.

"How can I afford another mouth to feed? Who will want to marry Lupita after he's been screwing her? I no can keep her around. And a baby? I no want another mouth to feed. I can't feed the mouths I have already!"

"No, no. We'll help." Brother Jime pleaded.

"Like Hell you'll help! You all live here and eat like kings, and me familia all go hungry." He waved the gun around.

An expression covered his face. "Perhaps he is changing his mind, I thought." He pointed the gun down.

"I no kill him today, but he no touch my Lupita again!"

Señor Sanchos walked away hanging his head low. All I could feel was victory. I didn't care about him or his family only Aleric Regallito.

Aleric paused and then began again.

Word spread that Lupita went to the city to have an illegal abortion.

"It was quite a scandal for the Sanchos family," the giant spoke, quietly. "Hush hush, but all the neighbors knew. Mrs. Sanchos stopped talking to her husband for months after. Lupita went away to live with her aunt and uncle."

It was Aleric's turn to hang his head low.

There's a cross in the back of the mission. It is my only memory of my child. God punishes. I sinned against him so he decided to let my baby be killed: my only child.

"You're more concerned about that fetus than the women you screwed?" Adrien popped in. "What about poor Lupita and her starving family? Instead you have a tiny memorial to some blob without a name. Lupita and the rest are just some faded memory."

"How many women did you screw, Mr. Inveres?" the giant interrupted.

Adrien shot a look that bounced off the giant like a ping-pong ball. Not getting any response, he sulked like a chastised cat.

"Aleric, continue, please!"

"After that, I wasn't interested in women. They tried to throw themselves at me...."

"Give me a break!" Adrien sighed.

"Again, why are you so surprised, Mr. Inveres?" the giant asked. "Women hung around your movie sets all the time, waiting, just waiting for your acknowledgement and then maybe a date. Then, you know what followed."

"I didn't brag about it."

"It is part of his story."

Women throwing themselves at men? Really? I prided myself on being a feminist, in control of my life and body. No man was worth throwing yourself at, or was he? Norm? Wasn't I going to throw everything away just for him?

Aleric continued with his story.

After that, vengeance for Gutierrez tormented my soul. Hate replaced any love. I had no more time for anyone, even Antonio.

"Aleric, why don't you play with me anymore?" my brother asked one day.

"Hah, Antonio, I'm getting too big for that stuff."

"Brother Jime plays with me. Did you know he played fùtbol in college?"

"Not real football," again, Adrien interrupted. "Soccer is what he probably played."

"Americans call it soccer; we call it fùtbol," Aleric smiled. "Americans, so absorbed in themselves. Where was I? Oh, yes. Antonio was telling me about Brother Jime and playing fùtbol in college."

"Brother Jime kicked the winning goal for his team's national championship," Antonio said. "He showed me his trophy."

"He shows everyone that trophy," I said to him, irritated. "Now, get out of here, I'm busy."

Aleric let the hat fall from his hands. He looked hard at the empty space beneath his feet.

"Antonio, Antonio, will you ever forgive me? I threw away your love for what? For hate? For a life full of regrets. No love, only hate."

"There was someone else who came into your life. You loved her," the giant almost whispered.

Pain covered Aleric's face.

"She comes in later." The giant stood up. What he was standing on, what any of us was standing on, I couldn't figure out. "I think I need some refreshment." A crystal bell appeared in his hands, in which he waved back and forth. Its tinkling

17

summoned Heavenly beings laden with food.

CHAPTER 4

The giant and Adrien bookended me on one side of the table. Ursula and Aleric sat across from us. Gold fabric draped over a massive table festooned with flowers, crystal goblets, sterling flatware, and paper-thin china. I picked up each piece of dinnerware and examined it carefully. It obviously hadn't been made or purchased on earth.

"Oh, yes, you used to sell this stuff, didn't you?" The giant chuckled.

"Yes, but never anything quite so lovely."

"It is beautiful," Ursula assented. "I never had anything except plastic for the last years of my life."

Aleric and Adrien inspected the dinnerware, and then began to lift up the filmy tablecloth.

"This is marble?" Aleric asked, running his hand over the cold, hard surface.

"Of course," the giant chortled again. "Only the best, the most magnificent up here. What's so great is that everyone can enjoy it, not just rich dictators, or movie moguls."

The two men squirmed in their seats. Food began to appear. Soup, perfectly hot, streamed down my throat. I had been bedridden for the last four months of my life. Very little food passed through my old dry lips.

Bread, wine, salads, and fruit arrived soon after. We were hungry and devoured the food greedily. Little conversation flowed from our lips. Plates of meats and unidentified side dishes appeared. There seemed to be no end to the delights. Finally, a cart rolled in laden with a sterling carafe and serving plates of desserts. I spied a cake that looked remarkably like the one my mother used to make for me on my birthdays. It was lemon chiffon layered with lemon curd and blueberry pie filling. I remember Mom whipping the cream for the frosting.

"Are you sure this is what you want for your birthday cake?" Mom had asked. "I can't decorate it with just cream on it."

"Can't you put something on top?"

She knew what I meant. Every year until I moved out of the house, Mom placed plastic ballerinas posed in various ballet stances on my cake. My girlfriends all loved my birthday cake the best. We were all in ballet, so the pirouetting figures wowed us year after year.

By my eighteenth birthday, the ballerinas' faces and dresses had faded. Many years later, at an old general store, I discovered a set of plastic ballerinas hiding on a back table. I left them in their plastic bag because I didn't want to spoil them. I had hoped one of my nieces would keep them and not chuck them into a rummage sale after my funeral.

"Ah, Kopi Luwak coffee," Adrien's voice cut into my reverie.

This time the giant chortled so loudly I jumped.

"We don't need to get coffee beans from civet cat feces."

Adrien appeared miffed and pulled off the cart a dark brownie studded with macadamia nuts. Aleric grabbed a plate loaded with fruit, and Ursula took a crystal goblet filled with chocolate mousse. It seemed like each confection had been created especially for us.

"Do you like your lemon blueberry cake?" the giant asked.

"It's better than I remember, though it's been years since I've had it."

Mom stopped making it for me when macular degeneration robbed her of her eyesight. Many activities became impossible for Mom. She stopped quilting, knitting, even piano playing. Once her eyesight left, so did her desire for living.

"Mom, you're not dead." I remember kidding her one afternoon in the nursing home.

"I wish I were." Her once smooth voice had been replaced with a sound that reminded me of a bumpy road. "I just want to go home and be with Dad." Her face turned toward the window, though she could not see outside.

"You have so much life left in you." I couldn't reconcile myself to her leaving us. She was such a vital part of all her kids' and grandchildren's lives. We would all be orphans without Mom. It cut into me like a knife.

"At eighty-seven? Really?" she laughed. Her hands reached out searching for mine. We clasped our hands together. "Catharine, Catharine. Why did you never marry? All the other kids have spouses to take care of. You only have an old lady. You never could find the right one, could you?"

The question pierced my heart again. It was a painful reality for me, even at fifty-two. "Spinster Aunt Cathy," was what I heard at all the family reunions. I firmly told everyone that I had chosen to be single, that this life hadn't been thrust upon me, yet even the little ones knew that Aunt Cathy couldn't find a man.

Nights in bed were often cold and filled with tears. Strangely, I found many men who wanted to share my bed, but none who wanted to share my life with me. I stuck to my principals, and wondered if perhaps I should have loosened them up a bit just to maybe catch someone. I knew it would have gone against everything I had stood for.

There was Grant. He wanted to marry me. The wife of Doctor Grant, everyone expected it. He was handsome, and I was beautiful. It would have made a perfect fit, except that I didn't love him. I couldn't love him as much as he loved himself. He drifted off and married Minnie, then Susie, then Catrina. After that, he just lived with women. None could maintain their worship of him.

Then there was Norm. He was one of our many store managers. I met him at our managers' meeting. He was tall, very tan, and had jet-black hair. Most managers kept their hair cropped short, but not Norm. He reminded me of a pirate. Oh, did I create the fantasies, especially being shipwrecked on an island with him. For a while, I thought the infatuation was all one-sided, but Norm soon let me know his feelings for me.

"Hey, let's go get a bite to eat," he said one day at closing.

"Sure," I fumbled.

"I'll drive, then take you back to your car when we're finished," he volunteered. He had a black Corvette. Looking back, I'm not sure if it was Norm or his car that I had loved.

We sat at the restaurant for what seemed like hours. The waitress hovered over us, trying to encourage us to leave. I talked. Norm listened, really listened, and seemed so interested in my stories. He laughed at all my jokes, nodded, added comments. Norm could have been a therapist, he was so good.

Norm took a different route back to the store.

"Let's drive by the lake," he said.

Mom's disapproving face hovered in my conscience. Apprehension coursed through me.

I really don't know this man, I thought. He could rape me, then throw me in the lake. All the news accounts of women murdered flashed through my mind. Norm must have sensed my nervousness.

"We don't have to go tonight, but maybe some other time. Are you busy tomorrow night?"

Soon, the entire store, then the mall knew that Norm Skeffington and Catharine Zimmer were an item. I gained a new respect from all the other employees. Even Julie, our HR manager, who lived on her own planet, decided I was worth coming back to Earth for. In fact, Julie couldn't talk enough about Norm.

"'Did you notice Norm looking at me? Isn't he cute? Doesn't he remind you of a pirate? He always lingers in my office after we work on the department schedules.' On and on she'd prattle. It was clear she was infatuated, but it was only one sided. Norm had only eyes for me, or so I thought.

Our dates soon morphed into make-out sessions in the Corvette. Norm knew all the right buttons to push, and I became pliable in his arms. My body so wanted to give him everything, but my mind stopped in time.

"You are so funny," Norm would tease. "What century are you from, anyhow?"

"I just want to wait until I'm married! I want to give myself to only one man. It might just be you."

Norm turned his face away from me when I made that final comment. I had gone too far.

The way Norm and I carried on, it soon seemed like Norm was going to get the goods. One Friday morning before work, I packed my suitcase for a weekend get-away with Norm. I had told no one of this historical decision. What would my family say? What would anyone say? Yet I loved Norm so much I would have thrown myself into Lake Michigan had he asked.

She appeared at the cash register. Thick, black plaits hung below her neck. Fringed bangs partially shrouded thick, black eyebrows. Her blue eyes contrasted beautifully with the sprinkling of freckles on the pale skin. She looked as if she had stepped out of a German traditional costume catalog, wearing cranberry colored lederhosen and a white blouse underneath. When I looked down, she even had hiking boots with thick socks rolled over the tops.

"May I help you?" I asked.

"Yes, leave my fiancé alone," she quipped as casually as if she was ordering a hamburger. Despite the costume, there was no accent.

"Excuse me?" I leaned over, unsure I heard her correctly.

"Norm Skeffington and I are engaged to be married. We've been living together for two years." She turned on her heels and sauntered away as quickly as she had appeared.

Was this woman crazy, I wondered? Then comprehension filled in the tiny gaps of my brain. Little situations I had thought were insignificant took on meaning..

"What are you hiding?" I'd tease when he'd forbid visits to his house. "Dead bodies?"

"Why can't you come tonight? I know you're not working?"

Norm was hiding something, and it wasn't a pet dog.

"Wait," I yelled across the sales floor. The Fraulein turned around. I followed her. "How did you know about us?"

"He always has a few girls on the side," she shrugged. "I'm the one he always comes back to. I must admit," she eyed me up and down, "he must have been pretty smitten with you because things at home have not been the same. I guess I could give him up, but I'm not willing. Besides, I give him what he wants, which is something I hear you don't." She sneered and turned away.

"What's your name?" I shouted, watching her descend down the escalator.

"Tracy Vera." Her cackle still rankled me even after many years had passed.

The heat from my face could have fried an egg as I stood watching her in humiliation. She was long gone, but I stood fixated on that spot.

"Catharine Zimmer, dial 295, Catharine Zimmer, dial 295." My reverie shattered, I ran to the nearest phone and dialed.

"Catharine Zimmer, here. How may I help you?"

"Hey, Honey, are you all packed?"

My heart stopped. I felt sick to my stomach.

"I'm not feeling very well," I stammered.

Instantly he turned on the care and concern button. "Do you need me to take you home?"

Take me home? I wondered. Yes, have him take me home, so I could give him what he really wanted and pry him away from Tracy Vera. That is what I resolved to do when suddenly my mother appeared at the cash register in front of me.

"I gotta go. A customer is here."

Mom's face looked grim as I hung up.

"Were you on the phone with that philandering lout?" she asked.

"Norm?" I asked innocently.

"Ah, yeah, Norm," she said. "I was at dinner with the girls last night and whom do I see with some blond, but your Norm! I knew I didn't trust him. He was practically making love to her in the booth."

For the second time in less than an hour, my face smoldered. I remembered the times Norm and I cozied up at different restaurants. Looking back now, he never took me to any local places, only out of town hideaways. Norm probably didn't want to run into Tracy or his other girlfriends.

"Did you need something, Mom?" I asked, trying to regain some composure, though how I was going to do it after being hit by not one, but two grenades, I wasn't sure.

"Yes, I need to make sure my daughter isn't throwing her life away to some sleaze bag, and, I need to buy some sheets. Can you help me?"

Mom could shift gears as quickly as a New York taxi driver shifting from first to fourth gear. I mechanically showed her the linens, rang her up, and then promised to stop by for supper after work. I couldn't tell her about Norm, but I knew Mom's cooking would keep the tears at bay for a while.

"Hey, hey, hey," Norm appeared as soon as Mom left. He avoided Mom, and now knowing everything, I understood why. Mom could spot a phony a mile away. "You're looking pretty good to me," he said. "Are we still on for the weekend?"

Oh, how I wanted to say yes to him, but I knew I couldn't.

"Norm," I faltered. I hesitated. He sensed something.

"What?" he said nervously.

"I waited on Tracy Vera today."

It stopped him cold.

"Also, my mother spotted you last night with a blond. Now I know why you canceled our movie night."

"That was just Vicky. She was an old friend who stopped in town for the night."

"Mom said you looked pretty chummy," I was stone cold. "Let's call off this weekend. Maybe you and Tracy need to sort out some things. I know I do."

I turned and walked back to my office. I packed up my briefcase and left my job for the weekend. Fortunately for me, Norm quit working at the store a few weeks later. I never saw him again, though ghosts of his image haunted me in my cold bed. He was like a sick addiction I couldn't shake.

CHAPTER 5

We finished our repast, and settled back into our chairs. Aleric, once again, took his spot. He cleared his throat and began.

I went north to live in the Tocar Cielos. The mountains bordered our tiny country of San Xavier with the even tinier country of Magellan. There I could go back and forth between the two countries to start building up my own little rebel group. Nothing could distract me from my goal to kill Gutierrez and assume leadership of San Xavier. Fortunately for me, Magellan's presidente despised Gutierrez. He became my ally and supplied me with guns and men.

In the mountains, we trained. It was easy because there were very few people up there. Though we had murder on our minds, I found a home in the mountains, a home I never had before.

Andes, Rockies, Appalachians, Sierra Nevada, Apennines, Pyrenees. These were only a few I had walked upon, their close proximity to the sky seeming to elevate them to sacred ground. Mountains were where I longed to rest my body. In all seriousness, I told my family my plans only to have them laugh in my face.

"Grandpa bought enough plots for the entire family," Jeremy joked.

*He was right. I would be buried, actually I probably **am** buried, at Holy Cross Cemetery. Did my funeral take place already? I wondered.*

In the Pyrenees I met another man, one I had hoped would relieve me of my thoughts of Norm. He hid his wedding band in his pants pocket. One day it fell out, ruining his secret.

"Catharine," the giant interrupted my thoughts. "Aleric is telling his story."

I gripped the quill harder.

One day, a man joined our group. He was much older than we were. I didn't trust him. I figured he was a spy for Gutierrez. He said we must use words not force for our revolution. We must speak to the people about democracy and freedom.

Bah, I thought. What do those words really mean? Our little country only knew war and tyranny. How were we to teach them about some foreign idea of freedom?

But he had contacts. We planned to hold a protest in the capital square. Thousands of San Xavierians would be there. I was to speak - to rile up the crowd and get them to accept the idea of freedom and democracy. I didn't accept it myself, how could I convince these people?

I remember that day as if it was yesterday. We took the train into the city, but not all together. We rode in separate cars. No one, not even the guards, suspected us, or what would happen.

The city square was about a mile from the train station. I walked, thinking I was alone, but others followed. It seemed as if each step I took I collected another group of followers. By the time I reached the square, a large crowded entered behind me. They pushed me forward. I was to speak.

Behind the podium, I could touch the faces, they were standing that close. When Gutierrez spoke to the people, he stood from a balcony. We must have looked like ants to him, which is why it was so easy for him to crush us. In front of me were the faces of hope, and at that moment I believed in those strange ideas of freedom and democracy.

Aleric's speech had been aired all over the world. His words sent chills up and down my spine. The television was on in the break room. I took another twenty minutes on my lunch to watch the young soldier inspire his country and the world. So did the rest of the store. Where he came from, I wondered as I watched.

"That was your shining moment, little man," Adrien pushed into my reverie. "But, soon the tanks appeared, and the crowds ran off, scared."

"Yes, everyone scattered. Gutierrez's men crashed into all the cameras. It became a blood bath."

While my co-workers and I were mesmerized, suddenly we were shocked to see big tanks roll in. There was screaming, and then black. Nothing. American journalists scrambled to cover the story, but the big news was how Gutierrez arrested and imprisoned those journalists, regardless of their native homes. Our president didn't act, until there was so much pressure put on him that he finally demanded the release of all the American journalists. Twenty-seven returned, but one was still missing. His wife appeared on any and every news show almost every day for about a month until people lost interest.

Gutierrez thought he had won, but we had stirred up the country. Revolution was in the air. Gutierrez knew it. He felt it. I was a wanted man. We hid in the mountains until things cooled down a bit.

I was getting impatient. I had decided we had to wage war. Of course, we weren't as equipped as Gutierrez, but we had to fight.

We started with tiny uprisings in the villages at the foot of the mountains. At night, we would come and set fire to the houses and government buildings. I told my men to kill anyone they saw. I knew these people were innocent, but someone had to pay.

Aleric held his head down for a moment.

I was storming through the streets myself, when I saw a young mother clutching her baby. "Kill everyone you see," the words wrestled with my conscience. "What will the men think, if you cannot destroy the enemy? They will think you are weak," the voice continued.

The mama's eyes pleaded with me. I hesitated. Then the dictator rose victorious and I plunged my sword into her heart, and then the baby's. They slumped down at my feet. From the alley, a little girl stared at me, then fled.

I clutched my chest. The image was as real as if I had watched the entire sordid event. I was stunned into silence.

Aleric fell to his knees. "I murdered them, an innocent woman and baby. I thought I was being heroic, but that was one of my most cowardly acts." Gut wrenching sobs tore out of him.

Adrien stared impassively. Ursula was at Aleric's side, trying to comfort him. There was no mercy in my soul for this vile man. I wanted his story to stop. I could no longer descend into the misery he created.

"I can't bear to hear anymore," I shouted.

The giant swung around and stared at me hard.

"His story is your story," he whispered.

What did that mean? I wondered. There was no way our stories were meshed together. I was a small-town girl, living a banal existence, with no thought of revolution in my heart. This giant had it all wrong.

"It is too painful now for you to understand," the giant answered my thoughts. "Continue with your story," the giant commanded, looking at Aleric.

Ursula moved back to her seat; Adrien folded his arms in derision.

With one more glance at each one of us, Aleric continued his grisly tale.

For two years, we caused trouble in the country. Gutierrez both feared and hated us. The bounty for my head grew larger and larger. I was very good at hiding. It helped when there were government officials who didn't like the fact that Gutierrez had been in power for over thirty years. I was offered hospitality at many a palace. They dreamed a savior would rescue them from the vice grip of Gutierrez.

Then *Capitán* Camerena, a so-called friend of Gutierrez, allowed me to hide out in his home. He didn't give me permission to sleep with his wife.

"Couldn't keep your pants zipped up, huh, little man?" Adrien quipped. "That'll get you into more trouble than anything."

Aleric ignored the comment and continued. "*Señora* Camerena came to me. It was like Joseph and Potiphar's wife."

"Joseph said, 'No,' little man. Obviously you couldn't resist the temptation."

We all looked at Adrien.

"Let him tell his story," the giant commanded.

Aleric continued.

She was very beautiful and desirable. Her husband was thirty years her senior. She would tell me that he was so cold, so unresponsive to her needs. We would meet in the garden house thinking we were safe until the gardener found us.

"You traitor! I protected you and this is how you pay me back, sleeping with my wife?" Camerena slapped my face.

"I am sorry. I won't do it again!" I pleaded

"*Sí*, you're right. We were friends, but now I despise you more than Gutierrez."

We fled, and the *señora* guided us down an underground tunnel. It didn't matter. Gutierrez's men were waiting on the other side. It was as if she had intended to trap me.

I tried fighting them off, but they captured me without too much struggle.

After several months in prison, Gutierrez decided to pay me a visit. "Here's the *diminuto* ant that tried to put me down." He smiled, but his voice rumbled like thunder before a storm. "Finally, I get to meet Octavio Isidro Regallito's little son. What shall we do with you, ant?"

"Kill me like you killed my parents," I spat out.

"And make you a hero?" He stared hard at me. "Ant, these four walls will witness the rotting away of your body!"

His laugh echoed as he left.

A few days later, my guard slipped me a very small trowel. Slowly I dug and dug. Each speck of dirt fueled my hatred even more for Gutierrez and his regime.

I'm not sure how long it took, but finally the tunnel was ready. I would escape and go to the summer palace and kill Gutierrez. There were thousands outside waiting for the coup.

"Rebel Fighter Becomes President." That headline had plastered itself onto my consciousness over sixty years ago, yet felt as vivid today as it did back then. I had read with great interest about Aleric Sampino Regallito, the underdog who would bring freedom to his oppressed people. I was especially impressed because he was young, younger than I was, fighting for a cause while I just rang up customers.

"Cash or charge? You don't have a Falls Department Store charge? Would you like to open one today? You'll get twenty percent off your total sale."

I didn't tell them I got two dollars for every credit card application they filled out. Some months I received an extra five hundred dollars in my check. My skill opened the doors to a manager's job. I had to wait until I was thirty before that happened.

"Why are you still a clerk at that store?" My Aunt Mimi would nag at every family gathering. "You're so beautiful. You could go into modeling, or acting. You should have gone to college, like my Evette. Now that's a life that has purpose."

On and on she'd ramble. She was like that bad cold you wanted to avoid getting while sitting next to a sneezing child. Everything in Aunt Mimi's existence was perfect - her home, her husband, her child, her garden, her cooking, her friends, her trips, her spirituality, which we never quite got.

"Don't listen to Aunt Mimi," Mom would caution. "She married into the family. She's really not one of us. My poor brother."

Everything horrible about Aunt Mimi, Uncle George was not. He was kind, friendly, humble, and generous. Why he married Aunt Mimi, we never figured out.

"He probably felt sorry for her since no one else in his right mind would wed her," Dad would say.

"If you can't say something nice, don't say anything," Mom would chastise Dad.

"My lips are sealed then," Dad would wink at us kids.

"Are you with us?" The giant's voice bellowed me back into the present.

"Sorry!" I grabbed the feather, poised to write.

Aleric smiled at me for just a moment, and then the pain of his story washed over his face. He continued with no trace of hope in his voice.

CHAPTER 6

He was sleeping when I chopped off his head. No more words, no more terror from this man who destroyed my family and my life. Years of torment gone in a moment.

There was a parade. Zealots carried his decapitated body through the streets. People reached to steal from his corpse.

I recalled the news footage with abhorrence. The headless body of Gutierrez bobbed from one group to the next, with people clawing at the corpse. I was dismayed that my hero of one day was threatening my home country the next.

"Today San Xavier, tomorrow, the world," Regallito's ominous voice echoed over the news channel.

"Hey, little man, the world was your oyster," Adrien mocked.

"Oyster?" Aleric's eyebrow furrowed.

"He means the world belonged to you, or at least in your mind," I told the dictator.

"I didn't pay too much attention to the news when I was young, but I remember the terror I felt when I saw your face," Ursula spoke up. "I was only seventeen then. My parents were glued to the television. I was going out, but stopped to watch. It was the creepiest thing, seeing that body go through the crowd. I never forgot that image."

Again, Aleric lowered his face.

Me, little Aleric Regallito, killing the villain who killed my parents. For so long I craved his revenge and my appetite was satiated, for a while. From the top of the palace, I looked out my windows. The people became ants.

The four of us were fixated on our own thoughts from that moment. The horrific memory created various recollections for each of us. My memory conjured up the Thanksgiving dinner that followed a few weeks after Aleric's takeover of San Xavier. It was a full house with my parents, my brothers and sisters, and the twelve grandchildren. We had just finished gorging ourselves on Mom's dinner and leaned into our chairs to settle the meal.

"What about that joker in San Xavier?" My brother John started. He relished politics and couldn't wait to bring it up at every family gathering.

"Can we wait until the kids leave the table?" charged Claire.

"What are you talking about, Mommy?" asked Gina, Claire's daughter, my parents' oldest grandchild. Nine-year old Gina pried into every adult conversation like an archeologist on a dig.

"Nothing. Just take the kids and go play."

"There's nothing to do," Gina pouted.

"You can do the dishes," piped in my father.

"All right." Gina sighed. "Come on kiddies. Let's go. I don't know why I have to be the babysitter."

"He's going to take over the world," Patrick began without waiting for all the kids to depart. Claire glared at him. Gina hesitated.

"Now, Gina!" Claire commanded.

"Well, if people don't start waking up, he could easily take over," Christina was our conspiracy theory family member. Every act of Congress was a covert act against the Republic.

"San Xavier is a tiny country. They're very poor. He could no more likely take over than an army of fleas," said John.

"That's what they said of Hitler," Dad said solemnly. He rarely participated in our political talks, preferring to play with his grandchildren instead. That day, however, it was different. "There's something about that man that is fearful. So young, but able to take over a country." He shook his head in disbelief.

"His father was a military man who worked for President Alvarez. It was in his blood," John said.

We mulled over the comments.

"Nah," said Tom. "He just can't."

"I wouldn't be surprised if Mr. President turned our country over to Señor Regallito," Mom, like the rest of us, had little use for the sitting president at the time.

"With the help of our Congress and Senate, I'm sure he could." Christina was spinning all sorts of conspiracy scenarios in her head. "We're not a democracy anymore. We're not much better than San Xavier."

"Oh, please! Give me a break," interrupted Claire. "We're bad, but not on the brink of total destruction. Let's be reasonable."

"All I can say is the guy gives me the creeps," I said. "Can we change the subject? Who's going shopping with me tomorrow?"

"You work full time at a department store, and on your day off you want to go shopping?" Mom asked. "Count me in. Where are we going?"

"Football for me," Tom answered.

"Me too," clamored the five other men.

Aleric's voice shook me back to the present.

Soon I realized being the leader meant watching your back. Enemies hidden, unseen, were working to destroy me.

I could not let my guard down. Emilina moved into the palace.

"Wait a minute," Adrien spoke up. "Who is Emilina?"

"Señora Camerena, of course," Aleric spoke as if we should have known that.

Her husband became my first and most formidable enemy. I had to act fast. I had to convince the people that my leadership would be the best for them. The rich were bad, I preached day in and day out. Gutierrez and the rich were the tyrants. The common people ate it up. What is that called? Class envy? I had plenty of it myself, remembering how the rich ate sumptuous meals while Antonio and I nearly starved.

"But you told us yourself that your parents were rich," Adrien smirked. "Didn't you tell us you lived in a house with more than twenty rooms?"

"Destitution erases the memory," Aleric replied.

"Aleric, you don't have to respond to Adrien's every comment. We'll never finish your story if you do," the giant glared at Adrien. "You will have your chance to speak."

Aleric twisted that cap again.

The people cheered as they watched the rich being dragged out of their homes and murdered on the streets. I told my men to let the people take what they wanted from the mansions.

The looting had been horrible. Camera crews caught thousands of people pilfering and fighting to rob the homes of their magnificent goods. Swarms trampled and killed children as they struggled to steal. I shuddered.

This went on for a couple of months, then things settled down. My main men moved into the empty mansions. They had to kick out the vagrants. The news people caught everything on film. That's when I realized the journalists had to go, at least the ones not sympathetic to my cause. Before I took over, most had supported me. Once they saw what I had become, they became my worst enemy. My tanks rolled over most of the newspaper and television buildings. We were going to start fresh. I had new offices built. I installed my own journalists. They were my puppets or else. I thought I had all the journalists taken care of, but I was wrong.

One day the most exquisite creature in the world came into my office. She was very petite, with fair skin and ebony hair that fell down her back. Her eyes were not the usual muddy brown of my people, but blue, very blue.

"Here we go again," Adrien rolled his eyes.

No one was permitted into my offices, but her beauty won over my guards and she appeared in front of me.

"Señor Regallito," she said. "My name is Verdad Quinn. What are you doing with our country?" she demanded.

"Who let you in here?" I stood up from my desk. "No one, not even beautiful women, are permitted into my office."

She ignored me. "Why are you killing all the journalists? We were all on your side. Gutierrez was an evil man. We had hoped you would bring change. Good change."

I stared at her. It was as if the statue of Venus had come to life; she was so beautiful.

"*Señor*, please listen to me!" she pleaded, her voice soothing music to my ears.

"Would you like a drink?" I asked her.

"I am here on business, *Señor* Regallito."

"*Capitán* Regallito," I corrected her. "We can talk business over a drink."

She didn't have the usual accent. In fact, it sounded foreign to me. I had only been to Magellan, and their dialect was similar to ours. To me, there was only one way of speaking. Anything else was foreign. Suddenly, Emilina entered the room.

She stared down Verdad. She walked around the younger woman three times, clicking her tongue. Emilina was jealous, it was obvious, and she wanted to hurt Verdad. I didn't want that to happen.

"Leave the room, now!" I commanded her. "We are discussing business."

"Sure you are! Just remember who got you here!" She stormed out of the room.

"She has nothing to fear," Verdad said. "You'd be the last man. No, you wouldn't even be the last man. If there were only you left, I'd become a nun," she spoke through her teeth.

I was filled with passion and grabbed her. I wanted to kiss her, but she slapped me. I shoved her away.

"You whore," I shouted.

"Whore?" She laughed in my face. "Look who's calling who a whore. Listen," she tried to change the subject. "I am only here to beg you to do what is right. You know in your heart what is right. You were taught it by your parents, then your aunt."

"What do you know about anything? My parents were murdered before they could teach me right from wrong, and *mi tia* died trying to keep my brother and me from starvation."

"Have you done the numbers yet? Do you know how many people have died since your reign?

"I'm not a king," I corrected her.

"You're worse than any monarch dead or alive. So far the count is over twenty-thousand. Those are just the reported figures." She shouted, "twenty-thousand! You've only been in power for nine months! One would have been too many, but people, *your people* have become easily dispensable. If they get in your way, kill them. You're worse than Gutierrez ever was."

"Those numbers are inflated, made up by people like you! Lies, all lies."

How dare she accuse me, the leader of a country, of being worse than Gutierrez.

I lunged toward her. I wanted to strangle her. She backed up, and I fell on my face. She began to laugh. If I wasn't so filled with hatred, I would have loved that laugh. It was beautiful like her, which wounded me even more. I wanted her, but I wanted to kill her, too.

"You've not seen the end of me," Verdad said. She kicked my face with her foot, then turned around and left.

She worked for a paper in Magellan. She was able to pass through our military boundaries to get reports. For about two years, her newspaper reported all the sordid, but untrue information of our country to the outside world.

One day, I was watching an American morning show, and there she was, Verdad Quinn. She was an American living a missionary existence to rout me out of office.

"I could not get her out of my mind."

"Tell us something new," Adrien interrupted. The giant glared once again at Adrien.

It was hard to concentrate on leading the country. Though Verdad only wrote scathing reports of me, I drank them up like strong coffee. Did they make me stop? No. Well, maybe a little. In my third year, people had begun to settle down. They accepted me as their leader.

"What were they going to do, risk getting killed?" I interjected.

Verdad Quinn - she was a contributing reporter for The New York Times. Luckily for me, the store manager brought the paper into the store every morning. Though I had a good salary, I was too stingy to purchase the paper myself.

I read Quinn's articles, probably as Aleric did. She was younger than I was, but doing something I had only dreamed of. She motivated the UN to investigate Regallito, but it led them nowhere. Quinn was persistent. Almost weekly, for about three years, I read her column. Then it stopped. Had things improved in San Xavier? Out of sight, out of mind. I quickly forgot about the plight of the people in that tiny country.

I stopped my nightly visits to Emilina. She left the palace and went home to her husband. I was interested in no woman, only Verdad. Looking back, I can hardly believe I lived the life of a monk those three years.

One night, I slipped out of the palace alone. I had heard Verdad worked late hours. In my mind, I imagined the scene. She would see me and throw herself at me. She would return to the palace with me. We would be lovers.

It was a five-hour journey over the border to our neighboring country of Magellan. They had no border patrol, so people could come and go from their tiny country without anyone noticing.

She was sleeping on a couch when I sneaked into the tiny building. It seemed even smaller since I had been living in a palace. I stared at her for at least an hour. She finally woke. She was terrified, but she pulled out a gun.

"I wondered how long it would take before you showed up," she said. "You're in dangerous territory right now. *Presidente* Fiorte has a price on your head: one million dollars."

"I am only here to see you," I said, staring, wanting, hoping.

"How did you get over the border? Everyone knows your face."

"*Diñero* speaks louder than words," I laughed.

She waved her gun. "I'd be a hero. It'd only take one bullet."

"You? Verdad?   Life is too precious to you." I moved closer. She raised the gun higher.

"Spare me the drama! Now, this would make a good movie. Why didn't this ever make it in the newspapers?" Adrien asked.

"Some of us would like to hear his story," Ursula said, quietly yet firmly.

"Is he telling the truth or making this stuff up?" Adrien pouted.

"Up here lies fade away. Only the truth comes out," the giant replied. "Please, Aleric, we need to hear it all."

At that moment, I knew she was the only woman for me. I wanted to grab her and make love to her, but she still had the gun pointed at me. I fell to my knees.

"Come away with me," I groveled. "You can have all the pretty dresses, jewelry, shoes, trips, food, whatever. It can all be yours if you come away with me."

I kissed her feet, but she recoiled from me, as if burnt. "Even if you don't love me, there must be something I can give you."

"Democracy. Freedom for your people."

I couldn't believe my ears. As the leader of San Xavier I did what I wanted, ate any food I liked, and slept on silk beds. It was like a drug, and I wasn't about to give it up.

"That is all my mother's people, my people want. Designer clothes, jewelry are nothing to me. Freedom to live how you want to live is greater than anything."

I laughed at her. "There is no such thing as democracy."

"In the United States, democracy thrives."

I laughed at her silly notions. "United States? That country filled with flag burners and freaks? I don't want a country like that."

"It is the greatest country on earth," she persisted in her stupid arguments. "Mother and her family fled San Xavier during Gutierrez's tyranny. I was born in America. I'm an American, but San Xavier flows through my blood. You, Captain Regallito, you could go down in history as the *Presidente* that opened his country up to freedom."

"Bah! That would mean death for me, death for my leadership."

"You don't know that."

The gun was at her side. I walked up and grabbed it from her. She was asking me to throw away everything I had killed for. The painful memories of my dead parents, my starving aunt, and the years living on the streets prevented me from seeing any other way.

"I could kill you right now," I said to her.

"Yes, you could," she said so quietly I wasn't sure I heard her. "You can kill all the people who represent the truth, but you'll never kill truth. Someday you'll have to face it, whether here on earth or in your grave, but it will come, no matter what. You have become an evil man. You have forsaken your God, your family, and your country. I am only one person. It won't matter if you kill me."

She was wrong. It would matter to me. I knew killing her would kill me, but I could take no more of her freedom talk.

"Stop!' I shouted. "From now on, my guards will be watching you very carefully. Forget about ever returning to your mother country."

"You'll never stop me. I will continue to write. I have my contacts. You have many weak areas," she taunted me.

I wanted to slap her smug face.

CHAPTER 7

She was right. People got in and out all the time without being caught. I stationed more guards on the border along the river, which I found out was the best place for escape. I also commanded that a wall be built.

"San Xavier Walls in Its People," the headline screamed. I could only think of China and its building of a thousand mile barrier to keep the Mongols thousands of years ago. The crazed dictator of San Xavier was trying to imitate the Asian country, and was just as successful in the high number of mortalities, but not so successful in keeping out its enemies and keeping in its people.. The dictator halted efforts due to pressure from outside countries. This was a crazy man, I thought to myself when I wasn't too preoccupied with my life. Only when his name popped up in the news did I give President Aleric Regallito much thought.

Verdad, my spies tried to follow, though mostly unsuccessfully. My men were to kill anyone and everyone who had anything to do with her. Verdad, I said, don't kill.

Soon word got around that cooperating with Verdad meant death. People stopped talking. The news leaks stopped. Finally, life was going my way. People respected me. I lived well, too well sometimes. Each morning began with *pulque* hangovers. Every day I ate a feast of food, especially fruit, any fruit I wanted. I had apples shipped to me from the United States until they imposed trade sanctions with San Xavier.

Aleric spat as if trying to remove a distasteful morsel from his mouth.

Then another enemy sprouted up: the church. I was surprised it took five years before fat, old Bishop Pandeles landed on my doorsteps. He would stand outside the palace praying on his rosary beads. He started with a small group of followers, but soon the crowds below my window swelled.

Bishop Pandeles was a U.S. citizen sent to San Xavier as a missionary. The Pope had put him there. Bishop Pandeles wrote every week, telling me my sins. My advisor told me to kill him. I couldn't. He was a man of God. Even though I despised him, I was superstitious. Worse yet, he was an American citizen. It would be bad policy.

As I tried to figure out what to do with the Bishop, my spies told me that he was escorting refugees out of the country. Thousands of filthy traitors were escaping San Xavier all because of him. Magellan and the United States welcomed everyone! That was grounds enough to have him executed. Not even the UN could stop me.

"Did you kill him?" It was my turn to interrupt.

"He'll get to that, don't worry!" the giant answered me.

Aleric looked at all of us again.

What goes through the mind of a dictator? What was his eternal fate?

"That is not for you to know." *There goes the giant again, reading my mind.* "Aleric, please continue."

Not long after, the Vatican called. Our country would host the Papa if we chose. He wanted to visit the tombs of the martyrs.

The mirth left Aleric's face as he continued.

Did I have a choice to allow this visit? I could have said no, but I saw this as an opportunity to polish my reputation a little. Maybe Verdad would come around to my side.

The Pope kissed the ground when he landed. The cameras flashed when we hugged. I thought it was going well. When we met privately, however, he lashed out at me for my terrible human rights violations. I told him that I was only trying to restore order in a country that had not seen order in years.

In his eyes was disbelief. After a strained hour, we visited   the tomb. There he knelt, bowed his head, and cried. I had never seen a man weep so. I felt ashamed, but only for a moment. I knew what the tears were about. So did the rest of the world. He was there, in my little Catholic country, to shame me. Why wasn't he visiting other countries with their problems? Why did he have to single out our tiny San Xavier? There were far worse rulers than I.

"You really believed that?"

"Catharine." The giant shook his head.

I decided then and there that San Xavier would no longer be the little Catholic country, bowing down to some remote Papa across the ocean. I was the commander, not some old man who wore funny hats and red shoes! When he left, I ordered all the monasteries, seminaries, convents, churches, and anything to do with the Catholic Church to shut down. Even the Catholic hospitals were forced to close. One day a bunch of angry doctors and nurses stormed the palace. They were shot down like rabid dogs.

Aleric shrugged his shoulders, as if he just talked about exterminating roaches.

We had the church buildings chained and locked. No one could get in. Why didn't I just smash the buildings? It was that superstitious feeling I had about destroying anything religious.

All bishops, priests, and nuns were to leave the country immediately or be killed. That didn't stop Bishop Pandeles. He still ushered people out of our country at night, while praying and chanting in my courtyard during the day.

"Why don't you kill him?" Eustaquio, one of my soldiers, asked. He pointed his gun out my window. He had a perfect target.

"No!" I

The Bishop continued until one day Eustaquio pulled me to my window. There he was, like a fat ant, with about a thousand protestors.

Rage overtook my superstition. "Kill them all," I commanded.

Soon the tanks, the very tanks Gutierrez had used, appeared in the courtyard. Many of the people fled, but I learned later that forty-seven had been killed. Bishop was not one of the dead. My men hunted him down and arrested him. I personally escorted him to his prison cell.

"*Presidente*," he scoffed at me. "How nice of you to show me to my rooms. You're not going to be very popular with the United Nations, you know!" The Bishop smiled like a cat that, what do you say, swallowed a canary? I pushed him in, and he fell on his knees and began shouting prayers. "God, save this man! Save this poor country! Help them in their time of great distress!"

The prisoners, including the Bishop, would be shot at dawn, or so I thought.

The next day, I was watching the news and it was all over the place. The United Nations tried to contact me, but I just ignored them. I couldn't execute the Bishop. Not right away.

General Peña, my right hand man, came into my office one day. "We have discovered where the leaks are coming from. Every word he spoke was crisp and sharp. "Should we send our men?"

"Let us surprise them tonight. We'll catch them in action."

Six army trucks left the palace around eleven o'clock. The trip would take some hours. It was in the mountains. The culprits would either be sleeping or conducting their illegal activities. It didn't matter to me. They had broke the law so they had to be killed.

It was two o'clock when we arrived at a breathtaking stone cottage snug in the mountains. The perfume of the wild orchids filled my nose. Stars studded the sky. It was a night for love, not for killing, I remember thinking at that time.

We knocked and shouted. No answer. I kicked opened the door. No one seemed to be inside. My soldiers, carrying rifles, marched through. They dragged women from their rooms.

"Women?" I shouted. "Who are they?"

They were silent; they fell to their knees bowing their heads. I finally went inside and looked around. There were statues and religious pictures everywhere. It was a convent!

Rage engulfed me, until I realized there could only be one woman that would defy my orders.

"Get out!" I shouted to the men. She would be my catch.

I climbed the stairs and stopped cold. On her knees was Verdad.

Her black hair was much shorter, but her beauty still mesmerized me. She didn't look up.

"You've finally discovered our little secret," she said. "I was wondering how long it would take you."

I just stared for a very long time until one of my men rushed in. He yanked her to her feet by her hair.

"Hey, here's a good lookin' one," he smirked.

"Leave her alone," I shouted back at him.

"Oh, you want her for yourself, huh?" He left the room.

I knew the soldiers would try to rape the women. I ran outside.

"Do not touch the women!" I screamed. Usually I let the men do whatever they wanted, but Verdad was there.

She sat in the front seat with me on the way home. She said nothing. I wanted something, even scolding, but she nothing.

Once more, the idea of forcing her to live with me ran through my mind, but I knew it would be like entrapping a wild animal. She would never be happy, but perhaps she would grow to love me. As we approached the prison, she finally spoke. "If you kill the others you must kill me, too."

I looked at her, shocked. She was right. I made the edict that any active Catholics remaining in my country would be killed.

"I can't kill you," I said to her.

"But you won't kill me, your soldiers will."

I escorted her down to the prison. The other captives reached out their arms, crying. Verdad would gently touch each and say, "God bless you."

Just her words and touch brought comfort to those miserable people. We passed Bishop Pandeles' cell. He was on his knees praying. He looked up. "Sister Veronica. You've come to join me. You must be special to have him," the Bishop pointed to me, "bring you down here."

"Yes, I am," she said. "I wonder if he'll be brave enough to escort me to my execution tomorrow."

The words stung. When we reached her cell, I went in. The prison guard stared at me. "Leave us alone!" I yelled. Verdad, or, Sister Veronica knelt by the bed.

"Is that all you people do, get on your knees?" I tormented her.

She bowed her head and said nothing.

"All your prayers are useless! No lightening striking, no sudden heart attack to kill me."

She continued.

"Say something!" I demanded.

Tears blurred the blue of her eyes when she looked at me, but she still said nothing.

I remained with her until the sun appeared in the horizon. As I moved to go, she stood up. She held out her hand. "Peace to you, Aleric. May your soul find peace."

A handshake. That is all. I wanted her, to possess her, but only a handshake.

I watched from the third floor of the palace. The blindfolded sisters were brought out into the square. Verdad was the third one from the left. There was a huge crowd for so early in the morning. Shots rung out in the air. The sisters' bodies slumped to the ground. I could hear wailing and chanting. The bodies were taken away, and the guards moved the crowd out.

Tears welled up in my eyes and fell freely onto the paper. I tried to wipe the moisture away with my hands, but the giant handed me a white cloth. As I dabbed away the tears, I noticed a change. Aleric's strong accent seemed to lessen, or perhaps I wasn't recording his words very well.

"Hell is too good for you," shouted Adrien.

"Yes, you are right, but there is nowhere else for a dictator, an evil man like me."

"Man's judgment has no place here," the giant said quietly, almost imperceptibly.

"What does that mean?" Adrien smirked.

"We never know the final outcome," the giant answered.

Adrien persisted, "Before us stands one of the most heinous men in history. There is no place, as far as I'm concerned, for him, but Hell."

"Maybe. But that is not how the final judgment is executed."

"Where is the justice in this? Innocent people died at his hands and they're supposed to spend an eternity with him? It screams injustice."

"Let God decide the justice."

"My husband had me killed, too," Ursula interjected.

We all stared at her, shocked.

"Yes, Ursula. Though many were too afraid to admit it, your husband had you murdered. Let us finish Aleric's story."

The giant's eyes were red, and tear stains mottled his cheek.

Who is this guy, I wondered again.

CHAPTER 8

In my grief, I failed to notice what was going on in my country. New rebel groups rose up to take my place, and there were bands of protesters throughout the country. They were demanding my death or at the very least resignation.

I would watch the protesters in the square for hours, but my mind was on Verdad.

One day I heard a commotion outside my door. A swarm of soldiers, led by General Pena, who was also my best friend, surrounded me. Apparently, he led the biggest opposition against me.

"We are arresting you," he said.

That was it. My paranoia of spies planning a coup was more frightening than reality. Limply, I held out my hands. They handcuffed me and dragged me out of the room. A crowd followed as the guards escorted me across the square to the prison. People threw all sorts of things at me. Some tried to grab me. One man with a knife attacked me.

As I approached my cell, Bishop Pandeles was leaving.

"So we meet again," he said. He made the sign of the cross on my forehead before he left for freedom. They put me in Verdad's old cell. That was the only request of mine that they fulfilled. Only seven years as leader.

Aleric shook his head.

"That's better than some of our presidents, loser," Adrien scoffed, "and you weren't even elected."

"Seven years?" Ursula asked. "Your story didn't seem that long."

Aleric shrugged and continued.

Surprisingly, the time went by very fast until my life was redirected, so to say, to cell number twelve. For the rest of the world, Aleric Sampino Regallito was dead, but for me, I was rotting away.

Shortly after the change, there was to be a trial for my regime. Most people, including myself, wanted death. It was going that way, until Bishop Pandeles testified. He was able to convince the jurors that if San Xavier wished to become a democracy, it needed to stop executing people. The public didn't really buy it, but the jurors feared the Bishop, and did what he said. The remainder of my life would be spent in a cage. No parole, like the American way, just prison, or should I call it a dungeon?

San Xavier's prison was built in the 16th century, underneath the palace. It was another imported idea from the Spanish invasion of our country. Like all dungeons, it was dark, damp, and intended to kill the prisoners. The floors were dirt, the walls stone. By 1950, little cots and sinks were added to show how progressive our country had become.

When it was built in 1573, they must have planned on a lot of prisoners, because it was like an underground city. When I took over, I ordered the cementing of the floors and blocking of all the hidden passageways. I didn't want the prisoners escaping, like I had during Gutierrez's reign.

My only visitor was a disgusting rat, which would crawl on my face in the morning.

"That's fitting," Adrien said.

I would scream and jump out of bed. This happened for weeks. I became afraid of going to bed at night because I dreaded waking up to the *gordo* rat on my face.

The pillow they had given me became *Gordo's* bed. *Gordo,* that is what I named it, used my pillow as a bed. He thought I was being a hospitable host.

We all laughed in spite of ourselves. Aleric failed to see the humor.

I complained to the guards. They laughed, too.

"You're only getting what you deserve," they'd mock.

I gave up the pillow and left for *Gordo.* I folded up my only blanket as a pillow.

"Poor, poor Aleric." There was no mercy in Adrien's voice.

One morning I awoke to find that *Gordo* was *Gorda.* No papa appeared, but eight *bambinos* squirming on the pillow. I had to kill them or they'd over-run my cell. I filled my little sink with water. One by one, starting with *Gorda,* I drowned them all. *Gorda* fought and bit me. I was still able to kill her.

"I've got some dead rats here! Come and get them out!" I shouted, but the guards just laughed.

"Dead rats, live rat. You're all the same," Peko, probably the meanest guard, said.

I kicked the furry corpses into a corner. In a couple of days, the cell really stunk. Peko said, "What smells so bad?"

I said, "Those rats you wouldn't take out of here!"

They assigned Hermin, the smallest guard, to clean up the mess.

"You killed these all by yourself? How?" Hermin asked.

I told him just like I told you. "There'll be more," he said. He was right.

Day in and day out, my life was the same misery. I didn't even bother washing or brushing my teeth. My teeth rattled back and forth until they started dropping out, one my one.

Aleric touched his teeth.

They've returned! They're all here, everyone of them!

The dampness from the stone walls sank into my joints. I started to move slower. I felt like I was a hundred, though I was only in my forties. Gray hair started falling out of my head.

I was lying on my cot one day when I heard someone speaking. It was a different voice, someone I vaguely recognized. Then Antonio stood behind the cell bars.

A sob caught in his throat. Aleric held his head down for a long moment.

Antonio and I had parted ways when I left the mission. It was many years since he and I had seen each other. He was a grown man, with whiskers, but very handsome.

The guards let him in. He hugged me. "My big brother, what have you done?"

We both sat on the cot. "Let's not talk about me. I want to hear about you," I said.

He was tall, taller than I was. When I had left him, he was still quite short. His shoulders were very broad and strong. I felt embarrassed to be next to this picture of health while my life was slipping away.

"Where should I begin?' Antonio asked me, still needing his big brother's advice, although I was a failure of a man.

"How much time do you have, because I'm not going anywhere?" I laughed at my own joke, but Antonio just looked sad.

"I'm only here for a week. I will stay as long as you need me to today. Oh, Aleric," he said, and then began to cry.

Aleric's eyes welled up.

"When you left for the mountains, I cried every day for at least a month. I wrote you letters, but I had no idea where you were. I prayed really hard, harder than I ever did before, that you wouldn't get killed," Antonio put his hand on my shoulder when he spoke.

"It probably would have saved a lot of people grief," I answered him. "Let's not dwell on me. I want to hear about you. It looks like you've been very successful and happy."

"When I finished high school, Brother Jime helped me find a college in the States. There I got my bachelors, went on to get my masters, then a doctorate in physics."

"My brother, the scholar? Remember, we couldn't even read?" I was so proud of Antonio for making something out of his life. Here I was stuck in this cold, dark, prison with a bunch of rats, both the four legged, and two legged kind.

"I met a beautiful woman there. We fell in love and wanted to get married. Her family thought I only wanted to marry her because of my wish to become a U.S. citizen. I did want to go back to San Xavier, but it was getting more and more dangerous."

"You could have lived in the palace with me," I said.

Now I wonder why I had never tried to contact him. I suppose my ego was too big for another Regallito.

"By then, I was long gone. America had become...is now my country." Antonio looked a little ashamed at his words. Who could blame him for wanting to leave his motherland filled with violence and terror?

In all my years of hunting, fighting, crawling to kill Gutierrez, then taking over the country, Antonio and my past life barely entered into my consciousness. What a monster I had become, abandoning my little brother with no thoughts or cares.

"I don't have to keep going on," Antonio said.

"Please, please. I want to hear it all. Your wife, your children - I want to know all of it," I told him, starving for anything besides these four, cold walls.

"On our wedding day, I remember watching Bertha, that's Jeanne's mother, shake her head as Jeanne walked down the aisle. Bertha told me she didn't think it'd work out. Today, she's like a mother to me. Both of Jeanne's parents are wonderful. I feel so happy to have parents now."

It was to avenge my parents' death that led me down this path. Would they be proud of me? Antonio chose the better path. I thought I was fighting for a cause, but vengeance was my leader.

Antonio reached into his back pants pocket and pulled out his wallet.

"Do you want to see the kids?"

"Sure, sure,' I said. The image of the cross in the back mission flashed into my head at that moment: Lupita and my child given away to death.

They were wonderful, healthy children. When I got to the last picture, I stopped cold. She looked like a miniature Verdad with black hair, blue eyes, and clear white skin. She was probably only five or six because several teeth were missing from her grin.

"What is her name?" I asked.

"Veronica," he answered. Was she to haunt me even in death or was it because I thought of her night and day that any resemblance became Verdad? I began to cry again. Antonio joined me. We were making a lot of noise when the guards rushed over.

"What's going on?" they demanded.

"I have not seen my brother in many years, and now he's married and has four beautiful children. Come look." I was like a proud father. The guards took the pictures.

"Ah, reminds me of my grandchildren," Hermin said. He handed back the photos.

We sat quiet for a long time before Antonio spoke again.

"I never told anyone in the United States that I was related to you. I just recently told Jeanne. It took some convincing. She wouldn't believe me at first. It was Jeanne who told me to visit you."

Antonio couldn't look me in the eye. "I didn't want anything to do with you," shame tainted his words.

"Who could blame you?" I said. "I wasn't really much of a brother deserting you. I was too busy with my own life to even give you a thought. Sure, once in a while I wondered where you were, but it only lasted for a moment."

"At the university your name came up frequently," Antonio said. "I told none of the other professors of my connection with you. Once, someone made a joke about me having the same last name as you. I told them it was a popular name in San Xavier. What would they say? What would they do if they found out I was the brother of the infamous Aleric Regallito?"

"Probably kick you out of the school," I joked.

I rubbed his head, much like I used to when we were kids. He hated it then, but didn't seem to mind it at that moment. We started to cry again. I cried for my parents, my old life...my lost life.

"I got special permission to have food brought in from Manuela's." Antonio said. "I had to pull some strings, but you're not getting prison food today."

Manuela was my favorite restaurant in the square. I had often had them bring food into the palace. The palace cook was always insulted when I did this. "Isn't my food good enough?" he would complain.

As if by just speaking about it, the food appeared. The wonderful fragrance of Manuela's crept in carefully to my dank prison cell. It was unsure of itself, but then came in strong. The guards carried in several bags and boxes of food.

"Why don't you help yourselves?' Antonio offered to the guards. I didn't want to share any of this food, but here was Antonio giving it to these men I hated. Before we knew it, there was a little party in my cell.

"I've often wanted to eat at Manuela's, but couldn't afford it,' said Rafael, the youngest guard. "This is better than my wife's cooking."

"Anything's better than your wife's cooking," Peko said. The other guards began to laugh.

Antonio stayed until evening. He looked at his watch, "I better go. It's already nine o'clock. I've been here for twelve hours."

I wanted him to stay longer, but there was no way I could ask him. He had already spent too much time in the dark hole of my existence, but he returned every day until the week was up.

"I leave tomorrow," he said very solemnly. "The time has slipped away."

45

"Our lives have gone by so very fast," I answered. "It just seemed like yesterday we were living with *Tía*.

"Yes, I even remember that, though I was so small. I sat on her lap, watching her cry."

"Was she crying?"

"Sobbing. My body jostled every time she'd weep. I almost fell off her lap."

The last day of Antonio's visit was very quiet. We had either talked ourselves out or were just too sad to say anything more.

Our good-bye was very tearful. When I hugged Antonio, it felt as if it would be the last time I would see him here on earth.

"Will you come again?" I pleaded. "Bring your family." I couldn't imagine little children coming down to this terrible dungeon, but I was hopeful.

Antonio didn't sound too sure about that idea. "Maybe," Antonio smiled. "We will see what we can do. Let's make sure we write to each other."

One more hug, then Antonio turned away. The guard let him out. I watched as he once again faded away from my life.

CHAPTER 9

We were all crying, except for Adrien. He sat passively, like a child not privy to the adult conversation around him.

"Have you no feelings?" I asked him.

"He's a fiend, a murderer. He's just trying to get us to feel sorry for him. He got what he deserved."

"No, I didn't get what I deserved. I should have gotten worse punishment for all the evil I committed, but for some reason, God had mercy on me."

"Oh, God. Yeah, I forgot about that." Sarcasm dripped from Adrien's voice.

"Finish your story!" The giant's voice boomed above us.

Antonio and I corresponded for many years. Those letters kept me alive. Once a week, they appeared like some miracle. No matter how many I got, each one was a brand new surprise. Antonio wrote better than any author could, bringing to me the lives of his family. I felt like I knew them personally.

Michael was the eldest, followed by Joseph, Maria and Veronica, my little Verdad. They all played musical instruments, something only the rich did, or so I thought. Veronica played the violin. My parents were going to have me play the violin, but that all changed with Gutierrez.

The guards let me hang their photos on the cold, cell walls. Soon the walls were covered. I would stare for hours at the images. Once, a cockroach crawled over Veronica's face. I swept it onto the floor stomping with my boot.

I longed to meet them all, hear them perform, and tell me their life stories, but I had made my choice. There would be no children's voices, only the hollow sound of the bars clanking back and forth with the entrance of a new inmate.

Then the letters stopped. Each morning, I waited but...nothing. I tried to remember what I had written in my last letter. Had I offended my beloved brother? Had the other professors found out about him? Had he lost his job? After a year or so, a letter arrived. The handwriting was different, more feminine than my brother's. It was from Jeanne, his wife. I still have the letter.

Aleric pulled tattered parchment from his pants. He tenderly unfolded it.

Dear Aleric, I am writing to let you know of the passing of your brother, Antonio. Aleric let out a sob.

"Sorry, this is so hard to read."

47

"Take your time," the giant said gently.

He had cancer and fought it for years," Jeanne wrote. When he visited you, he was in remission.

"Her Spanish was remarkable," Aleric said to us.

Aleric jammed the letter back into his khakis before he finished reading it. He looked back at us.

"She wrote about his treatment, how he struggled, and how he died. She then wrote how difficult it was for her and the children to live without him."

I let out a sob. I couldn't hold back the tears. Everyone looked at me. All I could think of was this mother with four small children, alone, without her husband. When Mom died, I had felt like an orphan. She was eighty-seven and I fifty-two. I cried the entire funeral. No one could console me. Looking back, I feel rather foolish and selfish. My other siblings suffered, too. Because they all had spouses, I assumed they could deal with Mom's death better than I could. Yet, I let them baby me. I soaked up their sympathies.

"Poor Catharine. Now who does she have?" People wondered. Others were cruel. "Now Catharine can get on with her life instead of taking care of her elderly mother." But that was never the case. Mom was generally independent until the very end. She only lasted in the nursing home for six weeks. It was me who Mom took care of, her youngest, most dependent daughter.

"Is there more?" the giant asked Aleric.

"I have only one more tale to add." He was quiet for a long time. He stared at each one of us.

There were no more letters after that. For over twenty years, my life became only the four cell walls again. No more joy, just rats in which I killed. In the morning, I'd awake, eat, take a nap, wake for lunch, sleep some more, eat supper, then go to bed. Day after day, that was my routine. Each morning I awoke, I wanted to die.

Then one day there was a lump, a small one, on the calf of my leg. At first I didn't pay too much attention to it, but it was growing. I thought maybe some vermin had bitten me, but it never left, just grew.

"Hey," I shouted one day. "Someone come and look at my leg!"

Of course, no one paid any attention to me. I was a prisoner. Who would care about my leg?

I ignored it, but then I started limping. "Look at the gimp," Peko shouted, while the others laughed.

One day there was a huge commotion outside the cell. It travelled through the tunnels until I beheld the figure of Bishop Pandeles. He ordered the guards to open my cell.

"*Presidente* Regallito, it is so good to see you!"

He spoke as if he were meeting me on the street, at the café or some shop. He hugged me tightly, as if we were good friends.

"Look at you! How long has it been? Too long!"

Age had not escaped the Bishop. Only a gray cap of hair encircled his scalp, and his plump body had grown even more rotund. His shoulders stooped.

"I've been living back in the States, but am here for a conference. Even though the current leader is still a dictator, he lets us worship freely." He grinned.

"Yeah, yeah. Why are you here?" I asked him.

"To see you, of course."

"To torment me, of course." I did not want to see a reminder of my past, especially this man who mocked my authority.

He looked like he had planned to stay, so I offered him the single, shabby chair. I limped over to my cot.

"You're limping." He sounded concerned.

"Yeah, yeah. Why do you care?"

He walked over to me and pulled up the pant leg. "That's quite a lump you have there. You got to get that taken care of," he said. "Guards, guards, come here please!"

The guards appeared, faster than any time I had summoned them.

"This man needs to see a doctor," he told the guards.

The guards began to laugh.

"'He's a criminal. He should be dead by now, but he's still here, taking up space, wasting good money," Grigio said.

"Isn't that a name of a wine?" Adrien piped up.

"I dunno. It was just the name of one of the guards." Aleric scratched his head. "Come to think of it, he did say his mama was a wino."

The giant once again turned derisively toward Adrian. "Please, can we get on with the story?"

The bishop said he would make sure I saw a doctor before he left. Sure enough, Doctor Ramirez reluctantly entered my cell while begging the guards to stick around. He was afraid of the evil dictator who had killed hundreds of thousands of men, women, and children. Me, who was getting so weak and tired.

He did all those things a doctor does. Then he looked at my leg.

"You need to get to the hospital to get that examined and taken care of."

Fear filled me. I don't know why. Every day, I wanted to die, but at that moment, the thought of death terrified me. I really wasn't ready to die.

An ambulance came to get me. I was chained down to a stretcher. As I left the prison, cameras flashed everywhere. People chanted and carried signs all along the street. In the hospital, guards stood at my door. Most of the patients had no idea who was in the room next to them, except for one.

Isabella Barrientos was in room 347.

Aleric paused. He stared, but not at us. Only he could see the invisible image.

One night, she entered my room while I was sleeping. I awoke to see her standing above me with a dagger held high above her head, ready to plunge it into me.

"President Regallito! You have no idea how long I've waited. I thought you were dead, but heard you were going into the hospital the same day I was, so I came prepared. This should have been done a long time ago. Why they let you live, I don't understand."

She lowered the dagger. My heart pounded.

"Do you remember the night when you killed my poor mama and baby brother?" She lifted her dagger higher. "You and your troops raided our tiny village, and then killed as many people as you could. We were all innocent, but you had to kill. There was no one left to care for me when they died. I did the only job a girl could do to make money to survive. You bastard!" she shouted.

Suddenly the guards ran in, grabbed her, and dragged her toward the door.

"Wait!" I cried out. The guards stood still, as if frozen in ice. "I beg you, please, forgive me for the evil I've done to you and your family," I pleaded. I so wanted her forgiveness. She stared hard at me for what seemed like an hour.

"Never!" The guards pulled her away.

In my sleep, all my dreams were of that terrible night. Fire everywhere, and from the flames arose the dead, pointing their daggers at me.

When I awoke the next morning, Doctor Ramirez stood grimly over my bed.

"Aleric," he said. I knew what he was going to say. "Your body is filled with cancer. There is nothing we can do. I'm going to discharge you today back to the prison. I will prescribe pain medicine. You can take as many as you need."

"What do you mean, 'Take as many as you need?'"

He shrugged. I understood. He was giving me permission to kill myself.

"How long do I have?"

"Not very long," he said. "Maybe a month, but probably less. I'm sorry."

He had done his job. He could leave.

There it was, my death sentence, given to me not by an executioner, but by a doctor.

Before the door swished shut, someone else entered, an old man shaking with palsy. "Aleric?" His voice shook along with his body. In an instant, I knew the trembling old man was Brother Jime.

"Brother Jime?" I said, and then began crying like a baby. He was crying too. After what seemed like forever, he spoke.

"Father Jime," he gently corrected me. "I was ordained shortly after you left."

Suddenly I felt ashamed, so ashamed. I turned away from him, like a child, thinking that perhaps if I didn't see him, he couldn't see me.

"Antonio died," I said.

"Yes, I know. I presided at his funeral."

We both began to cry. It was like when Antonio visited me.

"I guess I'm not much comfort, am I?" he asked.

"I am a terrible, terrible man," I said. "Where did I go wrong?"

"I asked that question many times myself," Father Jime said. "I saw so much potential for greatness. I feel like I had failed you."

"No, no. It was no one's fault but my own. I was rotten to the core."

"That, I will never believe. Have you had the last sacraments?" he asked cautiously.

"I haven't had any since I left the mission. I'm afraid you're too late."

"Never too late." Father Jime went out of the room and returned with a black box. When he finished, he hugged me good-bye.

When I returned to my cell, I was ready to die. I didn't expect God to forgive me, but Father Jime gave me hope. I left the painkillers on the ground, next to my cot. I didn't take any. I had caused so much suffering in this world that the little suffering I had would be nothing, or so I thought.

Never in all my life did pain wrack my body as it did for those weeks.

"Take the pain killers!" Pico demanded. "We can't stand the moaning." I refused.

Then, about three weeks later, I knew it was time for me to leave this earth. I asked Grigio what day it was. He said Friday.

"I'm leaving this earth today. I can feel it," the words forced themselves out of my lips.

"You should have left a long time ago," he scorned.

"I know," I whispered the words because to speak aloud would have been too painful. I lay there, panting like a dog. Nothing. For some reason, I had expected the Angel of Death to appear. He did not, yet my breathing changed. I felt pressure on my chest. My breaths were short and shallow. The guards must have noticed a change because they gathered around my cell door, watching, waiting. Hermin crossed himself.

"Can I go in there and bless him?" he asked.

"Him?" Grigio laughed. "We know where he's going already!"

All the guards laughed, except for Hermin.

"Then, I must go in there now!" I heard the urgency in Hermin's voice. Grigio reluctantly opened the cell door. Hermin looked me in the eye and marked a cross on my forehead.

"Thank you," I mouthed. I fell asleep. When I awoke, I was here.

CHAPTER 10

His death made all the major newspapers. Front page. Ironically, a little known nun in Yugoslavia died that same day. She founded twelve hospitals in her country and another twenty-five throughout the world. You could find very little news coverage of her death. Strange how humans are so attracted to evil, but repelled by goodness.

"Do you want to see what happened next?" the giant asked.

"I don't understand," Aleric replied.

The giant waved his massive arm into the air. Images materialized on some invisible television screen. Bars surrounded the dead Aleric. An old guard shrouded Aleric's face with the blanket. From the prison to a church, we viewed an elderly priest, his body shaking, at an altar. A large casket stood in the aisle, draped with a white cloth. Four solemn, but not sad, people stood while camera operators walked up and down the church aisles.

"Those are your nieces and nephews," the giant said. "They had your body flown to the States. They didn't want looters destroying the gravesite. Your body lies next to those of your brother, Antonio and his wife."

I remembered it. Human rights groups here in the States protested the stateside burial of Dictator Regallito. All dignitaries, the House and Senate, even the President, abstained from attending to avoid any association with this man. It would have remained a nonevent in the history books, except for one curious news reporter and his cameramen. Manuel Mendez, an exiled journalist from San Xavier, had some unfinished business to wrap up. The story hit the airwaves only a few short hours after the funeral, and it went viral on the Internet. Months later, Manuel Mendez published his first and only book, The Failed Dictator. Mendez died shortly after the book reached number one on The New York Times bestseller list. He was eighty-nine.

The image faded. We all sat in silence, pondering what our funerals were like.

Had anyone shown up at mine, I wondered? Did they serve fried chicken like I requested? Were my favorite songs played at the church?

"You were dead," the giant interrupted my thoughts. "What does it matter if they served fried chicken?"

I blushed. Center of my own universe, I could distort anyone's tragedy and make it my own. Empathy was lost on me, replaced more often with fear and dread of contracting the other person's malady.

"I have breast cancer," Claire said. She took a sip of her coffee as casually as if she had

just said, *"I like the color red."*

My heart pounded in my chest. Breast cancer. It runs in families. I should get checked. I wanted to check myself right at that moment for lumps, but couldn't because we were in a restaurant. Maybe I could sneak off to the bathroom.

"Hey, are you listening?" She interrupted my thoughts.

"Oh, yeah. So, how long do you have to live?" Dumb question!

"I'm not dying," Claire said in her matter-of-fact voice. "The doctor said we caught it early. The treatment is Hell, but I have a very good prognosis."

In fact, Claire, my mother's eldest daughter, is still alive at ninety-three. She probably arranged my funeral.

"It's time to eat again." Food appeared to be the giant's favorite pastime. The table was different, but still beautiful. Carts of fried chicken, eggs rolls, and various stir-fries, the staples of my life on earth, rolled in.

"Strange menu," Adrien said.

"Catharine picked it out. Not necessarily my choice, but very good, indeed," the giant said, as he lifted a chicken thigh to his lips.

House of Nanking. These eggrolls were from there; I was sure of it. Kearny Street, San Francisco. Discovered House of Nanking on my return trip from Asia. Weeks of Asian food only whetted my appetite for more. The cuisine exceeded any found in China.

"Catharine, do you think House of Nanking delivered our lunch today?" The giant guffawed so hard he began to cough, a loud, phlegmy cough.

Could he read the others' minds?

"No, Catharine. Only yours," he replied to my thoughts. "I was assigned to your case. These three other people are only here for your judgment."

We settled back into our seats. The table of food disappeared. I grabbed the feather quill. Who would be next?

"Ursula, it's your turn," the giant said.

"I, I'm not sure I'm re...ready," she quivered.

"You will be. Stand there." The giant pointed to the spot where Aleric stood. Ursula timidly stood up and began her story.

Since being all-together, I had not taken the time to study Ursula. There she stood, petite and very fragile. Her blond, pageboy hair gently swooped over her left eyebrow. When she talked, her large brown eyes reminded me of my sad Labrador, Abby. Chunky jewelry swirled around Ursula's short neck. I always noticed necks because mine was so long. Schoolboys had dubbed me Ostrich, and the name stuck.

"Ostrich, good luck! Be good to the world," Danny wrote on page seventy-three of my high school yearbook.

"Ostrich, get out there and do something great!" Samantha, page twenty-two.

Ostrich, this, Ostrich that. Even my teachers took to calling me that long-necked bird's name. Mr. Philomeno, our Shakespeare teacher, once stopped me after class.

"Why do they call you 'Ostrich'? Doesn't that bother you?" He pushed up his sliding, broken spectacles. His hair was always greasy. Mr. Philomeno was the oldest person I knew with acne.

I pulled down the neck of my sweater. "Ah," he responded. "Don't sweat it. There are worse things than long necks."

Turtle necks were a major part of my wardrobe. Spring and summer were killers. I had to find ways to disguise my neck without over-heating myself.

When I enrolled in a community college adult ballet class, Madame French-- that was what she called herself--gushed about my long neck.

"You're a swan, a beautiful swan! Too bad you can't dance like one, but don't hide your beautiful neck anymore, okay?"

"Okay, are you ready?" The giant bore holes through me.

"I'm just trying to depict Ursula's appearance," I defended myself.

"Her appearance or your long neck?"

I was feeling a little defiant. "My writing teachers said you need to describe your characters."

"Much good it did you," the giant growled. "Now, pay attention!"

URSULA'S STORY

M...my name is Ursula Bennett. Actually, I...I was born Ursula Rose Wojciechowski."

"That's a mouthful," Adrien said.

Ursula laughed.

"When I...I met my husband, I was very happy to take on Bennett," she said, but a frown of sadness deteriorated her beautiful looks. "I, I guess I'm getting ahead of myself," she shrugged.

"I...I grew up thinking my parents were too strict. Looking back, I... I think perhaps they were not strict enough. But at the time, I just wanted to get out. B... be... my own person. N... not... have to listen to anyone. I...it didn't work out that way."

"For Pete sake! Spanish boy over there with his rolling "r's" and leetle and preeson, and now we have a stutterer. Doesn't anyone know how to speak without crucifying the language?" Adrien spouted.

"What vernacular would you prefer, Mr. Inveres? Latin, Greek? Hebrew? Arabic?"

Suddenly words none of us understood, flowed from the giant's mouth.

"Did you understand, Mr. Inveres?" The giant motioned for Ursula to continue.

M... my friend Brooke called me one night. W... we were going to hang out at Ron's Bar. I...I was only seventeen. Mom let me walk over to Brooke's. Sh... she had no idea what, what w... we were, were up to.

That night is still so vivid in my memory. I remember walking past Old Lady Bergman's house on the corner. She rocked back and forth on her little wooden rocking chair hissing and moaning like a captive cat.

"Mrs. Bergman is crazy, crazy, crazy," the neighbor kids would often chant. Sometimes they'd run up onto her porch and spit on her. Sh...she'd say nothing.

That night was different. Th... there were no hissing sounds. It was the first time I heard her voice.

"You're up to no good," she said to me as I passed. "Beware. Tonight will be your downfall. Go back to your home where you belong."

I stopped. I had passed her house hundreds of times without looking, but that night I did. Sitting in the rocker was a beautiful old woman. Her blue eyes penetrated the darkness of the night. I expected a face with a river of wrinkles, but found instead a baby-smooth complexion. Her cheekbones were still high in her face, and she had wide, thick red lips. We stared at each other for a long time. I finally looked away.

"Ursula," she knew my name. How did she know my name? I turned toward her. "Ursula, if you go tonight, you will regret it for the rest of your life," she warned.

What horrible fate awaited me? Would someone shoot me dead? Would I get raped and murdered? I tried to act tough.

"My mom said never to listen to fortune tellers."

"I'm not a fortune teller. I've been having dreams. I didn't even know your name, but the dreams told me. Listen, don't go to Ron's."

"Okay! Dreams? Really? Tell me giant boy, could this be real?" Adrien was still eating an eggroll from lunch.

"You're not hear to discern the validity of her story. Ursula, you may continue."

Goose pimples covered my body as I skipped across the street to Ron's. When I entered, Brooke stared. "You look like you just saw a ghost," she said.

"Old Lady Bergman knew my name and warned me about coming here tonight," I told her.

"Really? That's so cool," Brooke said as she gulped her beer. "Let's go over there and see if she can read my future."

"She's not a fortune teller."

"Oh, poop," Brooke said. "Let's get some refreshment."

Seven beers later, I first noticed him - Ty Bennett. He stared boldly and smiled. My heart pounded.

"Hey, cutie. I was wondering how long it would take before you'd noticed me. Are you even old enough to be here?"

"Yeah," I lied. I... I pulled out my fake I.D. My brother Phillip had made it for me. Actually, he made all the fake I.D.'s in the neighborhood. He said it was his one talent. My parents were ignorant of his illegal operations. To this day I wonder why they never questioned him about all the visitors to his bedroom."

Brooke. That name spelled disaster in my dictionary. Brooke persuaded me to go to the liquor store before our high school dance. There was a robbery taking place when we entered. Brooke convinced me to sit in the back seat with Leroy. I thought he was just a bookworm, but he was a different kind of worm. Leroy ended up with a black eye. Brooke tried to get me to steal gum at the drug store. I put my foot down then. I could buy liquor, sit with sleazy guys, but I wouldn't steal. I vowed I'd never name my child Brooke.

"What's your baby's name," I remember asking Carrie.

"Aunt Catharine, you know what I was going to name her, Brooke!"

"Humph," I said.

Carrie laughed at her old aunt. "It's a beautiful name. Look at her."

"Baby Brooke redeemed the name Brooke. Baby Brooke, that is what I always called her, told me I was her favorite aunt, even though I had the most wrinkles and the least amount of hair.

"That's because I'm your great aunt," I corrected her.

"I know you're great," Baby Brooke said. "I tell everyone about my Great Aunt Catharine."

How could I not love the name Brooke?

"Catharine Zimmer!" My thoughts were once again blasted away by the giant's voice. "You are here to listen to Ursula's story, not daydream about your own."

"I know, but I had a friend named Brooke, too."

"Yes, I know. She was also a troublemaker, wasn't she? Able to get you to do things you wouldn't have thought of, like going to a liquor store when you were seventeen, right?"

"Miss Prim and Proper at a liquor store when she was underage?" Adrien piped in.

"How do you know I was prim and proper? I could have led a life of ill repute!"

The giant roared with laughter. It was infectious. We all began to laugh. We needed to laugh. Aleric's tale had left a mist of melancholy in the air, and we sensed foreboding in Ursula's voice.

Why must I listen and record these tragedies? How were they a part of my uncomplicated life?

Ty wanted to go out to his car to talk, he said. No way, I told him. I...I hardly knew him. Old Lady Bergman's warning seemed to echo in my mind. Was this the person who would seal my fate? Brooke didn't like Ty from the minute she laid eyes on him.

That was probably the only insightful thing she told me, but I didn't listen. I gave Ty my phone number.

He started calling.

"Where did you meet this guy?" Mom would ask over and over.

I gave her a vague answer, "I don't really remember."

"What do you mean? I know exactly the coordinates on the world map of where I met your father. The U. S. Post Office, 310 Oxford Street, Edison, Nebraska. I was mailing the invitations for Susie's baby shower. There he was, yelling at the post master."

Then my parents would get into their silly arguments. Dad said he wasn't yelling while Mom would say he was.

A smile of fond memories spread across Ursula's somber countenance, but the suffering soon returned.

We'd spend hours on the phone. Dad put a stop to that after the third time.

"You're never going to graduate if this Ty guy keeps calling. When are we going to meet him, anyway?"

Phillip hated Ty.

"You gotta stay away from that sleaze." Phillip couldn't bring himself to say Ty's name. "He is nothing but trouble. No one likes him. He's a liar, cheat, and he's very lazy. He won't even get a job!"

"How can he? The economy is so bad," I defended. In my heart, I knew Phillip w...was right. There was something I didn't trust about Ty, but he was so exciting, so thrilling, something I had never experienced in my dull life.

CHAPTER 11

I wasn't quite drunk from the vodka when he as...asked me. We were hanging out in the back of his '65 Chevy Nova. Then I understood why i...it, the back seat of his car, was so clean. No, I said. I want to wait until we're married. C'mon, he pressed. What if we don't get married?"

"Not get married?" I asked him. "I thought you wanted to marry me. Isn't that what this is all about?"

"You don't have to marry someone you sleep with," he said. "What era are you from? Everyone sleeps together with everyone else. That's no big deal these days."

It was so sho...shocking to my ears. Sure, he was probably right. The girls at school often tormented me because I was still a virgin at seventeen. I thought Ty was different. That's one thing I wanted to do differently than all the sluts at school.

"Listen." He was no longer Mr. Nice Guy. "I've been waiting for you for months. How long are you going to make me wait? Much longer and I'm going to find another girlfriend."

"Don't you love me?" I...I asked

"Sure, sure. But if you loved me, you'd really show me."

Phillip had warned me about guys like that. "Take me home, now!" I demanded. "Let's just call this off so you can go find someone else to sleep with," I said."

"Come on, Baby. Let's not get so drastic," he pleaded.

"You're the one getting drastic," I said. "Just take me home. I'm tired."

We drove home in silence.

"Don't call me anymore," I said as I got out of the car.

"Now, don't say that," he said. "I'll still call you. All good relationships have little disagreements."

"Little? Good-bye, Ty. I don't want to see you again. I have to focus on my schooling."

I slammed the door shut then turned toward my house without looking back. I ran into my bedroom and flung myself, like a typical teenager, onto my bed and cried.

Phillip heard me. He knocked on my door. "Hey, are you okay in there?"

"I just want to be left alone."

"That jerk didn't hurt you, did he?"

"No," I sighed heavily. "We broke up."

"Great!' He was happy. I...I was feel...feeling terrible.

Did I really do the right thing? Did I...I throw away the man of my life? Will I end up alone and lonely? Will my life be a tragedy? I fell asleep and woke up wearing the same clothes I had been wearing the night before. My mother was knocking at my door.

"Honey, wake up. There's someone here to see you." She didn't sound too enthusiastic.

The door flung open. Red roses camouflaged his face.

"Hey, Baby. I brought you a little something."

"Roses. I ne...never got flowers from anyone. Every year in October, our school celebrated Sweetest Day. Students paid for delivery of flowers to their girlfriends, boyfriends, or good friends. The vase on our dining room table had always looked so empty at that time of year. Phillip bought me flowers one year, but that wasn't the same.

"Why didn't you just order yourself some flowers and plop them in your vase?" Adrien again - so pratical. Ursula smiled.

"Every....everyone wo...would have known. It...it would have been very embarrassing."

"Who cares what others think?"

"That's easy for you to say, Mr. Hollywood. When you're a young teenage girl it's so different." I defended Ursula.

Every year my girlfriends carried my bounty home. Mom would scour the house for all the available vases, glass jars, and glasses.

"Catharine has a boyfriend, a boyfriend!" John would shout.

"Not just one, but the entire freshman class," Claire teased.

"All these flowers smell like a funeral parlor," John crinkled his nose.

"Miss Zimmer! How many times do I need to call you back to earth?" the giant exclaimed.

"We're not on earth," Adrien quipped.

"I'm using an idiom." The giant was losing his patience. "But then our author would know that, wouldn't she?"

Author. He called me author. Sunglasses, limousines, and long autograph sessions. Book stores would daily, even hourly, request my presence so I could meet my adoring fans. Photo shoots for my book covers and web site. The photographers would know the right angle to display my beauty in a way to make me look intelligent.

Adrien wouldn't have been the only one appearing on television as I would have bee-bopped all over the different networks discussing my profound works. Then the late-night shows - the host would ask me questions, and I would answer, displaying my great humor and wisdom. Mansions, several of them, would await my homecoming with flower packed, massive vases in the foyer greeting my entrance. My fame would attract suitors, but I'd huve to be careful they weren't gold diggers.

The giant stood up, carried a box over to me, and dropped it. He did this five times. "Keep dreaming!" He sat back down. "Ursula, continue."

I must admit, the flowers did the trick.

"Ty, you shouldn't have!" I took the roses and searched for that special vase. Strange, but when I placed them inside, they seemed wilted and not as beautiful as I had imagined them to be.

"Well, aren't you going to kiss me?" Ty asked, laughing.

My dad must have walked by. "What are you doing here?" Dad asked.

"Just trying to make up with your daughter."

"Make out with my daughter?" Dad asked in shock. "I think you need to go home."

"Dad, he said 'make up.' We had a fight last night, and he's trying to say he's sorry."

"What kind of fight?" Dad persisted.

"It's not important now," I stared at the roses. A pedal dropped.

We continued dating. There, there was always something about Ty that I didn't trust. It, it was just a feeling. Maybe it was his mother.

Ty's father had deserted the family when Ty was two. Left the Nova, that's it. Ty wouldn't recognize his father if he saw him on the street. Donna, his mother, could have left as well, since she preferred whiskey and Coke to spending time with her son.

"You're dating Ty Bennett?" An old elementary teacher asked while I was out shopping with Mom. "We used to dread parent–teacher conferences. Once, security escorted the screaming Donna out of the school. She didn't take advice for her son very well."

"That's confidential information," Mom told me later. "What kind of teacher tells all the dirty little secrets of their students? I wonder what she says about my kids?"

Ursula paused for a moment, sighed long and hard, and proceeded with what seemed like a tragic tale.

Once I made the mistake of calling Ty's mother, 'Mrs. Bennett.'

"Don't ever call me that." She always slurred her words. "I never married that bum."

"Mom, lighten up!" Ty said. "How would she know?"

"Just call her Donna," Ty said to me. "Everyone calls her Donna."

"Madonna is my full name," she interrupted. "Don't know why I got that name. Lost my virginity at twelve." She laughed hysterically.

She stumbled over to her throne. It was actually a beige recliner, depleted of most of its stuffing. Mom would have thrown it on the curb, but not Donna.

"Get off my damn chair!" she screamed when she discovered me leaning on it one day.

"Don't ever let me catch you near my chair again," she shoved her face into mine. I turned my face away from the stale whiskey breath.

"Mom, leave her alone," Ty came to my rescue, again. From then on, I waited in the Nova. I...I wasn't safe there either.

One day, Donna looked out the living room window and spied me waiting in the car. She staggered down the stoop and tapped on my window. I didn't want to open it.

"Open this damn window," she yelled.

I opened it an inch.

"Ain't my house good enough for you?" she snarled.

"No, that's not it. I just don't want to be a bother."

"Nah, you just don't want to be bothered by me! Well, I found you, didn't I? I'm bothering you."

A neighbor, who had stepped out onto his porch, watched the whole thing and shook his head.

"What are you looking at?" She asked me.

I pointed toward the neighbor. Her eyes followed my finger.

"That's the minister from the church down the street. He doesn't approve of my drinking, no drinking, as a matter of fact. Hey," she shouted toward him. "I'm drunk again! Are you going to pray for me?" She shrieked at her own joke.

"I pray every day for you, Donna. Have a nice day," he went back into his house.

Donna was once beautiful. She was gone one day so I waited in the house for Ty. The house was hot, so very hot. It was because Donna was stick thin, sickly thin, if you ask me. She was cold all the time, even in the summer. She had no use for air conditioning. I went for water and passed by her bedroom. She kept it very clean. There on her bureau was a photograph of a beautiful young woman.

"Is this your grandmother?" I asked, never thinking it could be Donna.

"Nope, it's my mother." He had such a sad voice. "That's before she met my dad and liquor."

Every night, Ty would go on cigarette runs for his mother. They were actually liquor runs, too. We came back once, and Ty pulled out two bottles of whiskey from his coat.

"You didn't buy those, did you?" I asked, shocked.

"Baby, did you see how expensive the cigarettes were? Really? They're overcharging on the smokes, and they expect me to pay for the liquor, too?"

"That's stealing," I said.

"Just call me Robin Hood. Baby, that guy owns a bunch of stores. He can afford to lose a few whiskey bottles here and there."

"To feed your mother's habit? You're willing to steal to help your mother stay drunk?"

I don't know why I stayed with Ty.

"I do," interrupted the giant.

Ursula looked down in shame. She knew, too.

Yes, we, we were sleeping together by now. Anytime we got into an argument, most of the time it ended up in bed. It's so odd. Though I didn't trust him, I felt like I needed to stay with him. Then my parents discovered my dirty little secret.

Mr. Ridgewood, my homeroom teacher, called one afternoon. He told Mom my grades were slipping. He asked her if she noticed any changes in me. He suggested looking for drug paraphernalia. So, after Mom hung up, she marched to my bedroom.

The only drug she found were my birth control pills. All Hell broke out when Dad got home from work.

"I guess if you're old enough to have sex, you're old enough to live on your own!"

Mom packed my suitcases. Phillip pushed to get them to relent.

"You're feeding her to the lions!" Phillip shouted.

"She doesn't follow our rules. And that's one of the most important ones. No sleeping together until you're married." Dad sternly said.

"What if she breaks up with the loser?" Phillip asked, his eyes pleading with me.

"Are you willing to break up with him and never see him again?" My mom was trying to find some way to keep me at home.

"No!" I was so defiant. My parents had given me everything, and this was the way I would pay them back. I grabbed my suitcases and called Ty to pick me up. I had failed to see that the road I was on was leading me to a cliff.

"I ain't having her live in this house," screamed Donna when I showed up. "If you 'n' her are shacking up, find your own place to screw. Not in my house!"

Lucky for us, or so I...I thought, Ty's friend, Sidney, had an apartment. Ty called him, and Sidney let us move in.

Sidney seemed great. He and I would play board games, watch television, and even walk his dog. I talked to Sidney more than I did with Ty. Unfortunately, Sidney wanted some compensation.

"Hey, Good Looking, when are you going to start paying rent?" He had waited until Ty was gone.

"I thought you and Ty had made a deal."

"Freeloader Ty? Right. I won't see anything from him." We were standing in the kitchen. He shoved himself right up to me. I turned away from his foul breath. "You can pay me back," he grinned.

I backed away. My heart started pounding.

"No!"

"Why not? You said yourself that I spend more time with you than Ty. Let's just complete the deal."

I stumbled over a kitchen chair. He yanked me up.

"Let's just say if you don't pay up, I'll call the cops and tell them you took my five hundred bucks. My word against yours. Whatta say?"

"You should have kicked him where it counted!" Adrien piped into the story.

We all glared at Adrien.

"Perhaps, Mr. Inveres, your life's vocation should have been a news commentator," the giant hissed. "Ursula, please, continue."

I pulled myself away from him and started running toward the door. Just then, Ty showed up. I was so relieved.

"What's going on here?" Ty said.

"Your girlfriend here just took my five hundred dollars."

"You don't have no five hundred bucks! Besides, she wouldn't take a penny. Baby, tell me what's really going on here."

"You tell him, and you're outta here."

We packed our suitcases and left.

It's your word against mine. Those words were the same ones I heard when I opened my house up to Adella, a woman from work. She and her husband were divorcing. She had no other relatives, so I offered to let her stay in my guest room.

At first, I didn't notice the missing items, such as my earrings, some loose change, or gift certificates. I assumed they were just misplaced.

Then her personality began grating on me. The bathroom counters were always wet and grimy. The kitchen sinks never emptied of dirty dishes. My living room, once a spotless haven from work, became a receptacle for her shoes, briefcase, candy wrappers, banana peels, poker chips, and old gum wrappers.

"Do you mind cleaning up after yourself?" I asked her one day.

"Touchy, touchy," she responded. The mess remained.

"If you're going to live here, rent free, I expect a little help around here," I said, ignoring her rude comment.

"Just throw me out into the cold?" she whined.

"Right now, yeah. Clean up your mess."

She shaped up, but not for long. Her downfall was her greed. I cashed my check one Friday night and had the money in my bedroom. I was planning a weekend get-a-way with my sisters. When I checked my purse for my keys, the bank envelope was missing.

"Adella, did you see a little bank envelope?" I asked her. I knew she'd lie, but I wanted to give her a chance.

"No. I didn't see your money," she said very calmly. She must have been a good poker player.

"How did you know there was money in there?"

"What would be in a bank envelope, an elephant?"

"You took it, didn't you?"

"How dare you accuse me?"

"Adella, I think you need to leave. Pack your bags and get out of here. Or, I will call the police."

"It's your word against mine."

"True, but I can have them arrest you for trespassing."

The news traveled fast at the store. Shortly after, Adella went to prison for embezzling twenty thousand dollars, along with stealing about three thousand dollars worth of merchandise.

One day, her ex-husband showed up in my office.

"I'd like to repay you."

"That's not necessary. Really..." I felt embarrassed for this man.

"Adella had a gambling addiction. She wouldn't get help. It was killing our marriage. I still love her."

I couldn't understand how anyone could love Adella.

"I visit her in prison when I can. I'd feel better if I could pay you back."

"How about if you give the money to a worthwhile charity? Maybe a group that helps gamblers. Wouldn't that be a good idea?" I said, feeling smug with wisdom.

"Miss Zimmer!" the giant's voice bellowed. "How does your little tale have anything to do with Ursula's?"

"Tell us, Miss Zimmer," Adrien smiled. "What's going on in that red-headed skull of yours?"

"I, uh, I let a woman stay at my house once."

"Did you ask her for sex?" Adrien laughed so hard at his own joke. My heavenly countenance reddened. "Then you threatened her? This is great. I can't wait to hear your story."

"I will have to throw you two out of here if you don't pay attention."

"Hey, I've been to Hell and back. What could be worse?" Adrien quipped.

"The next time you won't be coming back." The giant frowned. "Let's take a little break and we'll return to her story. Who would like a tour of the library?"

CHAPTER 12

It would have taken centuries for us to complete the library tour, so we returned to our seats.

"Please continue your story, Ursula," the giant said. He turned toward me. "Pick up your pen and write!"

Ursula smiled, but it was pained.

Eighteen and living the life of a homeless person with the man I supposedly loved was not what I had envisioned so long ago. Dreams of a princess wedding complete with a golden gown, six bridesmaids, and a horse drawn carriage from the church to the hall seemed so silly. A perpetual growling stomach and incessant fear of sleeping under the stars wiped away all my childhood delusions.

One day, I was alone, resting on a cot. I did that a lot. I didn't have too much energy to spare. Then, the most beautiful vision appeared - Phillip!

"How did you find me?"

"There are only two homeless shelters in town." He handed me three envelopes. "I thought you should see these," he said.

The first was an official letter telling me I had basically dropped out of high school and missed graduation. My scholarships had been rescinded.

"Can't you see you're ruining your life?" He sat at the foot of my cot.

He was right. I hadn't had a hair cut in months. My clothes were getting worn and dirty. The times between washings w...were long. Sometimes I brushed my teeth, most of the time I didn't. At home, I had always brushed my teeth at...at least three times a day and flossed them. I was a model for Dr. Greely, our dentist.

"Come home with us today. Mom and Dad said it would be okay."

"Really?" I didn't believe him. I wanted to. I so wanted to escape, but I felt trapped somehow.

"Yes. They're in the car waiting. They were afraid they'd scare you into not coming home."

I didn't believe him. I hesitated for a long time. Phillip eyed the clock on the wall.

"Come on. Don't take all day or Ty might show up!"

"Okay, I'll go." I grabbed what little items I had, said good-bye to Nanny, one of the helpers, and left. I blinked as I walked into the sunshine. Mom and Dad were standing outside of the car. Tears streamed down Mom's face. Dad's face was just a series of sadness. Mom hugged me, then Dad. It was a long hug.

Ursula wiped her eyes.

It all seemed so surreal, my family rescuing me from some evil villain. Dad pushed on the gas pedal and we squealed away.

Dad drove for some time without speaking.

"I'm glad you're coming home," he finally spoke up. "We should have come sooner. I'm sorry for anything I've done or said that made you leave."

My father apologizing? My head hung very low.

"I'm the one that should be apologizing. I'm sorry, so sorry."

The drive home was all tears. I wondered how I would get my life back before Ty.

Dad pulled into the driveway. Our two story, gray asphalt sided house appeared as a beacon, a lighthouse to my darkened life. Inside, Mom's china cabinet gleamed in the sun. Chocolate chip cookies, where were they? I could smell them.

"I don't deserve this," I said.

"We love you," Dad said. That was the first time in my eighteen years that Dad had ever said he loved me. He hugged me again. He had never hugged me before, but on that day, he hugged me twice.

I took a long shower - the first shower in months. Then I brushed my teeth over and over again. Phillip knocked on the bathroom door.

"Hey, are you going to stay in there all day? I'm hungry!"

My clothes hung on me. I lost ten pounds while I was gone. Mom complained I was too thin to begin with. I looked in the mirror to see a blond skeleton stare back. I forced a smile and was relieved to see my teeth still white and straight.

It was a warm, early summer day, but Mom still cooked my favorite - pea soup.

"Pea soup?" Dad complained. "It's eighty-two degrees outside."

"It's Ursula's favorite." Mom gave Dad 'The stare.'

How, how could I have overlooked all their love? How could I have shunned them? I began to understand what the phrase, "scales fell from my eyes," meant as I looked at each of them with a new vision: Dad, Mom, Phillip. They really loved me for me. There were no expectations, no delivering of the goods back to them to prove my love. It was too much for me to bear.

Ursula's hands flew to her face as she sobbed. It was Aleric's turn to comfort her. Adrien continued basking in his state of boredom.

After lunch, the doorbell rang. My family looked a little guilty. Mom looked out the living room window and then opened the front door to let in Mr. Casper, the principal from Case High School.

He was a great man. I always admired him. At that moment, I felt embarrassed to see him.

"Hi, Ursula!" He said it as if I was a celebrity. "I'm glad to see you back at home."

"Hi," I said shyly. "I know I totally messed up," I confessed.

"I'm not here to judge you," he said so quietly I wasn't sure he was speaking. "Just to tell you the story of a young man."

"Come, sit down in the living room," my mother said.

We all sat around Mr. Casper, waiting for his story.

When he finished he asked, "Do you want to know who that young man was?"

"Was it you?" I asked.

"See, I knew you were very bright. Yes, it was me."

I didn't say anything for a while. It was strange to hear that Mr. Casper once had a drug addiction. He didn't actually go back to college until he was in his thirties.

"Now, I don't want to push you, but I want you to know if you work really hard this summer I think you can graduate and get started onto college by the fall. Some of your old teachers are willing to help you."

His words overwhelmed me. I cried for a long time. I couldn't believe I had almost thrown away my life. I almost had a free ride at the college of my choice. Now I'd have to pay for school. Despite the overwhelming sense of disappointment in myself, an overwhelming sense of relief also filled me. No more Ty.

Brooke left to stay with an aunt in New York State. Fortunately, there were no distractions that summer. Ty vanished. I actually finished all my class work by the end of July and applied at the local college for nursing school.

Those years sped by. What I remember most are tests, tests, and more tests. I met some great friends, even dated, but not seriously.

This time I graduated with honors. The local hospital offered me a position right away in their emergency room. Thanks to my efforts, Phillip also married my friend and nursing buddy, Cecelia.

My condominium was close to the hospital. This way if they needed me, I could go in without too much time delay. Work was my life.

One Friday I was called in early. Twenty-car pile up on the Interstate. I heard about it on the news. When I got into the ER, it was pure chaos. People bumping into each other. Stretchers everywhere.

"Triage number three over here," Doctor Vadner shouted.

I pulled the curtains aside, and there, there he was, Ty Bennett. Scratches all over, but he didn't look too injured.

"Wow, look what the wind blew in. A breath of beautiful, fresh air," he said. "Wow, you're more beautiful than I remember. Come here, Baby, let me give you a kiss!"

He was drunk, not feeling too much pain. I found a scratch kit from the closet and started cleaning and checking his wounds. I said nothing.

"So, what do we have here?" Dr. Vadner came in.

"Just some minor cuts and abrasions, and probably a hangover tomorrow."

"Then I can send the cops in here? He's the cause of the pileup."

I felt sick for Ty. If anyone died in this crash, he would be going to prison, for sure.

Two officers appeared and shot out questions. "Did he get his blood drawn?" "Can we do a breathalyzer?" "When will the DA charge him?"

I left the room. "Where are you going?" Ty shouted.

Fortunately for Ty, there were only a few broken limbs among the injured. Most of them wanted to break Ty's limbs. The judge was too lenient everyone thought. Maybe if he had sent Ty away, he would have been out of my life forever.

CHAPTER 13

Some months later, a spruced-up Ty showed up at the hospital with red roses. He was still on probation, but out on good behavior. His hair was moussed up; he was clean-shaven, except for the goatee in the center of his chin. His denim shirt was opened to reveal a leather cord around his neck. A red carnation stuck out of his right pocket.

"Good description, Ursula." It was the giant's turn to interrupt. "Perhaps Catharine over there could learn from you."

I shifted in my seat, while Ursula smiled and continued.

"Hey, let's go out for lunch," he said. Ty's reappearance did nothing for my digestion, yet I knew if I refused, he would make a scene, so I agreed. I suggested the cafeteria because of my employee discount. Wrong suggestion - I paid for lunch. Ty's meal almost cost as much as my weekly grocery bill. Cecelia walked in.

"Who is Cecelia?" Adrien asked.

"My friend." Ursula answered and continued. "She married my brother, Phillip."

"Did you miss that part?" I gibed. "She was the matchmaker for her brother and Cecelia. It's here in my notes."

I looked down and my writing had disappeared.

"What's happening?" I asked the giant. "The pages are empty."

"Aren't they all empty?" The giant asked, pointing to the five boxes.

I recognized the cardboard. I had brought them home from work to store my writing. Inside, however, were sheets and sheets of blank paper.

"Where is it all? You had it earlier!"

"You will have to search for it, but not now. Ursula, I apologize for our rude guests. Please continue."

"That is okay. It helps me somehow."

Cecelia shook her head when she saw Ty sitting with me. I shrugged my shoulders. She headed toward Dr. Vadner and whispered in his ear. He headed toward our table.

"Is this your boyfriend?" he asked.

"No," I said quickly.

"We once were serious," Ty piped in.

"But not anymore." I liked Dr. Vadner, and I thought he liked me. "Hey, aren't you the dude who nearly killed off a bunch of people with your drunk driving? Shouldn't you be in prison?"

"No. The judge gave me community service."

"How did that happen? Did you pay him off?"

"Can we talk about something else?" Ty shifted in his seat.

"Sure, if you don't mind if I join you," Dr. Vadner said. I smiled.

Dr. Vadner, Thomas actually, and I did all the talking. Ty just ate. I don't think he even listened. He looked around, like a child, and generally showed no interest in our conversation.

"What's your favorite food?" Thomas asked. He hardly knew me, but wanted to know what I liked to eat!

"Pea soup," I told him.

"Ugh," Ty said.

"Pea soup is good," Thomas said. "Are you busy Friday night?"

"Yes, she is," Ty answered for me.

"No I'm not." There was no way I'd let Ty ruin this chance for me.

"Baby, you're going out with me"

"I'm not your baby! You and I called it quits a long time ago."

Thomas stood up. "I don't want to get between anything!"

"You're not!" I told him.

I quickly left my seat, returned the tray, and walked with Thomas to the elevator. "Bye, Ty. See you around!" I waved across the cafeteria.

"That was cold," Thomas said. "Do you treat all your boyfriends that way?"

My heart sank. I knew I had to tell him, but I was terrified of revisiting my past. Yet, if I didn't, there'd be no Thomas in my life. While we headed back to ER, I told him the abbreviated version of life with Ty.

"Sorry," he said when I finished. "I thought you were just being rude to him. I'll pick you up at seven Friday. Is that a deal?"

Thomas and I developed a great friendship. We went sailing, golfing, dancing, things I had always wanted to do, but had never done. He was everything Ty wasn't.

Sunsets on his boat were beautiful. We'd spend hours just talking about life. He always listened and asked all the right questions.

"Someday I'd like to take this rig around the world, just like Magellan. Actually, he never quite finished, did he? So, what are your dreams, young lady?"

He always called me young lady. It was so sweet.

"I think I'm living my dream now," I said.

"You mean you don't want to conquer the world, discover new things?"

I felt silly then because there was one dream I had, and had hoped he would be on board with me. "I want to have a bunch of children. Six at least." Did I scare him away, I wondered.

"Six kids! Wow! Who has that many these days?"

I was disappointed with his response, but I continued. "My parents wanted a large family, but when I arrived Mom just couldn't keep her babies. She had four miscarriages after me. She says she got her six, just not here on earth."

Thomas hugged me. "You have so much love to give. You'd be a great mother, no matter how many children you have." His answer confused me. I was hoping he'd say no matter how many children *we* would have. He didn't. After a while, I chalked it up to the insensitivity of men.

"I resent that!" the most insensitive person in our group spoke up. The giant turned toward him.

"Mr. Inveres, we're not here to pass judgment on the stories. Only listen. Judgment will come later."

Thomas Senior and Hattie Vadner loved me like their own daughter. I practically lived in their colonial mini mansion; that's what I called it. As long as we didn't discuss politics or religion, we were on safe terms.

"I'm a very progressive woman, you know," Hattie once confessed to me. "I caught it from my mother, who got it from her mother, and so on. We were way ahead of the suffragists. My grandmother got drunk the day the Pill came out. I haven't ever worn a bra."

"You never needed a bra!" Thomas Senior shouted. Because he couldn't hear, he shouted.

"Shut up, everyone will hear us." Hattie stuffed the olive from her martini into her husband's mouth. The country club members glanced toward us, wondering what the commotion was about.

Thomas had his own place, but I never stepped foot inside. Looking back, I understand. Thomas and I were a couple, but we *weren't* a couple. Strange rumors roamed through the hospital, but I was unwilling to listen to them.

"So, have you two had sex yet?" Hattie asked one afternoon.

My eyes bulged.

"You can be honest with me. Thomas Senior and I did it long before our wedding night. I'm very open-minded you know."

"He hasn't really kissed me," I felt like a Catholic in a confessional.

Hattie stood up, grim. "I was afraid of that." She sighed, long and hard. "I'm very open-minded. It shouldn't matter. It's his life."

Hattie babbled on like this for about ten minutes. She sat down next to me. "Honey, I think my son, my one and only son, is gay."

"No, no. That can't be." I wanted the floor to open and swallow me up. Then I thought maybe she was just trying to get rid of me. But she always acted as if she loved me as her own. Hattie broke down and wailed.

"My son, my only child. Why? No grand babies." After a while, she straightened her shoulders and dabbed her face. "This is not supposed to bother me. I'm very progressive. I'm very nonjudgmental," she repeated over and over.

"Why is this bothering me so much? Thomas should be able to choose for himself the life he wants. Let's go," she said, determined.

"Where?"

"I need to know for certain."

Thomas lived about forty-five minutes away from his parents. We drove in silence the entire way. Hattie pulled into a lush condominium complex. She knew exactly where she was going.

"I've driven here so many times, but never had the courage to go in." She parked, and we both got out of the car. She marched and I timidly followed to unit number 573. Hattie pushed on the doorbell. I heard the Westminster chimes echo within. Then there were footsteps.

A man, with muscles rippling over his taut body, wrapped only in a towel, answered the door. I stared. He had curly black hair and brown eyes. I had never seen a vision of manhood like this before. It was if I was staring at some Greek or Roman god. Michelangelo's David could not compare to this man's beauty.

"Sounds like you were lusting after the guy!" Adrien tossed in his two cents again.

Ursula blushed. "He was amazing. Even Hattie stared dumbstruck for a long, long time. Water droplets were splattered all over his chest like a work of art."

"You're making Catharine blush," Adrien smiled.

He was only half-right. The other half was my memory of Good Friday night. The girls wanted to take me to Park Avenue. Mom shouted I was going straight to Hell if I went out on Good Friday. The drive to Milwaukee was tortuous. All I could think about was Mom's warning.

When we arrived, we stood in line for a half hour. I looked around and noticed there were only women waiting. I didn't go to Park Avenue to look for women, only men, so I asked, "Why are there so many women here?" Susie, my friend, said, "Didn't we tell you? It's male stripper night."

What if Mom had followed me? That thought plagued me all night as I sat in the corner waiting for the strippers to finish. My back was turned away from the debacle going on in center stage when suddenly I felt a warm body pressed against mine.

"Hi," a virile male voice whispered in my ear. I turned to see probably the same man Ursula described, though only clothed in a thong, panting. He was gorgeous, but he repulsed me. "Put some clothes on!" I said and slid out of the booth to hide in the bathroom. My

73

girlfriends tormented me the rest of the night. I never went out on Good Friday again.

Ursula sighed.

He was not interested in women, only men. My man, or so I thought he was my man. I've had plenty of male attention to know that I was somewhat attractive to the opposite sex, but this guy wasn't interested.

"I'm Thomas's mother," Hattie said, grabbing his free hand to shake it. She pumped it up and down. He was trying to clutch his towel to keep it from dropping.

"So, he's finally told you about us," Nick, so I found out later, said. "Come on in. Let me get dressed, and I'll show you around."

I nearly fell over. I leaned very hard on Hattie. She sensed that I was about to fall apart.

"No, we don't have time. Besides, I need to get my daughter to the hospital."

"Thomas never told me he had a sister."

"I bet he never told you he had a girlfriend, either!" Hattie stated firmly.

Nick finally looked at me. It was a cold, impassive sweep of the eyes like a physician examining a patient, not the look of a man for a woman.

"Why did you come here?" his voice grew cold.

"We had to find out for ourselves," I told him. "Thomas and I have been dating for over a year, but, but...." I couldn't finish.

"Sorry for the inconvenience!" Hattie squared her shoulders, turned me around, then we walked arm and arm to the car. When we got inside, I wept. Hattie sat impassively. Was she in shock?

"I have to reconcile myself with this. Maybe I should ask him over for dinner. Maybe we should plan a family gathering. I could live with this. This is okay. This is what Thomas wants."

"Why are you tormenting me?" I asked her.

She shrugged her shoulders. "People break up all the time. So he has another love interest who is a man? Why is that so troubling?" Hattie suddenly broke down and wept deep, heart wrenching sobs. We were hugging each other and didn't notice a car pulling into the spot next to ours.

There was a tapping at my window. Thomas jutted his head into the car. He actually had tears in his eyes.

"I am so sorry. I am so sorry," he repeated.

Ursula stared hard at all of us, and then looked directly at the giant.

"Was I only born to be unlucky in love?"

Her words resonated with me. I was never to find the love of my life either. It is just the way life goes for some people.

"Perhaps it wasn't meant for you," the giant said.

"I know that," I answered. "It's obvious I couldn't find Mr. Right."

"That's not what I meant."

What did he mean? Was there someone waiting for me? I searched in single bars, single cruises, single dating services, but I could find no man waiting.

"You didn't have to look," the giant said. "Ursula, please."

CHAPTER 14

Innuendo became truth, and the flames of gossip swirled around me. Ursula was the jilted lover of Dr. Vadner, dumped for a man. I began searching for another hospital, especially one in...in a different city.

Did I work hard enough to avoid Tom? Probably not, because he always seemed to find me.

"I think I'm ready to take that trip," Tom said one day. "I've mapped out my route. I plan to start in the West Indies. Do you want to sail with me?"

"Why don't you take Nick?" I lashed out.

"Nick and I broke it off."

"I'm sure you'll find another man to take his place." I...I wanted him to hurt as I hurt.

"I want to sail with my best friend."

"I thought best friends knew each other's dirty little secrets."

"I thought best friends forgave each other." Then he walked off, but he wasn't finished with the topic. A couple of weeks later, he pushed himself next to me at lunch.

"Come on. Why don't you say yes?"

"Yes to what?"

"The trip of a lifetime."

"You're joking, right?" I said. In my mind, I was hoping to see him disappear so I wouldn't have to face him every day. "You can afford to take a year off to sail the world, but not me."

"Why don't we get married?" His gaze penetrated my whole being. Warmth flashed throughout my body. I wanted to say yes, but I couldn't bring myself to do it.

"What? Aren't you proposing to the wrong person?" I said instead.

He was mocking me; I was sure. I stood up so quickly I dropped my lunch tray. We bumped heads as we scooped up the garbage and dishes.

Tears stung my eyes. I ran off and hid in the bathroom. What kind of marriage was he asking from me? Maybe he wasn't gay. I quickly pushed that thought away. Before word had traveled about his sexual preference, we were the hospital's premiere couple. I had daydreamed about our children. Now, there would be no children, at least for Thomas and me.

Thomas Senior and Hattie Vadner hosted a going away party for Tom at the yacht club. Of course, the jilted girlfriend was invited. I called Hattie and told her I was busy that night.

"Honey," she said. "I've just accepted the fact that my son is gay. You have to do the same. I'll send a car around to pick you up at seven, okay?" The word 'no' belonged only to Hattie Vadner.

This scorned woman refused to look the part. Cecelia and I shopped for hours before I found the perfect evening gown.

Thomas turned and stared when I entered the room. His look kindled that old flame that just wouldn't expire. He stayed by my side the entire evening, putting his arm casually around me every so often. It probably meant nothing to him, but, for me, it sent electric charges all over my body.

"Let me take you home," he said when the party was over.

It was midnight, but Thomas drove along the lake for what seemed like hours.

"It's still not too late to say yes."

"It's too late for many things," I replied.

Ursula began to cry. We waited in silence; even Adrien had nothing to add.

"I'm sorry," she apologized. "I had forgotten all of this, until now. I didn't realize it would affect me so much."

"Take your time," the giant answered.

Ursula took a deep breath and continued. We were silent for a long time.

"I'm sorry," Thomas broke the silence.

I didn't want to make a scene, but I began to cry.

When we pulled into my driveway, he performed his usual gentlemanly ritual of jumping out and opening my door. I stumbled and fell against him. Before I knew it, we were kissing each other. Not just the usual little peck that was his trademark, but a passionate kiss, the most beautiful kiss I've ever had. He then stepped away, shocked, then walked backwards, still staring at me, to his car. He got in, looked at me once more, then drove away. That was the last time I had ever laid eyes on Dr. Thomas Vadner.

Ursula wiped her eyes.

About seven months later, at two o'clock in the morning, the phone rang. It was Hattie.

"You gotta come over! The Coast Guard just called. They received a distress signal from Tom's boat. They have not been able to locate him or his vessel."

When I arrived, Thomas Senior opened the door.

"I told Hattie not to bother you, but I'm glad you came." He hugged me.

"Any more news from the Coast Guard?" I asked, not really expecting much.

"They think they located a wreck on the Atlantic Ocean side of Martinique, but they're not sure. The guy at the Coast Guard said they find wrecks all the time, abandoned boats, just left in the ocean."

Hattie was smoking and pacing.

"I didn't know you smoked," I said.

"Times like these require action. This is the only action I can think of," she puffed.

Thomas Senior shrugged.

"Thomas, make some coffee. Make it strong." Hattie puffed and puffed. She reminded me of a dragon with the smoke billowing out of her flaring nostrils.

"You don't have to work tomorrow - or should I say today?" Thomas Senior asked. Cups clanged as he removed them from the cupboard.

"Nope, this isn't my weekend on." I didn't tell them my mother was picking me up at seven for breakfast, then shopping for Cecelia's baby shower.

Hattie took one final drag on her cigarette and then snuffed it out. "While you're at it, whip up some eggs or something!" she directed her husband.

"How can you eat at a time like this?" he asked her.

"How can you not eat? We're probably going to be up all night or the rest of the morning."

After we ate, Hattie pulled out twenty-seven photo albums of Thomas. Looking at those pictures stabbed at my heart. That is how I pictured our babies would have looked.

The sun was just peeking over the horizon when we got the call. We stared at the ringing phone. It rang eleven times before Thomas Senior picked it up.

"Yes," he said, his voice deep and somber. There was a long pause. He sighed as he listened. Tears began to well up in his eyes.

Hattie threw her hands up to her face. "This is terrible," she cried. "No, no, no." She shook her head. I tried to hug her, but she jumped up, grabbed another cigarette, and began her pacing. Thomas Senior gingerly set the phone down.

"They found his ship. It was capsized. They also found a body nearby. We need to identify it."

Thomas's funeral was surreal. People sent me flowers and sympathy cards, as if we had been married. My supervisor even gave me time off from work. At the funeral home, I stood alongside Hattie and Thomas Senior as the mourners processed through the grieving line.

"I should have married him, even if it would have been a sham," Ursula said. "Maybe, just maybe, if we had gotten married, he wouldn't have died."

I looked around and noticed Adrien had tears in his eyes. He caught my glance and gave me a dirty look. He quickly wiped his eyes.

About a week following the funeral, a lawyer called. "You are named as a beneficiary in Dr. Thomas Vadner's will."

I couldn't believe my ears. Was someone playing a joke on me?

"Are you able to pick up a copy of the will?"

After I hung up, I checked to see if the law firm actually existed. It did. I went downtown. The receptionist smiled when I told her my name. She pressed her phone and said, "Dr. Vadner's wife is here."

"I'm not his wife," I said, quickly.

"You are Ursula...however you pronounce your last name," she waved her hands. "You're in the will, so it really doesn't matter if you're married or not." She ushered me into the lawyer's inner office.

"Hello, Mrs. Vadner. It's so much easier than the name on this document." He stood up and shook my hands. "I am so sorry to hear of your tragic loss. So young. Your husband was very wise. He set up the will before he left."

I gave up trying to tell them that Thomas and I were not married.

The lawyer handed me a large manila envelope. "Do you want to read it here or take it home? If you take it home, just call me if you have any questions."

Did Thomas know something? Was he planning his own demise? Thomas frowned on suicide, but maybe he couldn't accept his life. No, they said a storm suddenly erupted, and there were other deaths on the sea.

"He perished from the storm, as many sailors did that night," the giant interrupted. We all jumped as his booming exclamation shattered Ursula's soothing intonations.

"Did he die?" she was afraid to finish the question.

"He made his peace and died quickly," the giant answered.

"Thank you." Ursula continued.

Thomas left most of his estate to me. I hadn't known Thomas was so well off. I assumed Thomas was making a doctor's salary, which was great, but certainly not what was there on paper. I could quit my job and live very comfortably. I was a very rich woman.

What a story Ursula had. It's strange; you look at people and never guess what lies behind their lives.

"Honey, I am so glad Thomas put you in his will," Hattie said when I told her. "My little Thomas was not only book smart, but street smart, too. When he was ten, he wanted to invest in my husband's new company. Thomas had two hundred dollars saved up. Thomas Senior did so well that Thomas became quite wealthy as a teenager. He paid for his medical school right up front, so no student loans. Of course he had scholarships, but they didn't cover the whole cost."

My parents benefitted from Thomas's gift. I bought them new furniture, new kitchen appliances, paid for house repairs, and landscaping around the yard.

"Ursula, you won't have any money left if you keep spending it on us," Mom said one day while we were painting her living room.

Mom refused to hire a painter. The room hadn't been painted since they had first moved into the house over thirty years ago. I saw the scribble mark I had made behind the couch when I was three. Mom thought it was so cute she never removed it.

"Mom, I have a great job. I should have done this sooner!"

"I bet you the taxes are killing you." Dad always worried about taxes.

I also paid for Cecelia's baby shower. Since I had the extra money, and was a new member of the country club, we hosted it there.

"Wait a minute!" Adrien again. "You keep bringing up this Cecelia woman. Who is she?"

"She was my best friend who happened to marry my brother Phillip."

"Didn't I already clear that up with you?" I looked at Adrien.

"There was nothing written down on that piece of parchment you pretend to be writing on," he answered.

"I can't help it; the words disappear."

"Yeah, right."

"You two make me laugh," Aleric interjected. "You sound like you're married."

"Heaven forbid!" I exclaimed. "Him? Never."

The giant sighed. "Thank goodness we have Catharine here to clear up Ursula's story, since we all know she was a great reporter."

Ursula smiled. She was right about her teeth, they were perfect. What a difference a smile made on a person.

"This was such a beautiful shower," Cecelia said when everyone had left. We were alone. "You didn't have to do this, but I will treasure it always." She laughed. "I can't believe everyone got me two of everything."

"You *are* having twins," I laughed. Even though my personal life seemed to revolve around a Shakespearean tragedy, Phillip and Cecelia were my life's greatest joy. Soon, there'd be more joy to go around.

CHAPTER 15

Ursula continued.

Gregory Patrick and James Charles were born April 27, my father's birthday. Dad couldn't contain his excitement.

"The twins have arrived," he called me at five o'clock in the morning. "They are the best birthday present a grandpa could have!"

"How much did they weigh? How is Cecelia?" I asked, still groggy.

"I dunno. Talk to your mom." Dad was never into details. Mom, on the other hand, told me play by play about the birth. Gregory was breech - James wasn't. They thought they would need to do a C-Section, but somehow the doctor maneuvered Gregory for a natural birth. Cecelia was in labor officially for eighteen hours and forty-seven minutes. Gregory came out before James.

I went up to the hospital as soon as visitors were permitted. I carried in two enormous stuffed animals. They were larger than the babies were.

"They have red hair!" I said in shock. "Where did that come from?"

"My two aunts had red hair," piped in my father.

"And red hair actually runs in my family," Cecelia said. She looked tired, but very happy. I recalled that at that moment there were many redheads at their wedding.

When I wasn't working, I spent most of my time with the babies. I was their favorite aunt, at least on their dad's side of the family. I especially went to visit them when I was thinking about Thomas.

"So, don't you think it's time you let go of the ghost of Thomas and move on with your life?" Phillip asked one day. The twins were already two years old. "You're not getting any younger." Phillip liked to tease. "And, you're not going to meet any men babysitting all the time -though I do like the free service."

"I've been dating, here and there," I lied.

"Sure you have," Phillip said.

"Leave her alone," Cecelia always defended me.

What would my life have been without such a dear friend?

Ursula's smile quickly turned into a frown.

One day, I was shopping at the mall. I was looking for a birthday present for the twins. They were turning three already. I was stepping out of the toy store when I bumped into Ty Bennett.

"Oh no," Aleric and I said together.

"He was probably stalking you," said Adrien.

"Mr. Inveres, you would know all about stalkers," the giant said. "You didn't have to chase women; they swarmed you like the paparazzi."

"Yeah," he sighed. "It's tough having woman fall like apples at your feet."

"Perhaps if you were forced to pursue a woman you might have actually loved one," the giant said. He bored holes through me.

What did that stare mean?

"It means some people were not in the right place at the right time," the giant answered my thoughts. "Ursula, sorry for the interruption."

Ursula seemed to welcome the break. It was a long moment before she began again.

Ty immediately grabbed my shopping bags to carry them for me. "Ursula! It's been forever! Let me help you," he said. This couldn't have been the Ty Bennett I knew. He never would have thought to help me carry anything. "Are you available for lunch or did you eat already?" Was he expecting me to pay the tab? I wondered.

He drove me to a cozy French restaurant near the lake. Did he have a job? Could he afford this? These questions kept running through my mind.

"I got my GED; then I went to the technical college. I got myself a great job," he said, breaking through my thoughts. He then got very serious. "I have really changed, Ursula. I hope you give me another chance. You're the only one for me."

"What's that phrase you Americans say, 'He's a bad penny that keeps showing up?'" Aleric interrupted.

We all laughed, though we knew that Ursula's story was turning a grim corner. It was almost too much to listen to, especially after Aleric's account. How could we endure this?

He was moving in too soon. In fact, I didn't want anything to do with Ty, so I tried to cut him short.

"We just bumped into each other. Let's not rush anything," I told Ty. I looked for the waiter to give me the bill. When he came, Ty grabbed it, then handed the waiter his credit card. That was a first.

Before we left, Ty asked for my phone number. I resisted, but he was very persuasive. He called me about ten minutes after I got home. I told him not to call me for at least a week. I left it at that.

At the twins' birthday party, I told my family I bumped into Ty. They all groaned in misery.

"When will that doofus get totally out of your life?" Phillip asked.

"When I picked up my dry cleaning on Monday I saw him waltzing out of

Everest Motel with a woman," Cecelia said.

I tried to enjoy the party, but Ty was like a bad corn on your toe.

Aleric laughed aloud. "Corn on the toe? What a strange phrase."

"It's a blister or pile of dead skin on the toe," Adrien defined for Aleric. "I suppose some of our American terms seem funny."

"I was literally thinking of corn - you know the yellow vegetable!"

We all laughed again, even the giant.

"But, from what you say about this Ty, he does sound like a bad sore on the foot," Aleric began. "And being a soldier myself, having sores on the foot is the worst thing. I remember one time..."

"We heard your story, already," Adrien said. "We don't care about your sore feet."

We all laughed again.

"My apologies." Aleric bowed like a Chinaman I had once seen in a movie.

Ursula smiled, but then it faded as memories of her tortured life flood her mind.

When he called a week later, I told him that my sources saw him with another woman, and he should just forget about us.

Ty was relentless. I had to give him credit for that. Flowers showed up at the hospital. Chocolates, expensive ones, came once a week. I gave them away. The other nurses loved it.

I was nurse executive by then. I made over a hundred thousand a year and still had a little over two million dollars left of Thomas's inheritance. I was a rich woman and was liking it a lot. There was a niggling feeling that Ty was only after me for my money.

"Duh!" Adrien said. We all looked at him. "I speak from experience."

"You certainly did have your gold diggers, didn't you?" asked the giant. "But, let's save that for your tale."

I decided to make out my will. I met with the same lawyer who had written up Thomas's will. If I should die, I wanted my nephews to inherit what I had. It just seemed like the right thing to do. If I did get married and have children, I could change it. I just felt better about it.

I went over to Phillip and Cecelia's house to tell them. They both began to laugh.

"Why are you laughing?" I was surprised at their response.

"We're expecting again! Isn't that great?" Cecelia beamed.

"Ah, man! Now I have to add the new baby to my will!"

"You're not planning on dying soon, are you? Is there something we should know?" Phillip wore his brotherly concerned face.

"Nope! I would hate to suddenly die, and then have all you wonder what should be done with Ursula's millions."

We all laughed again.

"You're much richer than we'll ever be," Phillip said. "Our kitchen ceiling is rotting out. Just got the estimate for that repair - ten thousand dollars." He stopped himself short. He tried not to complain in front of me because he knew I'd write out a check. I didn't offer this time because he'd only refuse. I'd give it to Cecelia later.

I shook my head. "No, I would trade all my money to have what you have."

John Paul was born on October 23. The red hair missed him. Actually, any and all the hair colors possible missed him because he was very bald, but he was very round and jovial. He seemed to laugh at the very moment of his birth. Gregory wanted him returned back to the hospital. He didn't like all the attention going to the baby.

"Auntie Ursi," he said to me one day. "When you go back to work, could you take Johnnie back?"

"Why?"

"Everybody loves him better than us," he pouted. "Look at all the presents he got! More than us!"

"We couldn't even walk into this room; you had so many presents!" I answered him.

"So what? Just take him back."

Cecelia took the boys upstairs for their naps. When she returned, she said, "Let's play a little trick on them. When they wake up, you hide in my bedroom with Johnnie. I'll tell them you took him back to the hospital."

When the boys awoke, I scooped up baby Johnnie and hid in the bedroom. I heard the boys come out into the living room.

"Where's baby Johnnie?" Gregory asked.

"You told Aunt Ursi to take him back to the hospital, so that's what she did," Cecelia answered.

Gregory suddenly burst out crying. "Call her right now and tell her to bring him back!"

I could hear his weeping in the bedroom. Cecelia could not console him. I felt terrible for playing a trick on him. I rushed downstairs holding the baby.

Cecelia laughed. "Gregory, here he is," she said.

"Baby Johnnie, I love you! I won't let Auntie Ursi take you to the hospital!" Gregory kissed him. The baby just smiled and gurgled.

CHAPTER 16

Nights were very lonely. Images of Phillip's family haunted me. I wanted to stay away because sometimes the pain was too great.

Maybe this yearning is why I finally gave in to Ty. I convinced myself that I loved him, in a strange sort of way. There didn't seem to be too many prospects out there, and Ty just seemed so devoted to me.

We set the wedding for March. Actually, Ty did. I wanted a June wedding, but he wanted to speed things up a bit. We were both in our thirties. He said why should we wait.

I contacted the priest from the parish I grew up in to do the wedding. I wasn't really going to church, but it seemed like the right thing to do. The priest said we needed to set our wedding at least six months from now and take classes. Ty was totally against this.

"Let's just get the justice of the peace, and be done with it," he said.

"Are you kidding me? No way, I want a big church wedding. I waited thirty-two years for this."

He found some hocus pocus minister on the Internet who would do the service for five hundred dollars, whenever we wanted. We had set March 17th for the date, but when he found out that having the wedding on a Friday saved us about one thousand dollars, he convinced me to change it to the 16th.

My family wasn't happy with the change.

"We all work late on Fridays," Phillip said. "I just started this job. I don't want to make waves."

I wanted my whole family there. I tried to change Ty's mind on this. Finally, he gave in.

"Sure, we can have it on Saturday, but isn't there someplace that's less expensive than the country club? You know my relatives. That's just too highfalutin for them."

The only place available at that short notice was a run-down tavern with a basement for large gatherings. I found out it was Ty's favorite hangout. It could only seat one hundred people. I was forced to trim down my guest list.

When Cecelia and I went to look at the place, my heart sank. It was dark and smoky. When the manager flicked on the lights, the walls were filthy. I didn't want to have my reception here.

"Doesn't your condominium complex have a gathering space?" Cecelia asked.

"Why didn't I think of that?" I said.

I spoke to the manager. She was thrilled to have my reception there. Surprisingly, it held over two hundred people. I was so excited to tell Ty. He wasn't so thrilled until I told him it was free.

"Are you going to register?" Cecelia asked.

"I have everything I need," I told her.

"Bah! A bride needs to register for all those pretty things, like china and crystal, especially if a rich relative buys the entire set for you," she winked. I had been the rich relative for my brother and his bride. Cecelia picked a pattern that was ivory with tiny blue flowers edging the rim of the plate. The flowers reminded me of Cecelia, sweet and delicate.

I went alone to the department store. Ty thought it was a stupid idea. The sales woman there...Ursula stopped. She stared at me. I wondered what she was thinking, and then suddenly, I remembered.

Ursula Rose Wojciechowski. It was such a long, strange name on the bridal registry. I was filling in for the bridal manager because she was sick that day. This beautiful, blond woman, who seemed to have so much going for her, appeared to be planning a funeral not a wedding.

"I had wanted a June wedding, but he wanted to speed things up a bit. Then I wanted it to be at the country club, but he said it was too expensive. I wanted a church wedding, but he didn't want to wait. I had a guest list of three hundred, but he wants a small wedding. He didn't even think I needed to register," she was confiding in me, just a store manager. I kept wondering what kind of woman marries a man like that. Professionalism clamped my mouth shut.

"Continue, Ursula." How many times had the giant said this?

"You're the woman from the department store. It was so long ago," Ursula began again. "Something inside pushed me to tell you everything. Maybe I had hoped you would talk me out of it. A stranger having more power than my own family? I wouldn't listen to my own parents or brother, but the advice of a stranger, some objective voice..." Ursula's voice trailed off.

"Why didn't you say what was on your mind?" The giant accused me.

"I was a store manager," I defended myself. "I had no business poking my nose into her life, even though I had thought she was crazy for marrying him. She wouldn't have listened anyway."

"Are you sure about that?" Adrien said. "I don't know what this bridal registry stuff is, but I do know I would have told that woman to dump the dude."

"Right," said the giant. "You would have asked her on a date."

"Maybe. Wouldn't that have been better than marrying Ty?"

"It would have been all wrong," I said. "You and she, it just doesn't seem right."

"Catharine, are you a matchmaker?" The giant smiled, revealing large, straight white teeth.

"I've been known to join a few people together."

The giant shook his head. "But not yourself."

"Whoa! Those are fighting words," Adrien defended me, or so I thought. "Spinster Catharine was too busy writing to take notice of men!"

"If she had only taken up the pen, she might have found who she was looking for." The giant bowed his head toward Ursula.

She continued, as if trudging up an insurmountable obstacle.

My cat woke me up on my wedding day. She was sick and left a pile next to my bed. Rain spilled out of the sky. Fortunately, I didn't have to leave the building. I could just walk down the hall to the atrium. You were there, waiting.

Ursula stared at me again. I shifted uncomfortably.

Yes, I was dropping off more wedding presents. She was the saddest looking bride I had ever seen. I had wanted to tell her not to go through with it, but it wasn't my place. Melancholy walked out with me. When I returned to the car, I thought very seriously about going back, but there was a downpour. I turned over the ignition, flipped on the wipers, and mused all day about Ursula on her sad wedding day. When I complained about being single, Mom always said, "It's better to be single and happy than married and miserable." Ursula was going to be miserable, I just knew it.

Ursula hesitated before continuing.

Cecelia arrived, and we put the finishing touches onto the decorations. The cake arrived. Florence, the condominium manager, arrived with the flowers. Her daughter was a florist. Maybe this day wasn't going to be so bad after all, I thought.

Ty's mother arrived. She had substituted her mother of the groom dress for green jeans and a 'Kiss Me I'm Irish' t-shirt. She had already visited four pubs, and it was only ten o'clock.

The quasi-minister showed up with a purple Mohawk. Ty managed to be on time and looked quite handsome. After a ten-minute ceremony and the signing of the marriage licenses, we were officially married. Hattie wept and shook her head through the entire ordeal.

"It's better to be single and happy than married and miserable," Hattie repeated over and over.

Donna flung her beer at Hattie during the luncheon.

"Why do you keep saying that?" Donna slurred. "Your damn son was gay and couldn't give her what she wanted."

Hattie flung her martini back in Donna's face.

"Your son is a lying, lazy, son of a bitch!"

"What does that make me?" Donna managed to ask.

"It doesn't take many brains to figure that out!"

Both women lunged at each other. Thomas Senior dragged Hattie home.

Dad didn't say much. Mom tried to be cheerful, but her red eyes belied her demeanor. Phillip drank - a lot.

"What am I going to do?" Cecelia asked after he fell over some chairs. She was crying. Dad drove them home.

People didn't stay around too long. Ty didn't want dancing, so most of the party dispersed by around two o'clock in the afternoon. I had visions of an all-day wedding with dancing into the night. After everyone left, we drove Donna home.

Back at the condominium, Ty was ready. I wanted to talk, get cozy, not just jump into bed.

"So, did you and that gay guy ever sleep together?" he asked.

Suddenly thoughts of Thomas crowded my head. He was the one I wanted next to me, not this man who seemed so foreign to me.

"Never. He was always a gentleman," I said.

"Humph. Not! He was screwing some guy behind your back," Ty answered. "I'm just glad you didn't sleep with him or you might give me AIDS."

Ty was matter-of-fact. When we were finished, I felt disappointed. There was no tenderness. After we were done, Ty didn't even want to hug me or be near me.

"This is my wedding night," I thought to myself. I rolled over and fell asleep.

Our honeymoon didn't improve matters. We stayed in an all-inclusive resort. Ty seemed more interested in the scuba instructor than his new wife. George, our tour guide, was interested in me. At night, when we should have been dancing with each other, we were couple swapping.

George was delightful, really delightful. He made my honeymoon so much more enjoyable. Ty didn't like him, but George's attention soon got Ty's attention. Ty dumped the scuba lady and became the doting husband. George backed off. Things finally improved when we got the call. Donna was in the hospital. The honeymoon was over.

CHAPTER 17

Ty's mother had had a severe diabetic shock. No one, not even Donna, knew she had diabetes. It partially explained her mood swings. After a few days in the hospital, surprisingly, she recovered. Despite this crisis, Donna's bad habits remained the same. In and out of the hospital, we would go after one of her crashes. No one could talk sense to her, not even Ty.

Things got much better between Ty and me after I told him how I felt. He did try to be a good husband.

"He had to behave. He wanted all your money." We all stared at Adrien.

"Thank you, again, for your commentary," the giant said. "Should we stop her story so you can tell yours?"

Adrien shifted in his seat.

"That's okay," Ursula said. "It is a dreary story." She smiled.

Ty was in and out of jobs. He couldn't seem to hold on to one for more than a few months at a time. For the most part, I learned to love him once again.

"Ugh!" It was my time to comment on Ursula's story.

"Miss Zimmer, now what is your problem?"

"I just can't understand how she could love this guy."

"Spoken by the card carrying spinster in...."

"That is very sexist! I can't believe they talk like that in heaven." I huffed.

"We're not in heaven," the giant said. "Continue, Ursula."

Then I started getting sick. Smells bothered me, and I threw up in the morning. I was pregnant. I couldn't believe it! Pregnant, finally! I wanted to tell everyone, but I was afraid. My mother had all those miscarriages. I wanted to wait until I was further along with my pregnancy before telling anyone.

Cecelia called one morning while I was at work. I had just returned from the bathroom. I think my workers knew what was going on, but they said nothing, at least not to me.

"Hi, Ursula! How are you?" Cecelia asked.

I lied and told her I was feeling great. I actually just wanted to lie down and sleep. "We have some news. I'm pregnant again!" She couldn't contain the joy in her voice.

"How wonderful," I said. We could have our babies together, I thought to myself. I wanted my baby to have a cousin his own age to play with. I almost spilled out my news, but hesitated.

"You're okay with this, aren't you?" Cecelia asked. She must have sensed my reservation.

"What do you mean?"

"I know you want to have children, and we already have three, and you don't have any."

I laughed. "Cecelia, always thinking of others. I couldn't be happier for you." The urge to reveal our secret was strong, but something still gripped me back.

Ursula shifted and hung her head. She began wringing her hands like Lady Macbeth.

The doctor said the test came back positive. The baby would have Down syndrome. "What do you want to do?" He was so cold, so clinical.

"What do you mean?" I asked.

"Most women choose to terminate their pregnancies if there's any suspicion of abnormalities in the fetus."

"No, no, no. I plan to have this baby, regardless!" I was firm. I picked up my purse and left.

Ty wasn't so sure. "Do you really want to bring a child in this world who already has problems? What kind of life will he have?"

"We will love him or her," I said. "A child is a child!" I was resolute, but Ty changed his tactics.

"It's cruel to bring a deformed child into the world. It's best they don't have to live in this messed up world. Think of how the other kids will tease him. His life will be horrible."

I don't know why I gave in to him, but I did. I went in on a Friday afternoon, the worst day of my life. I stayed home the entire weekend crying. Ty went fishing with some of his buddies. Sunday afternoon, my doorbell rang. It was Cecelia.

"I know it's the middle of summer, but I thought you might like some pea soup, since you're under the weather. Phillip took the kids to that new jumpy place so I could have some time to rest."

"So you make soup for me!" I laughed. Cecelia never rested. She thought of everybody, but herself. I started crying.

"Something tells me this is more than a cold."

Sobbing, I just shook my head no.

"What is it? Can you tell me?" She gently wiped the tears from my face with a tissue.

"Do you remember how you and I would talk about having our kids together?"

"Oh, yeah," she laughed. "We thought we could just decide when we'd get pregnant. That was so funny." She stopped smiling.

"Well, we *were* going to have our babies together!"

"You're pregnant?' she didn't get the full meaning of what I had just said.

"I was pregnant."

"Was? When? What? I don't understand." Then she stopped to think. "Oh, dear. Did you have a miscarriage? I am so sorry."

I shook my head. "No. The baby tested positive for Down syndrome. Ty didn't want that, so..." I couldn't finish.

"Ursula. I am so sorry." She sighed, the weight of what I just said crushing her soul. "What have you done?" She began to cry.

Her words stung. She didn't realize it, but they were accusatory. Didn't she understand the burden I was carrying? Didn't she realize that the child would be unloved?

Ursula bowed her head.

I would find out later that that decision was the worst one made in my entire life.

"I would say marrying that scum bag was the worst decision," Adrien said.

Ursula winced, but continued.

Monica Ursula was born on December 27th, the exact due date for my baby. When my mother called with the news, I just cried. Mom didn't know; no one, except Ty and Cecelia knew about the abortion. She just thought I was sad because I didn't have any babies.

"Ursula, I was married for five years before I had Phillip," she said. Mom tried to console me.

"You were only twenty-five. I'm thirty three. I don't have five years."

Every month brought more tears. Each monthly cycle became a punishment for my decision.

I resigned myself to being childless so I focused on my career. The position for hospital vice president opened. Mr. Lang, the president, encouraged me to pursue it.

"You're the right person for this job, Ursula," he said. "You have worked in almost every department, supervised the nurses, been on the ethics committee, as well as been very helpful in human resources."

"I'm not very financially astute," I said. "Don't I need an MBA for this position?"

"Nope. In fact, Harry was too much business, and not enough people, if you know what I mean."

Harry was all about the money. He and I had countless arguments about how I should staff my nurses. Harry wanted fewer nurses working more hours so we could shave off the payroll. I wasn't willing to overwork my nurses at the risk of patient safety. I still prided myself on running a tight ship, but there was no way I wanted over tired nurses trying to insert IVs or administer medication.

The interview for the vice president position lasted all day on a Friday. The board members seemed very excited about bringing me on as the vice president. After the interview, I felt confident the position would be mine.

I went home, and sitting in the driveway was a motorcycle. Ty held a red rag and was buffing it up. Why, I didn't understand, because I had to squint to look at it.

"Hi, Baby! Look what I got! Let's go for a spin!"

I had never been on a motorcycle. After working in the emergency room, I had never wanted to be on one.

"When did you get this?" I asked, pretty annoyed. "I thought we would talk before making large purchases."

"I saw an ad that said this cycle would be life changing! I figured since your life was changing, we needed a little celebrating!"

"The job isn't guaranteed. If you really want to celebrate, buy me a boat, not this thing." I ran into the house, dumped my briefcase onto the kitchen table, then went online to see how much Ty's toy cost. My secure nest egg had been dwindling for some time. Donna's frequent visits to the ER were draining my account. She no longer worked and collected a very small amount of Social Security. We also paid for her rent, utilities, groceries, and medical care. She was basically our child.

Ty tried to invest, but didn't have the skill. We lost some big bucks, and now I was down to about a quarter of a million dollars. Still not bad by most people's standards, but it was making me feel uneasy.

Ty plopped himself on the chair next to me. "Hey, Baby, you're always so worried about money. Life is way too short to be living so tight. What are we going to do with that money once we die?"

"I was hoping to leave a little for our children or my nieces and nephews."

"They can take care of themselves."

"Just like your mother."

"That's a low blow. You know she can't make it on her own."

"Because she's always drunk. Maybe we should pay for some treatment for her."

"Come on," he cajoled. "Just look at the bike. It's the top of the line."

"Never can go cheap if it's someone else's money." I stood up and followed him outside.

It was a beauty, I must admit, for a cycle. It should have been; he paid thirty grand for it.

"Where are the helmets?" I looked around.

"Worrywart," Ty said. He strolled over to the garage and returned with two helmets. "Let's go for a spin."

I wasn't sure about this, but I climbed on and held tight. He didn't drive too fast, at first. We toured the neighborhood. It was exhilarating. I was ready to get off, but Ty continued. He merged onto the Interstate 94. Ty maneuvered in one lane out another, passing cars as if they were standing still.

Ursula paused for a long time.

The last thing I remember is coming up to a semi. To this day, I have no idea why, but it started to jackknife. We were too close avoid getting hit. I screamed. We flew into the air as if in slow motion. Then thump, we landed and spun around like a top.

When I awoke, I sensed something was different, but I didn't know what. Voices, echoing voices, seemed to loom over my head. They were familiar voices, but I couldn't place them.

"Her eyes are open. She must be out of the coma!" Who was saying that? I know that person.

"Very unusual. The prognosis isn't good," said a very cold voice. "Even if she survives, she'll be a vegetable all her life." I didn't like that voice.

"We'll take care of her," a woman's voice said. I knew that voice, but who was she? Blurry, blurry. That's all that seemed to be in my brain. Nothing made sense.

"I can't believe Ty walked away with just a few scrapes and bruises," a man's voice said. Who was that man? Who was Ty? I closed my eyes. I couldn't make sense out of this.

"Go figure," said an elderly woman's voice. "Ursula's been carrying the brunt of all of Ty's bad decisions." She sighed, heavy and long. It was a sad sigh. Why did I understand that, but everything else seemed foreign?

The clinical voice spoke up, "Let her rest some more. We'll keep you posted with any further changes." The room darkened and became tomblike. It was too much for me. I started screaming, but what I heard was more like a caveman grunting. It was a horrible sound.

"She's saying something!" The lights went back on. I stopped grunting. A man's face loomed into mine. I knew him, but I couldn't put a name to him. "I think she wants the lights on," he said.

"That's preposterous," the clinical voice said.

"It won't hurt to try," the younger woman's voice said. The lights went out. They left. I started grunting. They rushed back in, turned on the lights, I stopped.

93

It was horrible. Right then and there I realized who I once was, and what I had become. Ursula Bennett, the nurse, almost vice president of a hospital, became an animal in a human body.

"Get me out of here! Get me out of here!" I screamed, but it came out in grunts, crude, uncivilized grunts. Drool fell upon my chin. A beautiful woman, with curly, long hair, found a tissue and gently wiped my chin. I knew her too, but who was she?

"Ursula, honey? You're okay," she gently touched my hands. "Everything is going to be okay. You're alive. You survived a ...." She stopped herself. Don't agitate the patient.

I wanted to be dead, not live like an animal. Something told me this wasn't temporary. This was to be my new existence.

CHAPTER 18

Sunlight! Noise! Jostling! They were transporting me to a regional rehabilitation center via ambulance. All these voices surrounded me like a hum of bees: the nurses, ambulance drivers, Mom, Dad, Phillip, Cecelia, and Ty.

"Hey, there's a cemetery over there. What a fine place for   dead people to go," Ty said.

I was still flat on my back, tubes bringing me sustenance for survival. After that comment, I grunted in distress.

"Do you always have to say such terrible things?" Cecelia asked. She tried to comfort me, but the tubes coming from every direction of my body made it difficult for her.

After weeks of endless, grueling therapy, I had improved enough to be restrained in a chair to prevent me from toppling over. Tubes were removed. With help, I was able to eat soft or mashed food. I was able to communicate my wishes through grunts. The humiliation of that never left me.

There was no more the rehabilitation center could do for me. Finally, one day, Dr. Sonova came into my room. Ty was sitting in the chair next to my bed. Dr. Sonova had his usual stern demeanor plastered over his face.

"The team met yesterday. We feel there is nothing more we can do for your wife," he said. "Our social worker will meet with you to help you set up your home to accommodate the patient."

I had been in the Walden Rehab Center for five months, and not once did Dr. Sonova say my name. I was the non-cooperative patient, the wife, the daughter, the sister, the vegetable, but never Ursula Bennett.

"I don't know why we keep this vegetable in here," I overheard him say outside my door one day.

Another voice spoke up, "Because we're getting tons of money from the settlement."

It was killing Ty that much of the 7.3 million dollars of the settlement went to my care. When Dr. Sonova gave him the discharge notice, Ty couldn't have been happier.

"She'll do so much better at home than here. I'll take great care of her. You won't be able to recognize her when I get through. She'll be a new person."

After about a week, my house was filled with the necessary hospital equipment.

An ambulance drove me home.

"It's costing over a thousand bucks to transport you. I could have thrown you in the back of the truck for nothing," Ty groused.

I grunted. I didn't want him riding with me. I wanted Cecelia.

"May I ride with her?" Cecelia asked.

"I'm her husband. That's my job," he said while jumping into the back.

My heart pounded in excitement! I couldn't wait to return to my home. Waiting for me when I arrived was Phillip and the kids waving banners and flags. I grunted and moved my head back and forth.

Monica, who was already three, came up and kissed me.

"Aunt Ursi, you look different," she said. She remembered an Aunt Ursula with soft blond tresses, a smooth complexion, and expensive outfits. The Aunt Ursi before her was a drooling fool.

"Look at yourself," Ty once said in the, in the rehab center. We were alone. "You're an ugly hag," he said. "I suppose if I want any of that money, I'll have to play the devoted husband."

The family decided, without Ty's full consent, to hire Cecelia as my home care nurse. They hoped this would encourage Ty to find a job. Ty was all against this, but he didn't want to look bad in front of the rehab team, so he agreed - for a while.

My beautiful home changed almost as I had. A hospital bed and a large wheelchair were plopped in the center of my recreation room. Cecelia thought I'd enjoy looking at the fireplace. I could also look outside from the French doors. Sometimes deer came out of hiding in the woods to prance along my yard. Before the accident, it was my breakfast room. Now, it would be my home. Much better than the rehab institute, but not the way I envisioned my life.

Every morning Cecelia and Monica would arrive around seven o'clock. Ty would leave around 7:30 to go to the career placement center downtown. They were helping him with his resume. If I knew Ty, they were doing all the work. I couldn't wait until he left. I grunted with pleasure the minute Cecelia and Monica arrived.

Cecelia would begin the long process of bathing me. Monica would go play or watch television. Then we'd all eat breakfast together, Cecelia spooning food into my mouth, me gobbling it, and Monica watching.

"She sounds like a pig," Monica said one day.

"Shush," Cecelia said. "She can hear you. You don't want to hurt her feelings."

"Sorry, Aunt Ursi. I didn't mean to hurt your feelings," Monica went off to play.

She was right. Pigs probably ate neater than me. If I wasn't so hungry, I would have stopped because it was so humiliating. First, the bib, then the long, slow process of feeding me. Once, at the rehab center, Ty was shoving food into my mouth. I started choking. He stood and watched. A nurse ran into the room.

"What are you doing?" It was Rosie, my favorite. She lived in the States since her family's arrival from Jamaica twenty years ago. On her shifts, I could expect a long visit after her normal working hours. She'd chat and chat, oblivious to the drooling idiot in the bed next to her.

"You're a special woman," she said to me once while we were alone. "Don't let anyone tell you different, especially that fool of a husband of yours. The good Lord has a purpose for all this."

If he did, God didn't let me in on the secret. I was miserable, lonely, and uncomfortable most of the time. My family helped ease some of the pain, but my greatest joy was Monica.

One day, she decided to have a tea party. She set her tray onto my belly. She put the plastic teacup to my lips. I grunted in pleasure.

"Mommy, Aunt Ursi likes this! You like this right?" She moved her face right up to mine. Her sweet breath caressed my dry face. I grunted louder. Monica took the cup again to my lips. We would do this for hours.

My chair was the other great love of my life. Ty and Cecelia would lift me into it, and then Cecelia would strap me down. She would roll me throughout the house. Not upstairs, but through the main floor. When the weather warmed up again, a ramp replaced the front steps. Cecelia would roll me down outside and take me for long walks. Monica would ride along on her tricycle. We'd go to the park where Monica would play, and we'd watch. Cecelia would talk. I could only grunt. For Cecelia, that didn't matter. She could talk to a tree and still have a conversation.

"Monica starts school next year, already," Cecelia said.

I grunted. This time I barked like a seal. It was my sad grunt. Cecelia and Monica were the only two who could decipher my way of communicating.

"Yes, I'm sad, too," she said. "The kids are growing so fast. Before you know it, they'll all be married with kids of their own," she sighed long and hard. Then she jumped up. "Why am I so melancholy today? I have so much to be thankful for."

"Like not living in a wheelchair. Not being a drooling idiot. Not having a terrible husband," I loved Cecelia, but the resentful thoughts raced through my mind. I barked again. Cecelia fell on her knees, facing me.

"You're right, Ursula. I'm so sorry for being so insensitive. Maybe I'm so sad because I remember our conversations from college. We were going to marry and raise our kids together. That's all gone now. Every time I feel joy, it's tinged with sadness because I see you suffering. It feels so unfair. I have so much, and everything has been taken away from you.

"Did you know I used to envy you? Oh, I loved you, but in my mind, you were the beautiful one, the successful one. I'm so ashamed of myself, wasting our valuable friendship."

Envy? Never once did I sense Cecelia's envy toward me, only her love. I grunted my, "It's okay," grunt. Cecelia hugged me.

One warm summer day, we were sitting on my front porch. It was hot, but windy. The wind chimes clanged. I snorted in approval.

"Mommy, Aunt Ursi loves this!" Monica said.

Every warm day after that, Monica would insist on taking me outside to hear the chimes. If it wasn't windy, she'd climb on the wicker chair and push the chimes. I'd squeal in delight. When they stopped, she'd push them again and again.

My family tried to schedule visits when Ty was gone. Phillip and the boys would often come over during the summer. Many times the twins played too rough. I'd bark in anger when they'd knock my wheelchair.

"Boys, stop it!" Phillip would shout. But, after they left, the loneliness would always return.

It was getting harder for my parents to visit. They were both in their eighties. Mom was determined to drop in every Tuesday and Thursday, and on the weekends Ty was gone. She played cards the other days. Mom could always elicit sad moans from me. She would hug and rock me like a baby. It was probably strange looking, but it was so comforting. Then she'd leave and promise to come back soon.

Ty's mother, Donna, never showed up. She died about two years after my accident.

Some of my visitors were former colleagues. They would come into the house; Cecelia would lead them to my room, chatting. Many could only stare, words failing them at that moment.

"Say something to her," Cecelia would remonstrate. "She understands."

Most of them remained mute. There was only one person from the hospital who actually tried to communicate with me. Her name was Ursula, also. She was the housekeeper for my office. She was so intrigued with someone else having the name Ursula since it's not very common. I remember the day she first spoke with me.

"You're Ursula Bennett?" she asked.

I was very busy. I was always very busy. "Yes." I remember answering her crisply to prevent any conversation.

"I'm Ursula, too!" she said with such joy in her voice, I looked up from my paperwork. I smiled briefly and looked down. She wasn't finished.

"Where did you get that name?" she asked.

"My mother's favorite aunt." I had to get this report done in an hour. Why is she bothering me?

"It was my mother's favorite aunt, too! What a coincidence," she said.

I looked up and said, "I'd love to chat, but I have this report due in an hour."

"Oh, oh, I'm so sorry. They told me not to talk to the employees while cleaning. I just couldn't help myself."

Her arrival at my home was like a fresh bouquet of flowers. "What a magnificent house," she said. "Do you need a cleaning lady?"

Cecelia told her that we'd think about it.

"Hello, my fellow Ursula," she said. She knelt on the carpeting and touched my hands. She wasn't afraid of me! Ursula stayed for over an hour. She told stories of her grandchildren, of her dead husband, and her pet guinea pig. I laughed and laughed, but, of course, it sounded like grunts. But, she knew.

"I'll come back, if you'd like," she said as she was leaving. "I could even clean around here." Ty was thrilled to hire a cleaning lady. That left him off the hook.

Ty had his own visitors. After Cecelia and Monica would leave for the day, women started appearing at the house. Sometimes Ty would bring them into the den to stare at me.

"This is my wife," he said once, bringing a blond who looked like a younger version of me into the den. "This is what I have to come home to every day."

The young woman just stared, repulsed. She turned on her heels and left the house. After that, he just took them right upstairs to the bedroom. I knew what was going on. In my dark loneliness, I would groan. It was a low moaning. My heart was breaking inside of me, while he was upstairs breaking our covenant.

Cecelia must have suspected something because one day she and Phillip arrived, without the kids, around six. Phillip bounded up the stairs and pounded on the bedroom door. A half-dressed woman bolted out of our house. Phillip dragged Ty to the steps.

"I should throw your sorry ass down these steps right now!"

"Phillip! Stop it!" Cecelia shouted. "Ty, why don't you just divorce Ursula? Then you can move on with your life."

"And leave all the precious money to *that*?" Ty pointed at me.

The very next day, Ty changed all the locks, fired Cecelia, and pretended he was caring for me. Fortunately, he let Ursula, the cleaning lady, in every Saturday. He would disappear to let her clean. When she finished, she'd spend the rest of her time with me. It was the only bright spot of my week.

Ty would get up around ten or so in the morning. My diaper was usually full and soaked through onto my bed. He never once changed my bedding. Occasionally, he'd wash my hair, but it usually hung in greasy locks over my eyes. Bedsores were developing all over my body.

When he left for the day, the drapes remained closed. I lived in a dark cave. Often I didn't eat anything until six or seven at night, when he decided to show up. All day long, I whimpered like a starving puppy. Is anyone there? Will someone help me?

One Friday, the doorbell rang, and rang, and rang. Ty finally woke up. It was eleven in the morning. He squeezed his head through the door.

"We're not interested," he said. He started closing the door when a foot jutted itself through the entry.

"I'm Rosie, Ursula's old nurse. I just want to see how she's doing." When Rosie wanted something, there was nothing going to stop her.

"Hello, Ursula! How are you?" Then her eyes bulged open wide, along with her mouth. She grabbed my bedcovers and flipped them off to reveal a full, soggy diaper and bed rash. She gently turned me over and saw the bed sores.

"Young man, get over here, right now!"

Within an hour, my bedding was changed; I was bathed and fed. I felt like a new woman.

Rosie must have known the right contacts because within the same day, I was admitted into the hospital for treatment of the bed sores. Cecelia was reinstated as my nurse. Monica would come back!

CHAPTER 19

After that incident, Ty didn't hang around the house much. He only slept and ate there, then left all my care up to Cecelia. Monica was now in kindergarten. I only saw her on Saturdays. She was faithful, never missing a Saturday. She even skipped taking ballet classes because it meant she'd get to see her Aunt Ursi.

"I can take ballet anytime, but I can't always see my Aunt Ursi."

Friday night sleepovers ended early on Saturday morning. Sometimes she'd bring her friends over. They'd play with my hair, give me facials, paint my nails.

"Why does she do that?" one of Monica's friends asked.

"She grunts when she's happy. And she's very happy. You should hear her sad sound," Monica said.

The last Tuesday I saw my mother alive, she seemed to linger at my house longer than usual. Cecelia had left for the day to pick up the children from school.

"Ursula," Mom started, her voice quivering, "I don't know if I ever really told you I love you. When you arrived, there was so much love wanting to burst out of me, but I was afraid to show you. I guess it was just something we never did in my own family. My father was never very emotional, and Mom left us when we were so young."

That was news to me. For all our lives, we were always told grandma had died. We had never questioned it.

Tears streamed down Ursula's face.

Mother talked for a long time. She told me how difficult it was meeting a man that seemed so happy when life with her father had seemed so grim. My mother's father died before we were born.

We only knew Dad's parents - lovely, jolly people. Cookies, candies, cakes were the staple at Grandma Mabel's house, though she had diabetes. Often she'd serve Phillip and me cookies before supper. It was Grandma's special ritual, she'd tell us.

"When Phillip was born and you arrived, I never knew there could be so much happiness in someone's life. You were so tiny and had black hair. Black hair! Soon after, the blond hair grew in. My little angel."

Mom stopped talking and just hugged me for a very long time. "I better get going. Dad will be here in a few minutes. Good-bye, Ursula. See you on the other side of Heaven."

Ursula wiped her eyes. Tears were in all our eyes; even Adrien couldn't hold them back.

The next morning, Cecelia knelt by my wheelchair. "Honey, Mom passed away in her sleep last night. Do you understand me?"

Tears and moaning. "Now, why did you have to tell her that?" Ty came into the room. "I won't be able to control her anymore!"

"She is a human being," Cecelia said. "Did you forget?"

"Really, that grunting, groaning pig is really human?" he asked sarcastically.

He could have stabbed me; the pain of his words crushed me. I moaned even louder.

Phillip wanted me to go to the funeral. Ty was against it. No surprise there.

"How are we going to get her there?" Ty asked.

"Part of the settlement money was to go for a special van," Phillip accused. "For now, the woman at the county said there's a special bus that can take her to the funeral. Ursula can stay with us for a few days."

"No, no, no. If she stays with you, that means she won't be coming back here."

"Wouldn't that make you happy?" Phillip asked. "In fact, now that you mention it, I wonder why I didn't think of it in the first place."

They screamed and shouted. I groaned louder and louder. Finally, Phillip stopped himself.

"Let's not talk about this in front of Ursula. She's getting upset."

In spite of Ty, Phillip won that battle. I was going to Mom's funeral.

"The drive to Mom's services was amazing. The only time I left the house was on walks with Cecelia and Monica. Now I was traveling a great distance. I chortled and snorted in pleasure despite the loss of my mother.

"You like this?" the old driver asked me. "You got a little extra time. Let me drive you somewhere I think you'll like." He pulled into the Rotary Gardens. Mom and I practically lived there before my accident. Azaleas in the spring, roses in June. Roses, roses, roses. How did this driver know? More snorting! There they stood, as if waiting for my arrival, in full bloom. I could feel Mom's presence.

More roses awaited me at Mom's funeral. I must have looked like some bobble head the way I looked up and down at the beautiful stained glass windows, the statues, the pews, the people. The choir! I hadn't heard voices singing for so long. It's so strange to say this, but my mother's funeral was the highlight of my dark, dismal existence. Aunts and uncles, cousins and friends all touched and hugged me. Uncle Bert even kissed me on the head! So much joy! What a legacy my mother had left. I could see Dad was sad, but buoyed by all the love and comfort.

"Why don't you ever come to the family reunions?" Mom once asked while I was still healthy.

"I hardly know any of my cousins or second cousins. We have nothing really in common."

"How will you get to know them?"

"Missed opportunities are more painful when they're taken from you," Ursula said to us, as she wiped her eyes.

More delights waited for me as I stayed at Cecelia and Phillip's for a whole week! This was living. Gregory fed me breakfast every morning, until Jimmy complained.

"Why do you get to feed her all the time?" Jimmy grabbed the spoon, spilling cereal all over the floor.

"I'm going to be the doctor, that's why!" Gregory stated while wrestling the spoon from him.

"I'm going to be a chef! I know all about food." Jimmy yanked the spoon away from Gregory.

"Behave, you two!" Phillip's voice boomed from the kitchen. "Jimmy, you can feed her tomorrow."

"That means Gregory gets more time!"

"Do you want to feed her or not?" Phillip threatened.

"All right!" Jimmy kicked a ball out of his way. I grunted for him to come back. He turned and looked at me. I wanted to play ball. Would he understand?

"Do you want to play ball?"

More grunting. "Yes, yes."

The children played every day with me. They would push my wheelchair around the neighborhood; introducing me to anyone they met as if I was a celebrity. In the afternoons, they would place me in the middle and play *Duck, Duck Goose*, *Pickle in the Middle*, or *Ring around the Rosie*. Monica learned how to bathe me. She'd scrub too hard, or scratch my ears, but I grunted nothing.

"Honey, you missed a spot," Cecelia pointed to my leg.

Cecelia tried different foods and beverages with me. Lemonade, ice tea, milk, soda. I was in Heaven. At home, it was water or prune juice to keep me regular.

"Mommy, let's give her an ice cream cone!" Johnnie said. "I'll hold the cone for her."

Ice cream! I hadn't tasted its cool sweetness for years. It dripped on my chin, in my lap, but I didn't care. Like a dog savagely attacking a bone, I devoured the dessert within minutes.

"We'll enter you in an ice cream eating contest," Phillip joked. I grunted.

It was the best week of my life. Then I had to return...

"Do we need a break?" the giant asked.

"I...I need to finish," Ursula said somberly, tears welling up, ready to spill.

I was home for about two weeks before I noticed I wasn't feeling right. When Cecelia tried to feed me, I coughed up the food. Cecelia called Phillip right away. "I think she's sick," she said.

Phillip thought maybe I had the flu. They waited a few days, but I still wasn't eating.

"She needs to be seen," Cecelia told Ty a few days later. "I called the doctor's office. They'll see her this morning."

"Why are we wasting money on that?" Ty said.

Cecelia ignored Ty. She bathed and dressed me, and we waited for the van to show up. It was raining. The driver was the same man who drove me to Mom's funeral. He carried an umbrella and shielded me while Cecelia pushed my wheelchair to the van.

The doctor admitted me into the hospital. "Bowel obstruction," he said. For most people, the words are serious, but not necessarily life threatening. For me, they were my death knell.

CHAPTER 20

"No feeding tube," Ty said. "If she can't eat on her own, too bad."

The shocked doctor had no comeback for Ty. Phillip stepped in. "If we don't do this, she'll die."

"She never wanted to be like this in the first place," Ty said.

He was right, for once. We were jogging through a park one day, when I saw a young man strapped from head to toe in a wheelchair. His blank stare and drooling lips repulsed me.

"Just shoot me if I ever get that way," I said casually, without any thought to what I was really saying. My fatal error - because at that moment, I had wanted to live. I had so much to live for - my niece and three nephews. I wanted to see them grow up, meet their future spouses, maybe even see their children, my grand nieces and nephews. I wanted to live for my father, brother, and Cecelia. I wanted to embrace life so I could be with the many new friends who loved the drooling, grunting fool I had become. I was fully human to them, never a burden. Their lives engendered in me a desire to live that was greater now than when I was the sophisticated, beautiful Ursula Bennett.

"Everyone says that, but when it comes right down to it, they want to live. Ursula, you want to live, don't you?" Phillip's face was in mine. I grunted yes.

"We might have to take this to court," Doctor Lee stepped in.

He was my favorite doctor at the hospital. He was probably in his seventies by the time I was his patient. The nurses often joked about how long it took Doctor Lee on his rounds. After the checkup, he'd stay and chat with the patient and family.

"Each patient has a story to tell," he told me one day while I was charting. "I learned that as an intern. Back then, it was go in, see the patient, get out as fast as you can. One day, I went into a room. Sunk into the bed was a tiny Chinese man. He spoke very broken English, but I still understood him. I did his check up and turned to leave.

"'Please, Doctor, stay,' he said to me. Five minutes, only five minutes of my time. And in those five minutes, I was transported to another land, with walls, mountains, and noisy streets. Next day, he was lost forever. Mr. Lu taught me, in his own way, to spend a little extra time with my patients."

I had heard this story at least a dozen times. At the moment, I was so backed up with charting I resented hearing it once again. I remember snapping the chart closed to rush to another patient's room. All these people were pointing me along a different path, but I was too busy, too, too busy to stop.

"If she's a patient here, we must put in a feeding tube! We're a hospital for Pete's sake, not a killing field!" Dr. Lee was passionate.

"Then we'll take her out of the hospital," Ty said.

"You'll need a doctor's order for that!" Dr. Lee knew he really had no authority, but he was playing all his cards.

"It's a free country. I don't need to keep her here."

"We'll see about that," Dr. Lee strode out of the room.

"I'm going to the newspapers with this," Phillip said. His face looked into mine again. "Honey, we're going to take care of you. I gotta go now."

An elderly person wearing a red jacket came into the room. "Who are you?" Ty demanded.

"Dr. Lee asked me to sit here and wait until he came back."

"I don't need a damn babysitter!" Ty screamed. "Get the Hell out of here!" The poor, frightened man jumped and limped out of the room.

Ty looked at my IV hookup. "Let's see if I can get this out of you."

I started grunting as much as possible. Suddenly, a nurse and two security guards appeared. The guards grabbed Ty and hustled him out of the room. The nurse checked my IV and me.

"Ursula, are you okay?' she spoke to me in a normal voice. Many of the nurses shouted, thinking I was deaf. I grunted.

"We're going to get you prepped for surgery," she said in her quiet voice. "You'll just start getting sleepy." She was shooting the medication into the IV.

When I awoke, I was still in the room, but something was in my stomach. Though coming out of surgery makes anyone feel groggy, I noticed a change, a better change already in myself. I wasn't as weak, and the pain in my lower stomach was gone.

Dr. Lee was checking my vitals. "Hi there, Ursula. How are you feeling?"

I tried grunting, but my stomach felt a little sore from the surgery. I gave him my smile, which was a bunch of teeth jutting out.

"We'll get you feeling great so you can go home as soon as possible."

This time I grunted, even with the pain.

Phillip brought Dad and the kids later in the evening. Monica crawled onto my bed almost pulling out the G-tube.

"Monica! You can't get on the bed with Aunt Ursi!" Cecelia scolded. "You don't want to hurt her!"

"I just love her so much! I'm sorry, Aunt Ursi!" Monica scrambled off the bed.

"Would you like to come and live with us?" Cecelia said. I could spend time with my favorite people! Their house was one-third the size of mine, but they had a hundred times more joy than in my lonely castle. It was a happy day, even after surgery.

The next morning, however, I couldn't shake the sense of gloom permeating all my thoughts. I didn't know why, but I awoke feeling impending doom.

"What's the matter, Ursula?" Susie, the morning shift nurse, asked. "You'll be going home in a few days. You'll have to wear that funny thing in your stomach for a while, but then we'll take that out too!"

Susie was pushing out the blood pressure cart when the door to my room swung open. In stepped Ty, the hospital president, and a man I didn't recognize. Dr. Lee ran in after them.

"You can't do this!" Dr. Lee shouted.

"Our hands are tied," said the hospital president. "We have no legal grounds. The hospital could face a lawsuit."

"Damn the lawsuit! We're talking about human life here! I refuse to write the order for the removal of this tube."

"You don't want to lose hospital privileges, do you?"

"Her life is much more valuable than any damn hospital privileges. If I write this order, I'm writing her death certificate!" He looked at me. "Ursula, I will do all I can to stop this!" He spun around and left.

"He was a great doctor and a great man," the giant said. "Very heroic. Your case spurred him on to become a patient advocate."

Ursula nodded, then resumed.

The tube was removed, and I was discharged from the hospital. Thus began the short, but tragic, journey to my demise. Every day, my family would pound on the front door, trying to get in. Ty had a restraining order placed on them. At the end, Ty allowed Dad to visit. He must have sensed it would be my last day. They were talking in the foyer.

"We don't want any of the money. You can have it all. We'll sign anything just so we can have our daughter back," Dad pleaded.

"It's not about the money anymore," Ty said. "It's so much bigger than that."

"Can I see her?" Dad hated groveling, especially to Ty, but he wanted to see me.

"Suit yourself." Ty went to the kitchen. Dad knelt down by me and grasped my shriveled hands. I hadn't been able to eat or drink anything since I had been discharged from the hospital. Dad gasped.

"I'm so sorry, so sorry." He kept repeating.

It was I who should have apologized for all the agony and grief I put my family through.

"Ursula, I love you." He said.

It took me back to the moment my parents picked me up from the homeless shelter. I grunted, "I love you too, Dad."

Dad noticed my very parched lips. He didn't want to arouse any suspicion so asked to use the rest room. He found a washcloth and soaked it with water. When he returned, he gently touched my lips. Oh, how sweet it was.

"Hey, what are you doing?" Ty screamed. "Get out of here!"

My father stumbled to his feet. He kissed me one more time. "Good bye. See you on the other side of Heaven," he said – the very same thing Mom had said.

Ty went out for the evening without turning on any lights. I had always feared death, but that night I welcomed it. The pain of starvation engulfed me.

"Forgive me, God," I whispered as life ebbed away.

"What did you need to ask God forgiveness for?" Adrien shouted. "He should have been asking for your forgiveness. What kind of God does this, anyways?"

Ursula smiled. "It is not something you can see with your eyes, only your heart."

"And you are now here with us," the giant finished. "Do you have any more to say?"

"I was surprised at how fast it happened, my death, that is. I simply fell asleep. Then I was here."

"For some, that is how it is," the giant said.

"It wasn't like that for me!" Adrien said.

"We'll learn about that when you tell your story." The giant frowned.

"One more thing," Ursula interjected. "The will I made out before my marriage to Ty remained. It never occurred to him to ask about a will. All the settlement money and my inheritance went to my niece and nephews."

We all began to laugh, a loud hearty laugh.

"So, there is a little justice on earth, huh?" Aleric said.

"Unfortunately, Ty tried fighting the will, which was a headache for Phillip and Cecelia," the giant said. "But your lawyer was one of the best. The kids will be very well off. As for Ty, he inherited his mother's debts, broken down trailer, and hundreds of empty liquor bottles. Maybe he'll come up with a creative way to use them."

"Will he make it up here?" I had to ask.

"Is it your concern?" The giant gave me a doleful stare.

I set down the quill, miffed. The giant grated on my nerves.

"The attitude needs to disappear if your destination is Heaven," he admonished.

"Maybe you should stop reading my mind." Mind reading was a quality I had always desired, but having someone butt into my own thoughts irritated me.

"What's good for the goose is good for the gander," I looked up to see him smiling. "But we must continue. Even though we have an eternity, we do have a deadline for your stories. Adrien, you're next."

"I don't think I'm ready." For the first time, he sounded unsure of himself.

"Just start at the beginning."

CHAPTER 21

My earliest recollection of life was sitting on a floor, a dirty floor. My hands were sticky, snot ran down my nose, and I was blubbering. For hours it seemed I waited, but nothing, until Mom scooped me up. She threw me into a broken down crib, thrust a baby bottle into my mouth, and left. I lay down. I must have fallen asleep for a while. When I awoke, I was still sticky and wet, *very* wet. I started crying again. My bottom was not only wet, but sore.

It's an unhappy memory, but was not an uncommon occurrence. It was my life for what seemed like forever if a baby can measure forever. I loved my mom, I craved her attention, but I spent most of my very early life in a crib until I learned how to crawl out.

"I don't remember anything from my infancy," I interrupted.

"Catharine, up here the memories are unlocked." The giant shook his head. "We will never finish. Adrien, please."

Then I'd showed up in her bedroom, unannounced. Usually, a man was there with her, a different man most of the time. It didn't make sense to me. Man didn't mean father to me. I didn't even really know what the word father meant.

One day, an elderly couple showed up. I was actually clean. I remember that. There were two blue suitcases at the door. I and the suitcases...

"You mean the suitcases and I," for some reason this man, like the giant, irritated me.

"Catharine! Perhaps we should give you a little taste of what Adrien experienced?"

Adrien smiled and winked at me. My face reddened.

The suitcases and I were scooped up for departure. I cried and grabbed for my mama. She withdrew to her bedroom without a glance. The older woman tried to soothe me, but I struggled, bawled, and almost fell out of her arms as she carried me down the stairs.

A man stood next to a very long black car, and opened the door when we appeared. It was clean and smelled fresh, not like cigarettes. My eyes wandered from the old man, to the old woman, and to the driver. My eyes grew heavy, and soon I was sleeping.

I awoke to the car driving slowly along a tree-flanked drive. I still recall the noise of the car tires spitting out rocks. How long will this take, I wondered, as the car crept along slowly. I wiggled in my seat wanting out.

The driver pulled up to enormous brick mansion. To me, it was just a giant house with green plants growing on its walls. He pulled around a circular drive. A black suited man opened the door for us.

"Hello, little chap," he said, clipping my nose.

Inside, people bustled about. Someone grabbed the suitcases, and another took the jackets of the old man and woman. Soon a group surrounded me, tweaking my cheeks, smoothing my hair, and making a general fuss. I hid my face into the old woman's chest.

"Let me take him to his bedroom," said the old woman who I found out later was my grandmother.

There was no end to the stairs. Panting, she finished the climb on the third floor. She shifted me in her arms and she carried me to the end of the hall. We entered a room. Bright colors everywhere - blues, reds, and yellows. My bed was a miniature car. I squirmed out of Grandma's arms and waddled toward it. I crawled right into it. The room was clean, no toys on the floor, no torn curtains, just clean and wonderful. I fell in love right away.

"Come here, darling. Are you hungry?" She reminded me of my mother, just more kind and loving. I remember liking her a lot, right away. I had no fear of her. I went right to her and let her carry me downstairs. Memories of my mother and my terrible childhood faded quickly.

"Cherubs couldn't have been more beautiful than baby Adrien," the giant interrupted. "Surprisingly, you didn't always act so angelic." The giant flashed a baby picture in front of us.

I gasped. Here was the baby in my dreams - curly blond hair, blue eyes, and smiling fat cheeks. There was no baby more beautiful than this child was. Once asleep and in dreamland, he would lead me to various places such as parks, zoos, or carnivals. We'd spend the day together. I remember my strong desire to hold him. He was capricious. Sometime he would hold up his arms while at other times he would just laugh. The minute he was in my arms, I would awake. I stared at Adrien's baby picture. It was the baby of my dreams; I was so sure of it.

"Did you see a ghost?" Adrien asked me.

"No," the giant answered for me. "But, she knows this baby."

"How?" Adrien asked.

"Don't worry about it. Just continue with your story, please."

I was about ten years old when my grandparents took me into the library. That was where all the important family conferences were held.

"Adrien," Grandpa said. "Your grandmother and I need to talk to you."

"What did I do wrong?" That was my usual response because I was usually in trouble.

"You need to know you have a mother. She gave you up when you were a baby; we've been caring for you ever since."

"Didn't she love me?"

"She loves you, dear. She just has a problem with drugs. We felt we needed you to know."

After that meeting, I worried about whether they were planning to send me back. I didn't want to go back, but the thought haunted my every waking moment. One day   I finally had the courage to ask.

"Am I going back to my mother's house?" I asked.

"Why, do you want to go back?" Grandma's eyes looked hurt.

"No!" I said it so quickly, she laughed. "I thought when you told me about her, you were shipping me back."

"We would never do that," she said. "I miss our daughter so much. I am so sad about her life, but you need to be protected, and we're here to do that."

They did that very well, in fact, maybe too well. I was very spoiled.

"That's putting it mildly," the giant interjected. We laughed. Adrien looked sheepishly at us.

"Can I tell the story, please?"

"I don't understand your accent. Would you please speak in English?" I interjected.

"Ah! That's very funny, Catharine!" the giant roared. "That's priceless."

Adrien stared and smiled at me. I blushed. Dead, I was dead, and yet some strange sensation coursed through my body as if I were some teenager on a date.

"The heart's inclinations are not silly." There goes the giant, reading my thoughts. "There is a purpose for those feelings. Unfortunately, men and women never learned to use those emotions correctly. I should know." A hint of sadness shaded his face. "Adrien, continue. Catharine, try to pay attention."

Whiz kid, that's what they called me. I finished learning the middle school curriculum by sixth grade. Grandpa knew I wasn't ready for the kids in high school. So, Mr. Simmons, my tutor, was hired. England was his homeland. His wife had recently died. The Simmons were childless, but not without means. Mr. Simmons, after teaching for ten years, dabbled in the stock market and left teaching behind. Money woes didn't bring him to America, just a desire for a change of venue.

When we picked him up at the airport, I wanted to meet him first hand. There he was tall, dark, and skinny as if he hadn't eaten for years.

"I'm dying for a fag!" He shouted right in the airport! Passerby stared.

Imagine my sixth grade mind. "Grandpa and Grandma hired a gay guy to be my teacher!" I shouted.

"He wants a cigarette, Adrien," Grandpa translated. "Mr. Simmons, we don't permit smoking on our property. Will this be a problem?"

"Depends on how large your property is. Hardly an hour goes by when I don't need my fix. Something tells me," he stared at me, "that I'm going to need to shorten the space between the smokes."

"I see," Grandpa sighed. "I'll talk to Marylyn. She'll just have to get used to it."

Mr. Simmons loved his mother country. He sprinkled my lessons with his memories of boat rides down the River Thames, bike rides along the rolling hills, and gardening the plethora of roses.

What about the moorlands? I wondered. Vast, empty land - the perfect setting for a mystery novel. I had traveled through most of Great Britain, but never once saw the moors.

"Catharine, Adrien's story is not a travelogue. Don't worry, you'll have you chance to visit them."

What? Didn't he know I was dead? What a strange comment.

Adrien smiled, and continued.

"Tell me again, how you met your wife!" I always wanted to hear more.

"Only if you finish your history assignment." He would barter.

Back and forth we'd go; I would interrupt begging for more stories, and he would use them like treats for a hungry dog.

"Teach me some swear words," I begged Mr. Simmons one day.

"What will your grandparents say? Nope," he said, resolute.

"I'm going to tell Grandma you smoke in the back garden."

"You cheeky little bastard. The answer is still no."

"I'm going to tell Grandfather you're taking nips of his cognac and you called me a bastard."

"You don't know anything, young man."

"I've seen you kissing Eleanor. You know how Grandma feels about that kind of stuff."

"You're a bloody little snoop."

"Bloody! That must be a swear word." I was going to get it out of him one way or another.

"Bloody means damn," he said, frowning.

After that, I said nothing without including the word, "bloody."

"Give me a bloody glass of milk. I want to go for a bloody drive. I don't want to go to bloody bed!" Bloody became my favorite adjective. The maids tittered, but Grandma wasn't pleased.

"Adrien," she said one day. "If you don't stop using the word bloody, I will have to wash your mouth out with soap."

"I don't give a bloody damn!" I answered back.

Everything tasted soapy for a week. Bloody was scratched from my vocabulary. Grandma hovered in penitence.

"Why are you apologizing, Marylyn?" Grandpa asked. "His mouth should have been washed out a long time ago!"

"I just feel terrible. He had bubbles floating out of his mouth!"

I did that for effect, but I didn't tell Grandma that. I pretended I was a bubble machine and was trying to spit bubbles out of my mouth.

What a personality. Adrien probably kept everyone on their toes. He would have been a blast in school, if the teachers hadn't kicked him out. Would I have liked him? Probably not. I was always very serious in school. I had no use for the class clowns.

The giant's eye skewered me back to the present.

"Adrien, Bob's your uncle!" Mr. Simmons said one day.

"I don't have an Uncle Bob!" I corrected.

"Oh, chap, that means life is going swimmingly. Swell. You know, great."

Not only did Mr. Simmons introduce me to some fine words, but he also launched my love affair with movie making. Mr. Simmons' brother, Roland, was an independent filmmaker in London. He invited us all to stay with his family for vacation. Every morning, early, the crew would arrange the set. I would watch ignoring all the chaos of the London streets. Roland said I was very well behaved, and could observe while they filmed. To my grandparents' dismay, I didn't want to see anything of London! Often they went sightseeing on their own. I'd only join them if the film couldn't be shot on a particular day.

When we returned two weeks later, Grandpa's dream of having a doctor in the family was lost to Hollywood, but he wasn't bitter. Whenever he would travel, he would return with a book for me. On my twelfth birthday, my grandparents gave me a video camera. I filmed everything!

My first movie was *Ants*. I sat, with my camera poised on an anthill, for eight hours. Eight hours! It was amazing what I captured in those eight hours.

The giant laughed the loudest, but we chimed in also. *Ants*? The famous Adrien Inveres' first movie was *Ants*?

The summer before high school, Mr. Simmons bid farewell. He wanted to tour the country in a caravan, as he called it. It was just an RV.

"America is a jolly country. There's quite a bit of it, not like Great Britain, though I'd put the United Kingdom up against America any old day," he said.

"But you still lost the war!"

"That's because the bloody French had to get involved!"

It was a tragic goodbye. There I was, fourteen years old, and crying like a baby.

"Here, here, boy! You sound like a prissy girl," Mr. Simmons said, his British accent stronger than usual. "I'm not dying, you know. I want to see a bit of the world. Besides, it just wouldn't do for an American teenager to have a live-in British tutor. What would the other kids say?"

He was right, of course. I was going to miss him. He had taught me a great many things besides swear words. He promised to write, and that he did.

About a year into his travels, he wrote that he had remarried. Lola was half his age. Mr. Simmons found her in a strip club. They settled in New Mexico. They invited me to visit during the summers.

When I was sixteen, my grandparents put me on an airplane to New Mexico. It was great until Lola decided to make a move. One night she entered my bedroom wearing a flimsy negligee.

"You're so strong and handsome," she thought she cooed, but it sounded more like a cackle.

"You're old and wrinkly and way too fat," I answered her back.

"You're rude!" She jumped off my bed and left the room. She was cool the rest of my visit. I didn't care. It was Mr. Simmons that I had come to see.

Lola filed for a divorce shortly after and fled with half of Mr. Simmons' fortune. Lola, what a name.

Adrien shook his head in disbelief.

UCLA promised me a full scholarship, which I grabbed, though my grandparents had enough dough to finance most of the students' tuitions.

After my undergraduate studies, I completed post-graduate work in film directing. My career blasted off. Fate must have smiled on me because I was making movie deals all over the place. Most people struggle for years to get into the industry, but not Adrien Inveres.

He was on the cover of some magazine almost every week. How could such a young man be so successful?

The giant stared at me, and smiled. "I know it's difficult for you to concentrate, Catharine, but you're here to listen to his stories, not make a judgment." He sighed. "Adrien, keep going."

It was all going so great, but it didn't last forever. First, Grandpa died suddenly of a heart attack. Not too long after, I lost Grandma.

Adrien wiped his eyes.

It was the night of the Oscars when it all began. I was feeling so high that night. Before the awards, I, like everyone else in that town, was drinking champagne as if we had already won.

When I arrived at the auditorium, I missed the seat and fell on the floor. I laughed like a maniac. Do did all the other drunk celebrities. I wanted to stay down on the red carpet, but what if a photography snapped a picture?

Flash! I was too late. That picture would end up appearing in *The Glossy*. I flipped the guy off and sat down.

Friends walked up and down the aisle, shaking my hand, telling me I was going to win tonight. I tried telling myself the other directors were more qualified to win. I had wondered if Grandma was watching on television. I didn't really care about the other actors, directors, or movies, except for mine.

"What movie was it?" Ursula asked.

Adrien looked at her, shocked. "The Cutting Factor," he answered.

It stole the academy awards: Best Picture, Best Supporting Actress, Best Actor. After seeing my heartthrob Jeremy Colton win best actor, I turned off the television and went to bed. I didn't really care to see who would win Best Director. The next morning I had read about Adrien Inveres claiming the prize. I remember spilling coffee on the picture of his face in the newspaper.

The giant pulled out a newspaper. "Is this it, Catharine?"

I blushed to see the smudges mottling the image of Adrien.

"Give me that," Adrien shouted. "You mean you didn't cut this out and put it in a picture frame?"

"If it had been Jeremy Colton's face I would have framed it."

"Oh." Adrien frowned.

It was almost too much – the crowds, bright lights, the announcement: "Best Director, Adrien Inveres." I stared out at all the people and flashing cameras. It was heady like a powerful drug. I was leaving the auditorium when I got the text – *Get to the hospital.*

It was a stroke for Grandma. She never came out of it.

"Grandma, it's me, Adrien. Can you hear me? I won an Oscar. You gotta get better so you can see the ugly statue."

Could two days be as long as the two I spent by her side? She looked dead, but I held my hand over her mouth and felt her breath. It was shallow. It was about seven o'clock on the second night when I heard a gasp, and she was gone.

Was she able to watch me on television? Would she be proud? Did she know how much I loved her?

Life is a bunch of highs, then lows. So low, it's hard to rise above that awful oppressive feeling of loss.

After the funeral, I wandered around a bit. I reneged on a movie deal, and rejected requests for new projects. What was the point?

Mr. Simmons wrote, inviting me to travel with him. I spent the summer out East. I learned about history and the female anatomy at the strip clubs.

"Wait a minute," I interjected. "Learned about the female anatomy? Besides making movies, you were making love to every woman in Hollywood."

"You shouldn't believe everything you read in those trashy magazines," Adrien answered.

"Where there's smoke, there's fire."

"Aren't you supposed to be a writer?"

"Maybe," I answered tentatively, wondering what his point was.

"Clichés, Catharine, should be avoided in good writing."

"I'm not writing, I'm listening."

"Actually, you're butting into my story."

"You would think that you two are lovers," Aleric quipped.

I almost gagged at the suggestion. "Never!"

"Never say never," the giant said. "It's my turn to use a cliché. Are you two done duking it out?"

"No! I want to know why Miss Zimmer over there would never consider me as a viable contender for her affections." Adrien's eyebrows arched.

"First, we would have never met because I lived in Wisconsin all my life. Second, you're too blond, and I don't go for blonds...."

"Ah, yes, Jeremy Colton, dark hunk, stud muffin."

"This is getting a little out of hand," the giant said.

I ignored him. "At least Jeremy had some principles."

"You never had to work with him on a movie set!"

The giant leaned back into his seat and folded his arms.

"Besides, you would have never met Jeremy, either! So, Miss Zimmer, what else is defective in me?"

There was pain in that question. At that moment, I glimpsed a man searching for something he would never find.

"Nothing," I could only reply. "I'm sorry I interrupted."

I must have imbibed more alcohol than a distillery produces in a year. Hangovers greeted me the moment I opened my eyes to the day. Then, one morning, I woke up without a hangover. I decided Mr. Simmons was a bad influence. We said our good-byes. I would embark upon a new adventure - to find my long, lost mother.

A private detective located her about three weeks after I had hired him. Chicago was her hometown. With my flight booked, suitcases packed, I was delving into the second worst day of my life.

CHAPTER 22

Not much had changed from the day I left as a baby to that moment. She had still surrounded herself with filth and decay. A bulb in the hallway dangled from a cord and knocked me on the head when I passed under it. I waited and knocked for about ten minutes, but there was no answer. I heard voices inside, so I kept knocking. Finally, someone from Apartment C opened his door. He was wearing only his boxers.

"Hey, she's gone. She left around six this morning. She leaves her television on so no one breaks in. Who are you?"

"Her son. What time does she usually get home?"

"It's hard to say. It really depends on how lucky she is."

"Lucky? What? I don't get it." I didn't know what this man was trying to tell me.

"You haven't seen your mom for a while, I take it? I suppose you're the one that hired the PI," the man laughed. "The PI didn't tell you what your mother did for a living? She turns tricks for her livelihood. She's pretty good, if I do say so myself."

I charged over to him and grabbed him by the throat. He slammed the door and squeezed it hard on my arm. I let go. The door shut. I kicked it hard.

I stood in the hallway for what seemed like hours. My mother, a prostitute? I lived the life of gentrified wealth while Mom tainted her body in Chicago? Then it all clicked: the memories of childhood, the sticky floors, the wet diapers, the men, one after another coming and going like we had a revolving door. All her life, or most of her life, my mother was defiling herself for a bunch of scumbags.

I scanned the hovel they called apartment complex. Some goon had scrawled, "Help me" all over the walls. Apparently, Mom wasn't too successful. A cat scooted past me. I kicked it hard, and it screeched. Then I descended the rickety steps. I counted them - five floors, twelve steps per floor, sixty altogether, not including the landings.

That was one of my habits - counting steps. At home I would ascend or descend the staircase, one-step at a time, counting. I drove Grandma crazy. Sometimes Grandpa would join me and really make Grandmother mad. We had thirty seven steps in the old mansion. Mr. Hentges, the original owner of Hentges House, built a rather quixotic home. There were no even numbers in that house, no symmetry, no balance.

Mr. Hentges was an inventor. That was, of course, after he made his millions in lumber back in the Northeast. Once he was rich, he took his five children, wife, dog, and other animals to California, "to seek an untouched, unblemished world," or at least that's what his gravestone said in the backyard.

I left the apartment and slid back into the stuffy taxi. "Hey, man, what took ya so long?" the cabdriver asked. "Ya know I had this 'ere meter on all this time. Seventy bucks ya owe me. Pay up before I move this car."

I grabbed a hundred dollar bill and pushed it through the cage.

"Ah! I get it. Ya was seeking the services of Crystal."

I suppose all the Chicago taxi drivers knew of my mother. They called her Crystal? The driver speaking her name enraged me further. "Do you want me to kill you right now?" My teeth were clenched.

"No, no, no. Is ya a politician? Wait a minute. I know ya. You is Adrien Inveres, the big movie guy! Ya gotta come all the way to Chicagee to get a woman? I'd think ya'd have 'em a dropping like flies all ova the place. I ain't saying a word! How much ya willin' to pay me to keep my mouth shut? I is sure the *Inquirer* would love this."

"She's my...." Adrien looked at us. The giant nodded.

"That's right. No need to add the expletive," the giant said.

"She's my mother," I told the driver.

"Right, right. She's ya motha. And I is the pope," the driver chuckled. I scooted out of the seat and hurled the door shut.

"Get the Hell out of my face!" I screamed.

Then I walked and walked and walked. All day I walked. I saw Lake Michigan. I went through museums. I walked down Rush Street. I rode the Ferris wheel on Navy Pier. People swarmed around me. Not like New York, of course, but there were still people all over, smiling. They were smiling as if they were in on the joke. I wanted to smack their faces, even the little children.

Things started shutting down around sixish or so. My stomach was growling. I hadn't eaten all day. I found a hole-in-the-wall Chinese place. Ordered about one hundred dollars worth of food. I thought I'd take some over to Mom's, if she'd let me in.

I found her place again and banged on her door. This time the yahoo from C didn't bother checking me out.

"I'm not seeing anyone tonight," her voice was harsh and cruel.

"I have Chinese delivery," I said.

"I didn't order any Chinese food!"

"Open up. It's your son, Adrien."

After a few minutes of silence, the door opened slowly. There stood a horrible representation of womanhood. Dry, over-frosted hair shot out from all directions. Roots, about two inches of them, revealed dirty gray. It seemed like her face was covered with mini potholes. Her eyes bored into mine.

"I gave at the office," she laughed at her joke. I just stared.

"Are you hungry?" I shoved the Chinese bags at her.

"Hell, yeah. How did you know I love Chinese? By the way, this is the best Chinese in the whole world."

"Maybe it's genetic," I said.

"I hope that's all you got from me, love for Chinese food."

She hunted for some plates, flung them on the table. She found two dirty forks in her sink. She quickly washed them. Plastic. I could have bought paper plates and they would have been better than what she had. What did she do with all the money she earned?

She devoured the food – six egg rolls, two portions of egg foo young, one of cashew chicken, and the other of broccoli and beef. There was nothing on her. No fat. Nothing. She would make herself sick eating so much.

"Mom, slow down. You're going to get sick."

"Don't call me that."

"What?"

"Mom. Don't call me your mom. I gave that up over forty years ago."

"You can't deny biology," I said.

"Like Hell, I can't."

I stared at her for a long time. She didn't even notice. She was too busy eating her Chinese. She didn't care that her words hurt like Hell. That she was more than killing her own son. But, she was numb, so numb. What made her like this? I looked around. I noticed little brown paper bags stashed throughout her apartment. What was in those bags? I went over to one and started to open it.

"Get your hands off that!" She stopped eating, her plastic fork in the air.

I ignored her and opened up the bag. Cocaine. Lots of it. I had been at enough Hollywood parties to know she had a good $20,000 worth in this bag alone. My mom, an addict. I suddenly remembered the conversation my grandparents and I had so many years ago.

She grabbed the bag from my hand. "You're not addicted, are you?" she asked, terror in her eyes. She did love me.

"Been offered, but never touched the crap myself."

She patted my cheeks. There were tears in her eyes. "Good." Then she went back to her Chinese.

"Who is the father?" I didn't dare say, "*my* father."

"You don't know?" she asked, incredulous.

"Nope. Grandpa and Grandma never told me."

"That figures. Your father is...." She paused for a long time. "You're the son of Gary Creston."

CHAPTER 23

Adrien Inveres the son of a televangelist? I couldn't believe my ears, but only for a moment. It started to click together. Most people who met me said I was the spitting image of Gary Creston.

"Who is Gary Creston?" I once asked my journalist girlfriend after someone came up to me at a restaurant telling me how much they loved me and my television show.

"Gary Creston is that televangelist with that huge building he calls his church. Didn't you ever watch him, just for a second, to get a good laugh?" Carly ate her arugula salad with gusto. "I think he wears a toupee, and his wife is a nightmare of makeup."

One Sunday as I pressed the remote, Gary Creston appeared.

"Is God speaking to you?" he asked the audience. Gary was wearing a Chester Barrie suit. I knew because I had a closet full of them. He tried to hide his diamond cuff links, but every once in a while they'd flash in the camera.

He sickened me. People, who apparently were not as rich as Creston, came up and gave their testimonies. Some heard the voice of God telling them to give their lives to Jesus and their money to Creston Ministries.

"He sure made it hard for the legitimate ministers to do their jobs." It was the giant's turn to interrupt.

"There are no legitimate ministers as far as I'm concerned," Adrien answered. He paused for a moment. "Well, there were maybe one or two."

"I am sure the hand of Father Jime brought me here thus far," Aleric said.

"Humph," was Adrien's reply.

After watching the show, I started doing some research. I wanted to see how much Creston Ministries earned. They had amassed more wealth than a Fortune 500 *for-profit* company had.

That's when I blew his cover. I contacted my then ex-girlfriend with the information. It made a nice cover story for *The New York Times*. I also sent a letter to Creston Ministries.

His wife sent me a scathing reply. She called me an atheistic Hollywood type who hated Christians. She was right. I never got the religious thing. Even though as a kid I had to go to church and Bible school every Sunday, I got nothing out of it. But turning in Gary Creston had nothing to do with my antipathy toward religion. He was a criminal that was it.

It was quite a blow to learn in one day that my mother was a prostitute, and my father was a swindling, religious con artist. I wanted so much to have real parents. I don't know why. Most of my friends had divorced parents, single mothers, two fathers, all sorts of different family arrangements. Many of them didn't even really connect with their families.

"Get over it, Adrien," Ralph, my good friend, said to me one day. "It's no big deal. What are you looking for, *My Three Sons*? That just isn't real."

Right then and there, I knew they were right. What did they used to call them, the nuclear family? I finally sat down to eat Chinese. I almost ate as much as Mom or should I say - Crystal? That was her new name, the name she christened herself with after turning tricks for a while. Found out that night her real name was Patricia. Looking back, I can't believe my grandparents never told me her real name. I couldn't call her Mom or Pat. It had to be Crystal.

"Why Crystal?" I asked her. I had already eaten four eggrolls.

"I took on my good friend's name after she was murdered. We worked together. Well, not together, but let's say we knew each other from the streets. She was the only one that really showed me any love. If I was sick, she'd bring me her famous chicken soup. She'd say, 'When I get enough money saved from this job, I'm gonna open me a restaurant.' She could have, she was a damn good cook. Did you know at Christmas she'd bake up a storm and take boxes to all the neighbors? Really, how many prostitutes do you know bake cookies?"

I started laughing so hard; it really sounded funny. Maybe there was a movie in there somehow.

"And fruitcake! She made the best fruitcake. I don't know how she found the time because Crystal was, let's just say, very busy with her job. She was a good-looking woman. When she wasn't working, she was baking. Now that I remember it, she even took food down to the homeless shelter. Can you believe that?"

No, I couldn't believe it. Mom was probably so tripped up on drugs that she didn't know what she was talking about. "Really, Mom, you expect me to believe that?"

She took a chopstick from the table and knocked my head with it. "Sure I do. There was a reporter who actually interviewed her and took her picture. They couldn't run it because, well, his editor said the police would be all over them."

Mom ate for a while in silence. I watched her greedily scoop up the food. Then she set down her fork.

"Come to think of it now, she was murdered shortly after that reporter guy came snooping around. It was terrible. Of course, not too much was done because of her station in society."

She stopped, closed her eyes for a moment, and then flicked them opened. "I was the one who found her body. It was horrible. It was a Saturday morning. I was gonna pay her back for the two eggs she had loaned to me on Friday. I usually got up early Saturdays and did my grocery shopping."

Grocery shopping? It just sounded so mundane, so suburban housewife, yet there she was talking about doing her everyday chores.

"What?" she looked at me.

"I just didn't think women of the evening did that kind of stuff."

"What do you think, I have a maid? Huh. I knocked on her door. It was around nine or so in the morning. I yelled, too. The neighbors got really pissed off at me, waking them so early on a Saturday. I didn't care. She was always home on a Saturday morning. It was her baking time. She didn't answer. I tried the door."

Mom stopped for a long time. Then she stood up, fumbled for a cigarette, and lit it. I had hoped my asthma didn't kick in before I heard the rest of the story.

"I turned the doorknob. Surprisingly, it opened. I didn't suspect anything because she always left her door unlocked. I just figured she was in the bathroom or something. I walked through the apartment. It looked like an earthquake had hit it. Crystal always kept her apartment very clean. She wouldn't even let me smoke. I started screaming her name. But no answer. This wasn't right; I just felt it. I looked for the note. She always left a note on the kitchen table if she had to leave. No note. I should have run away from there, but something pushed me inside.

"It was more horrible than anything on TV. She was in her bedroom, all bloody. Her beautiful body was contorted in some bizarre position."

Mom put her hands to her face and shook her head over and over again. Then she finished her grisly story.

"I stood there for so long. Who could have done such a horrible thing? Then I remembered something from a movie. I made the sign of the cross on her forehead. Crystal would have wanted that. I called the police. Soon the apartment was swarming with police and reporters."

It was all over the Trib's front pages. "Serial Killer in Chicago?" the headlines read. At work, we talked about it because we lived less than one hundred miles away. Would he come to our small town? I was especially drawn to the story because of the woman's name, Crystal Clear. What a name, I thought to myself. The report said nothing about her life's work.

Mom grabbed another cigarette. She lit it from the first one. I had to get up and find some fresh air. I went to the window. It was nailed shut.

"How do you breathe in here?"

"Some days I don't really wanna breathe. I promised Crystal, or her dead body, that I would take on her name in her honor. So, that's when I stopped being Pat and became Crystal. Some of my clients stopped coming to me because they thought it was bad luck, but I started getting some of Crystal's old customers. It was like she was takin' care of me, even from the grave."

Mom took a long draw from her cigarette, then continued droning on about her friend Crystal. "I also promised her another thing, something I haven't been able to fulfill. Now that you're here, maybe you can help me."

"The only help I want to give you is to get you out of this place and get you in some treatment program. You can live with me. You won't ever have to go grocery shopping again. You won't even have to clean. I have enough maids for that."

What was I saying? I couldn't believe my ears. Here I was inviting this woman to live with me. What would the papers say? I knew what they'd say. They'd eat it up. It would actually be good publicity for me. I would look like some humanitarian hero, rescuing Mom from the projects. Who knows, maybe there was a movie in all this.

"I don't wanna live with you. I hate California. I hate all those filthy-rich people thinking they're better than the rest of the world. I need you to find Crystal's killer."

"No." I was equally determined. "If you don't come back with me, I won't help you."

"Okay, okay. I'll come back with you, but only if you find Crystal's killer." I knew she was lying to me.

"You have no intentions of coming back with me," I called her bluff.

"You know I can't go back. Besides, I'd probably ruin your life."

"I don't care! Look at you. Is this what you wanted from life? Is this the granddaughter of Herman and Althea Inveres, immigrants who made something of themselves?"

"What? What are you saying? Don't you know what Herman did for a living?"

"He was an insurance salesman; that's what Grandpa told me."

Mom laughed hard. "He was a bootlegging mobster, that's what he was. That was how they could afford the Hentges House. Insurance broker, really?" She threw her head back and laughed. "Maybe I should keep you around, I haven't laughed this much for a long time.

"Herman Inveres distilled liquor during Prohibition. Yes, he did sell insurance, that's for sure. That was his cover. At night, he and Althea worked on their special brew. His cover was foolproof because he was also a good insurance salesman. He made his millions by light and at night. Hah, I'm a poet!" She went over to one of those brown bags. "Do you mind?"

"No! Mom, stop. Don't do that! You're ruining your life with that garbage." I ripped the bag as I grabbed it, the toxic powder spilling to the ground. She kicked me. It felt as if a baseball, flying ninety-miles-an-hour, collided with my shin.

"What the Hell do you know?" she screamed. "My life was ruined a long time ago – back at Hentges House."

CHAPTER 24

Adrien looked at each of us, making sure we were paying attention. The giant nodded for him to continue.

"What do you mean, Mom? Hentges House has been my home since I came to live there with Grandpa and Grandma." I didn't like the tone of her voice.

"Sit down, and listen." I spotted a green dingy couch that should have been thrown out on the curb.

What happened to my mother? Why did this wealthy, young woman from an upstanding family leave her home to live like this? It was going to be a long night.

"Do you have any coffee?" I asked.

"That's the other drug I can't live without. In the cupboard by the fridge are the beans and the rest of the stuff."

She crawled on the floor like a cockroach as she tried to scrape up the cocaine. I pulled her up and forced her to sit down on the couch. Then I took the remaining sweet and sour sauce and poured it on the white pile.

"You bastard!" she shouted.

"Yep, that's what I am." I went to the kitchen to dig out the coffee.

Mom's java was almost as expensive as her drug habit. "Wow, where do you get this stuff and how do you afford it?"

"Look around you. I don't waste my money on things I don't really need. Go look in my bedroom." I thought that was rather strange, but I did. The redolent scent of gardenias assaulted my nostrils. It transported me back to Grandmother's funeral.

"French Provincial didn't strike me as Mom's style, but it was all there. Silky cream gushed over the wicker bed frame. Nightstands stood waiting to serve. My eyes found the gardenias spilling over the lips of a two-foot sterling silver vase. A round ottoman, with some clothes carelessly tossed over it, stood at the foot of the bed.

"Mom and Dad left me money." My mother stood behind me. "I don't really have to work. They took good care of me, but for some reason I can't stop. I have to work to pay for my habit. The coffee is ready." The harshness left Mom's voice. It sounded sad, almost wistful.

"We drank two cups of coffee before Mom began her story. Can I tell it now?" Adrien looked at the giant.

"Of course, we need to hear it to understand your story."

Adrien began, "This is Crystal's story."

It was obvious she didn't want to tell me what happened. She hesitated, grabbed a smoke, then motioned for me to sit across from her.

"Mom and Dad were having one of their famous parties. It was Saturday night. I was sixteen and wanted to join the celebration. Mom said no, Dad said yes. Mom never argued with Dad. She helped me dress. I must admit, I looked beautiful, not like the hag you see before you."

"Grandma and Grandpa had all sorts of pictures of you throughout the house. I always admired my beautiful mother," I said to her.

"They didn't throw out my pictures?" Mom was surprised. She sat thoughtfully for a while.

"Back to my story," she began. "While Mom was helping me, she warned me not to go into any rooms alone with a man, especially Uncle Glen. I was very surprised. Uncle Glen was my favorite. I asked her why. She never told me. When we came down the stairs to join the party, who was standing there waiting, but Uncle Glen? Instead of a friendly face, I now saw a leering old man. Was it my imagination, I wondered. Was it because Mom told me about him? He took my hand right away. I loved Uncle Glen, but I didn't want to spend my entire evening with him. I was hoping Gary would see me."

"You mean the televangelist?" I said incredulously.

"He wasn't that when he was seventeen. He was just a good-looking, athletic boy who I happen to have had the biggest crush on. He was our pool guy. That was his side job while going to school. Gary never noticed me. I was just a kid in his eyes. On that night, I wanted him to notice me, but not while I was sitting next to Uncle Glen."

This was going to be even longer than I expected. I got up and poured myself more coffee. I grabbed Mom's cup and poured her some more as well. I looked at the wall clock: 12:16.

"I finally ditched Uncle Glen by telling him I wanted to help in the kitchen. That wasn't true. I had just seen Gary go in there. When I entered, Gary looked up from his plate of food. There was a piece of cheese stuck on the corner of his chin. He quickly wiped it off. "Wow, is that little Pat? You're not so little, now," he said. "Look at you. You're ready to meet a man." He finished eating, set down his plate, and then left the kitchen.

"I was so disappointed. That was it? Was that all Gary would say? This wasn't going to be as wonderful as I thought. Just then, Uncle Glen came in. "There you are," he said to me. "Are you trying to hide from me?" he asked.

I interrupted her. "Who's Uncle Glen? I don't ever recall meeting him."

"He wasn't really related. He was just a close friend of Dad's. I called him Uncle Glen. Now he's one of California's U.S. Senators."

"Glen Gauthier? I voted for that man. I couldn't imagine Glen and Grandpa agreeing on politics," I said.

"You're right." She hesitated, not wanting to continue. I nudged her a bit.

"I think Gary left the party early, and there were no other young, single guys, so I just let Uncle Glen tag along. He started getting me champagne. Mom said no liquor, but I was so sad that Gary left, that I wanted to get drunk."

I interrupted Mom again. "What was this Glen's problem? Couldn't he find a woman his own age?"

"He was recently divorced. Everyone knew why, but no one wanted to say. I didn't know any better. I was just a sixteen-year-old girl. He was better than nothing, or so I had thought."

"I had never drunk alcohol before, so, after the second glass, I was feeling tipsy. Mom noticed right away. She took me upstairs to my bedroom. She was happy to get me away from Uncle Glen. Little did she know that taking me to my room was the worst thing she could have ever done."

My Mom, or should I say, Crystal, chewed on her knuckles, a habit I thought only children did. She sighed as she continued.

"Mom tucked me in and kissed me. I was sixteen, but she still tucked me in. We even said prayers together, even though I was tipsy."

I couldn't believe my ears. Here was a lady-of-the-evening telling such a sweet story. Nevertheless, I knew it was going to get grisly.

"I was sound asleep when my bedroom door creaked open. I just figured it was Mom checking in on me. It was not my mother." My mother sighed again and took another sip of her coffee.

I figured it was hard for my mother to tell this story. She probably had never told it to anyone else before. I could feel anger rise inside me. I had guessed how the scenario would pan out before she even began. How many other young girls did Senator Gauthier rape?

"After everyone left the party, I went to my parents' bedroom. I told them what happened. Mom wanted to call the police right away. Dad didn't want it all over the news and said that it wasn't necessary. He would talk to Glen. I had never seen my parents fight like that before." Mom started crying. "I hated Dad for that terrible decision and hated Mom for going along with it. But I was so young and didn't really know what to do.

"Uncle Glen never came around again. My parents refused to talk about him or the incident. I started feeling guilty, as if I was the one who instigated it. I also started getting promiscuous. I flirted like crazy with Gary. I must give him credit. He really tried his best to focus on his job, but, like any red blooded American boy, if you throw fresh meat at him, he's going to gobble it up.

"I was pregnant before too long. Mom was devastated. Dad was furious. I spent the last four months of my pregnancy at the St. Gerard's Maternity Home. The baby girl went up for adoption. The minute I gave birth, she was whisked away. I never got to see her."

Mom began to cry, really cry.

"I wish you would leave, Adrien. This is getting too painful," she said, wiping her eyes. "Go get me that brown bag."

"No! I won't. I don't need to hear the rest. It's getting late."

Mom seemed resigned. "No, let me finish. After Amber was born..."

"Who is Amber?" I asked.

"Your sister. I saw her head as they were taking her away. Her hair was golden orange or amber colored. Which is why I named her Amber."

"So, I have a sister?" I couldn't believe my ears. Somewhere out in this vast universe was my sister. I don't know if my heart palpitated from the coffee or from this great news. "Have you ever seen her since?"

"She's not like her brother, apparently, not leaving well enough alone," Mom said dryly. "There are days when I wish that she'd pop in and say, 'Hi.'"

"The adoption was closed. Unless she hired a private detective, she wouldn't find me. She might not even know she was adopted."

After taking care of Senator Gauthier, I promised myself that I would find my sister. I would bring her back to meet her mother, our mother.

"Mom, I'm going to find her," I said.

"No, no. Let her live her life in peace. What a mess I am. Why would I want to ruin her life?"

Adrien Inveres really has a soul. Here he is trying to help his mother, the mother who left him as a child. Maybe he's not all that bad.

"Gary didn't want to sign away his paternity rights for the adoption, but he felt forced. Dad waved the word 'statutory rape,' around. Gary didn't want a record, so he signed on the dotted line.

My parents fired him, but we found ways to meet. Before we knew it, I was pregnant again. This time with you. I didn't want to go through what I did with Amber, so I decided to have an abortion. Mom talked me out of it."

Adrien looked at us all.

"What's the matter?" the giant asked.

"It just dawned on me that I wouldn't be here if my mother...Oh, forget it."

Adrien shook his head and continued.

Mom got off the crummy couch and poured herself a fifth cup of coffee. She was never going to sleep that night.

"Adrien, remind me tomorrow to make out a grocery list."

"Would you finish your story?"

"Where was I?" She had forgotten.

"You were pregnant with me."

"Yes. I wanted to move far away from Hentges House. The evil of that night lurked around every nook and cranny of that place. I couldn't even bring myself to call it home. I was eighteen and wanted to make a clean break of it. Gary proposed.

"His parents threatened him. They told him that he would ruin his life if he married me. They put a lot of pressure on him to break off our relationship. There I was - a single mom - not knowing a thing about babies, trying to raise you.

"The first three months of your life, you cried and cried. Then one day this guy Huey stopped by. He lived in the apartment below us. He wanted to tell me to shut my kid up, but when he saw me, he wanted... Well you can guess what he wanted. It was Huey who lured me into this nasty little habit. When Huey left, there were others, men willing to pay for what I could offer. When Mom and Dad found out, they reported me to Social Services. That's when they took you.

"I had to leave the room when they carried you off. I couldn't watch it, the pain was too great. In my heart, I knew it was the best thing for you. After you were gone, I packed up and moved to Chicago. I had seen an ad for modeling. I thought I could clean up my life, and then try to get you back. When I got here, I only found a porno shop. That was the last thing I wanted to do. The guy promised me big money, and he said I didn't have to do anything that bothered my conscience. I did that for a while, but they fired me because I wouldn't give them what they wanted. Then I started the other nasty habit.

"I was broke but didn't want to go back. Mom wrote every week, begging for my return. Hentges House held too many horrible memories. I tried to look for work, but jobs are scare for high school dropouts. I fell back on the only thing I thought I could do. I was just fine with my career choice, until you appeared."

She stood up. "I'm going to bed now. Sleep on the couch if you want."

No ceremony with Mom. She had told her story, now it was time to go to bed. She found some blankets and a pillow.

I eventually drifted off to sleep. When I awoke, she was gone. Had she left forever? Had I found her only to lose her again?

CHAPTER 25

"I believe it's time to eat a little something." The giant stood up.

I stretched my legs. It felt good. I was also hungry. What would we eat this time? It was breakfast this time. How much time had elapsed? There was no time here, no night, no day to tell us what passed. Just stories.

I had lived such a dull existence. How did their lines of life intersect with mine? Was I here only to be a court reporter? A South American dictator, a successful nurse vice president, and a movie mogul, then me, just plain Catharine Zimmer.

True, I had often fantasized about living a life of excitement and glamour, or at least something more meaningful than management meetings and store displays. That was my specialty; the front store displays. We had an in-house designer, but she loved my ideas so much that she allowed me this rather large job.

Each project was an opportunity to display my talent. I chose a theme usually based off one of my fantastic imaginings. Often, I'd skip nights out with my girlfriends to design the background and set. Each display was better than the one before it. The newspaper even ran a special feature on my store displays. Macy's got wind of my talents and contacted me. Here was my chance to get out of my small town, to live a life of excitement in New York City. I turned it down. I had all sorts of reasons then, but now those reasons escape my memory. All that's left is a deep sense of regret.

Everyone was back in their places. I looked up, they were waiting for me. The giant handed me the quill.

Adrien continued.

Mom did say she didn't want me around, but I had thought she was getting used to me. Then my phone chimed. Craig was texting, asking where I was. We had a production meeting on Monday, and he wanted to make sure I was going to be there. I told him the entire situation. For a while we texted back and forth. We decided to postpone the meeting for a week.

After that conversation, I returned my focus on Mom and Chicago, wondering where she was. Suddenly, she was kicking the outside door, and shouting, "Let me in." I ran to the door. She had bags and bags of magazines. Strange, I thought.

"I've been all over town buying up these filthy things." One of the bags spilt on the floor. There I was, on the front cover of *The Glossy*. They had interposed Mom's image next to mine. It was rather comical. I split my gut laughing.

"Ah, the taxi driver!" I said.

"What taxi driver?" Mom asked.

"The guy who drove me to your place. He recognized who I was and who you were. He wouldn't believe that you were my mother. This is really comical."

"This is not funny," Mom said. "They're going to ruin your beautiful career! My son actually made something out of himself, and I'm not going to let some sleazebag ruin it for you! We need to get the rest of these off the shelves!"

Mom was determined, but maybe not using her brains at that moment. "Mom, there are probably millions of these things out all over the country. Besides, every time you buy one of these things, you're helping their business. You don't want to give money to these creeps do you?"

Just then, my phone buzzed. I looked down and Craig had texted, "Great pix, ha, ha."

The news had already spread to the West Coast like some bad virus. All that day my friends sent me nasty texts.

"I need you to go down to Harry's Market and pick up my groceries. When I saw these filthy magazines, I left my bags there and went on a buying rampage!"

I walked down to Harry's. Twelve bags of groceries were waiting. Mom failed to tell me that I had to pick up the tab. How much could one woman eat, I wondered?"

When I returned, she had breakfast waiting. Mom placed a spinach and cheese omelet in front of me. Then she started in on finding Crystal's murderer. She wouldn't relent.

"I can't do that, Mom. I just want to get you settled somewhere out of this nightmare of an existence. You don't have to move back to California, but I want to take care of you."

"You are a good son, but you'd be better son if you'd did me this one favor."

I agreed, at least, to try. The first place I went was the newspaper office that interviewed the real Crystal. Maybe the reporter knew something. It was a small outfit, not the *Trib* or the *Sun*, but some South Side paper squeezed into an abandoned mini mall.

There were no reporters who fit the description that I had given to the editor. He was positive, but I didn't believe him. I told him about Crystal.

After a few more minutes of denial, he furtively looked around the newspaper office. He led me down a dark hall to a back office. When we entered the cramped space, he locked the door and crawled under his desk. I heard the sound of tape ripping away. When he resurfaced, he handed me a manila envelope.

"One of my reporters was working on this story," he said. "She was mysteriously murdered, too."

"But it was a male reporter. I am sure that's what my mother said," I told the editor.

"Funny you should say that because I had a few calls from various ladies of the evening asking me about this so-called male reporter. He didn't exist. Or should I say, he never worked for me?" The editor sat down on his chair. He offered me a seat, but I didn't really want to stick around.

"When Crystal was murdered, I remembered those phone calls. I sent Lucy out to flesh out the story. Maybe there was a stalker or serial killer on the loose. Lucy went under-cover. One night, she called me and told me to come to her apartment ASAP. She had some news. Before she hung up, she told me she was going to hide this envelope in case I didn't get to her on time. Good thing. She had been stabbed like Crystal. I should have gone to the authorities, but I was too afraid. This was more than some pervert killing prostitutes."

In that dingy office, I opened the envelope. Glen Gauthier, the most powerful U.S. Senator, was going down, and I had the evidence to do it.

"There's enough information in here to indict Glen Gauthier for life. Why didn't you go to someone with this?" I asked the editor.

"I was at a few of the homicide scenes. Those women were butchered like cows. Who would notice if some smalltime editor was killed? Adrien Inveres? That would be different."

There was no fear in me, only hate for such an evil man. He raped my mother, probably countless other women, then murdered like a Mafia Don. This was almost too easy. Crystal's murderer and Mom's rapist would be arrested and maybe even executed.

I couldn't wait to tell Mom, but something was wrong when I arrived back at her place. The door was slightly ajar, and I heard tussling and wrestling, then a gasp. I kicked open the door. A man, wearing a black mask, was standing over my mother with a bloody knife. He charged at me, and I backed up in time for him to stumble and fall. He landed on his knife. It was a bloody scene all around.

"I thought it was you, when someone knocked at my door," Mom told me later at the hospital. "He didn't say anything, but I didn't think anything of it."

The assailant turned out to be a paid hit guy for Gauthier. Strange, but his attack helped our case against Gauthier, who was actually connected to the French Mafia Gauldheri family. Of course, Gauthier was an American citizen, but he was pulling strings for his family across the Atlantic. It was worse for the Americans knowing that the CIA had no idea this guy was a lethal enemy to the State. Gauthier headed the Senate Select Committee on Intelligence. To think I voted for that guy. I even attended many of his fundraisers. It sickened me.

I figured that Adrien would have voted for Glen Gauthier. I know now that Adrien and I would have clashed. Gauthier, from California, was loathed by his enemies, his power on the U.S. Senate often stretching the Constitution. After the Gauthier incident hit the airwaves, it was clear how Gauthier had been able to work outside the usual constraints. I often fantasized about working on a campaign against him, or even running against him. There I'd be, in a heated debate on CNN articulating my position against a befuddled Gauthier, while the crowd cheered me on.

"You never even wrote a letter to the editor," the giant said. "Were you really hoping to overcome an evil man or just prop up your ego? Catharine, pay attention."

The humiliation I've had to endure under the giant was almost too much. I stood up and dropped the quill.

"I won't do this any longer," I said, firmly.

"Fine," the giant said as he pressed something on his desk. The flames reached up to grab me.

"No!" Adrien shouted. "Take me, not her."

The giant smiled as the flames receded. "Adrien, you are capable of more love than you realize."

I looked Adrien in the eyes, grateful and humbled. "Thank you," I said.

"I guess that you wouldn't have voted for Gauthier; am I correct?" Adrien's voice was clear. Aleric and Ursula were smiling. My face burned.

"I'm so glad we have you here for some amusement, Catharine, even though you're eating up time." The giant chuckled. "Good thing eternity is forever. Give me a minute to let Peter know we need more time. Your life sentences can wait."

The giant turned back to Adrien. "So, Adrien, once again, you ratted someone out. You were probably getting more famous for your investigative abilities than your movie making skills."

Adrien shifted his shoulders. "Whatever."

I flew back to California to continue filming the worst movie of my career and to check out places for Mom to stay. I had just booked a flight back to Chicago when I got a call from Gary. He was dying, so wanted to say good-bye to his biological son."

Fact is stranger than fiction, they always say. This was more than strange. I couldn't have conceived of such a fantastical plot line, let alone believed it. Adrien had to be telling the truth or the giant would have called him on it. Wow, my parents were so normal.

"Wait a minute. Señor Creston contacted you?" Aleric tried to clarify the story. "Did he know that he was your father?"

"Don't you remember? He signed off his paternity rights, but he always kept tabs on me. Apparently, some of my parents' employees kept Gary up to date on my life. One of his deathbed wishes was to meet his and Pat's daughter and son."

CHAPTER 26

The craggy orange Sedona hills surrounded me as I drove up to Gary's estate. He had moved to Arizona after college and never set foot back in California. When I reached the summit, gates magically slid opened at my approach. A large sign, 'This is God's Country,' stood to the right of the gate. This could have been mine, maybe, if things were different. Arizona had never really appealed to me, though I had never been in Sedona before this meeting. I could live with the idea of a hidden estate.

I was greeted by a gurgling fountain surrounded by cacti. A double hung, mahogany twelve-foot door with brass fixtures opened at my approach. Gary's wife appeared. She was a much better kept woman than Mom, but she wasn't selling her body every day of the week.

"Come in," she said, not too warmly. "He's waiting for you." I guess she hadn't forgotten what I had done to her husband.

When I entered the bedroom, there were three men and one woman, whom I assumed were his children, sitting around his bed. They scowled when I entered. I smiled.

"Don't worry. I'm not here to take your precious inheritance. I don't need Daddy's money," I told them.

"Kids, this is your brother."

"Half-brother," one of the men said, the frown etched on his face.

"Yes. You also have a sister, but I haven't been able to contact her."

I saw tears in the guy's eyes. Were they real or part of his televangelist gig, I had wondered.

"Please leave the room," Gary's voice cracked. It was only a shadow of that booming voice heard over the television airwaves. His right arm moved out from under the blanket, and he tapped the chair next to his bed.

"Sit, here," he said. "Thanks for coming. I didn't think you would."

"I didn't think I would be welcomed after what I did to you. Your wife didn't seem too happy to see me."

"You did the right thing."

The irony of that incident was not lost on me - his own flesh and blood ratting him out.

"You knew I was your son when all that happened, right?"

"I didn't want to expose the secret. I was afraid it would hurt you somehow being connected to me."

"Or hurt you by being the father of the biggest atheist in Hollywood."

He smiled. "Would you hand me that water?"

I propped him up. He needed my help to hold up the glass while he sipped.

"Thank you. So, you know everything by now?"

"Yep. Terrible life for Mom, you know."

"I visited her many times, not like I used to, but to urge her to stop living her life as a prostitute."

His words stung. Prostitute. What a life for Mom. How many other women were suffering like my mother?

"We wrote back and forth. This was before I was married. I proposed to her seven times."

"Seven times? Are you telling the truth? She didn't tell me that."

"You can ask her."

"Why didn't she marry you?"

"She told me she was tainted, that she was not worthy of me."

"Shit, I thought it was the other way around," I said.

Gary smiled again. "Yes, you're right, but your mother wouldn't see it that way. She wanted me to make something out of my life. I did, for a while, but greed seeped into my heart."

We conversed back and forth like this for what seemed like hours.

"So, when do they expect you to, you know..."

"Die? Soon. Very soon. They didn't expect me to..." He hesitated. "The will to live is very strong when you have unfinished business."

He began to cry, loud, heart-wrenching sobs. His wife ran in, but he motioned her to go away. She backed out cautiously. I had a strange urge to comfort him, but I was afraid. Adrien Inveres was not an emotional guy. Then I did something I hadn't done since being a child, cry. Two grown men blubbering like babies. I found my father, but it was only to be a temporary blip in my life.

"I'm not sure my visit was a good idea for me," I told him. "Saying good-bye so soon after meeting sucks."

Sure, my father was a weak charlatan, but there was goodness in this man. I would only get an appetizer, so to speak.

"You were a beautiful baby," he said.

Then I remembered his visits. He was the only man that didn't end up in bed with my mother. Instead, he played with me, changed my diapers, and even took me on walks. How could I have forgotten that?

"You were that man that came every week."

"Yes, until your grandparents took you away. It was for the best, though it broke my heart not to see you anymore. I kept up with Gayle until she moved away without leaving me a forwarding address. When I found her again, she begged me to leave her alone."

He motioned for the box of tissues. I handed it to him, and took a tissue for myself.

"Can you find it in your heart to forgive my weakness? I wanted to be a part of your life and should have tried harder, but it seemed like it wasn't meant to be."

"Dad." The word sounded so strange on my lips. "Let's not dwell on the past. Instead, I will come back and visit. Right now, I'm trying to get Mom better. I'm also trying to find Amber."

Gary cried again. "I tried, but the investigator told me she was dead."

"Dead?" I couldn't believe my ears. "Dead?" I repeated.

"He didn't tell me how she died, but just told me he found records of her death."

My heart sank. That explains why Mom never had some strange girl show up on her front doorstep. Amber was gone forever. What was I going to tell my mother? How was I going to cope with being the only one left of my family?

This was more melodrama than I had anticipated. I had just wanted to meet my mother, maybe my father, but not get too emotionally involved. Grandpa and Grandma loved me, this I knew, but they were never touchy-feely. Outward forms of affection were signs of weakness. Meeting my parents was pushing emotional buttons I had never known existed.

"Can you forgive me?" Gary repeated.

"I was never angry at you," I said. "Honestly, finding out that Gary Creston was my father made me angrier than not having a father. I guess you can't choose your parents."

Before this visit, I had believed it was going to be more about making Gary Creston feel better than healing some long-forgotten emotional wound. I would pretend for his sake, I told myself, though it went against my brutally honest nature.

"Dad," I choked out the words, "though we have just met, I..." I couldn't bring myself to say it. How could I admit to loving almost the worst man on earth? He was my father!

"I love you, too," he said. "I want to leave something to you, a part of my estate."

"No, no, no. Your four kids don't want a five-way split."

"Go to that bureau," he pointed to a Chinese marriage cabinet. "Pull out the top drawer and look way back." My hand searched and searched when it finally touched a worn, leather satchel. I pulled it out and handed it to Gary. It stuck as he tried to unzip it. He yanked and yanked. I grabbed it, yanked, and finally the zipper opened. He pulled out a pair of baby shoes and a faded envelope. I reached for the envelope and opened it to a lock of blond hair.

"Your grandparents sent these things to me after returning every one of the letters I sent to them. I wrote every week when I found out you were living back with them."

He handed me the rest of the envelopes, *Return to Sender* stamped on the outside of every single one of them. I peeled opened one after another and read how this twenty-something young man wanted to marry their daughter and reunite their family.

"Dear Harold and Marylyn," he wrote. "I have a job now. My salary is $30,000 a year. I can afford to marry your daughter and be a father to our children. Here is a $500 check"

The check had never been cashed.

Letter after letter he wrote how he regretted his terrible decision. My grandparents returned every single one. I was feeling an emotion I had never felt toward them before - anger at my grandparents who mistakenly tried to shield me, while pushing away my father.

"I clung to those tiny memories of you. At least I had something. I have never showed these to my wife or kids. They'd be too jealous. They never even knew I had two other kids somewhere out there until recently. They wanted me to forget about it, not bring up the past, but how could I die in peace? Would you do me one more favor?'

"It depends," I said, afraid he'd ask some crazy request like Mom had done.

"Would you find out how Amber had died?"

"I don't know if I can go through this again. It's probably better we don't know."

"Please, for your mother's sake, if not for mine?"

"I don't even want to tell Mom that Amber is dead. That would crush her."

"Yes, you're probably right."

He fell back into his pillows and sighed.

"I'm going back tonight, but will return on the weekend. Do you want me to bring Mom back?"

Gary lifted himself up in excitement. "Would you?"

We hugged. It was awkward, but felt good. He was very weak, but I felt his inner strength.

Gary died three days after my visit. He and Mom were never reunited. We didn't get to say our good-byes. Gary's son, I guess my half-brother, called to give me the funeral arrangements. I skipped it, but sent flowers.

I returned to Chicago only to discover Mom back in the hospital. Cancer. It had invaded her body.

"Go back to California, honey," Mom said. "I don't want you to see me in this condition."

"I wouldn't exactly say you're a beauty queen now, Mom," I said.

"Adrien! What kind of remark is that to make to your mother?" Ursula said this time.

"It was true. I had told you all before how awful she looked."

"But, you don't say that to her," I added to the conversation.

"Catharine, I believe you're happy it was Ursula who spoke up this time." The giant smiled.

Adrien shrugged his shoulders and continued.

She was released from the hospital with the prognosis of a few weeks left on earth. She tried to convince me to go back to California.

"I've been an absent mother for all of your life. How could I expect you to be here for me? I'm not that selfish." She grabbed my hand in terror. "But, if you really want to stay, I won't object."

Once she was released, she informed me that she had a lot of unfinished business.

"I want to say good-bye to all my friends."

Every day she'd give me directions, and I'd drive her to a house or an apartment. One day we visited a nursing home. Frank, one of her former customers, was now a resident at Fairhaven Home.

Adrien shook his head, but resumed his story.

The nurses smiled when we entered.

"Hi, Pat, how are you? Frank has been asking about you."

"You don't...." I didn't want to finish the question.

Mom slapped my arm. "Of course not. We're friends."

"Hi, Frank," Mom shouted. It was a good thing they weren't doing anything besides talking or the entire nursing home would have heard them. "I brought you some fruit."

He nodded, but said nothing.

"I got some bad news," Mom continued. "They found cancer in me."

"What?" he asked.

She shouted it again, her voice probably echoing all the way into Wisconsin.

"I'm constipated," he answered.

"He tells me that all the time," Mom said. "Frank, I have to go now. I won't be coming back."

"Tell the nurse I need prune juice."

"Yes, Frank, I will." Mom kissed his forehead. "Good bye."

For three weeks, Mom and I bummed around Chicago. Every day she'd ask me if I found Amber yet.

"No, Mom, my sources aren't pulling up anything."

"Keep trying. I want to say good-bye to her."

I started disbelieving the doctor's predictions, until Saturday morning of the third week. It was early. Mom wanted to go grocery shopping and then buy me some new clothes. The coffee was brewing and I plated her breakfast burrito.

"Mom, breakfast is ready," I shouted.

There was no answer. "Mom!" I tried again as I knocked on her bedroom door. Nothing. I listened. She was breathing. I pushed the door opened quietly.

"I'm going to die today, I'm sure of it."

"You want room service, today," I said. Mom tended to be a fatalist. "People don't really know when they're going to die," I said. "You might suddenly recover and live another fifty years!"

"Lord help me if I do!"

She ate, but felt like she needed to go back to bed.

"How long do you plan to lie here?" I asked her. "Didn't you have some shopping today? There's that flower show tomorrow. You wanted to see it."

She rolled over onto her left side. Later, she called me into her room to help her walk to the bathroom. At about six that night she said I needed to call a Catholic priest.

We weren't even Catholic, and Mom wanted a priest!

"Mom, what are they going to say when I call and tell them what you've been doing for a living?"

"They don't care. Call St. Adrian's. I stopped in there once because it was the same name as yours, only spelled incorrectly."

"Maybe my name is spelled wrong." I said, while checking the phone book. "It's not very near. I don't think they're going to send a priest over here. Hey, there's a church two blocks from here."

Mom was stubborn and determined. "I had met a Father Murphy. He's very friendly."

"He might not even be there anymore." I started thinking about all the relationships my mother had had, and wondered if perhaps this priest knew her better than he knew most of his parishioners. "He wasn't one of your..."

"Adrien! How disrespectful! Of course not! Occasionally I would stop after people left the church on a Saturday night. I had time on my hands because I didn't work weekends."

"That's convenient."

"I could pick my own hours."

"I see that was a great job benefit. Mom, why would a priest you don't know come here?"

"He'll come if you just call him."

I got an answering machine, but at the end of the message, it gave a number for emergencies. I wrote the phone number down.

"Is this an emergency?" I asked Mom when I hung up.

"I'm dying. I think that's an emergency."

I called the number. Father Murphy answered. He was at a wedding reception, but would come immediately.

After that call, I sat down and looked at Mom. What would the priest think if she didn't die today? Would he be mad for a wasted call?

I honestly didn't think it was Mom's day to depart this earth. She actually seemed very vigorous for a dying woman. About forty minutes later, Father Murphy showed up. It was awkward.

"Hi, I'm Adrien," I said while shaking his hand.

"Your mother has told me all about you. I visited her at the hospital."

All these secrets Mom had failed to tell me.

"She told me she met you at your parish."

"That's right, but when I read about her in the newspaper, I had to stop by for a visit. How are you holding up?"

Did he want my confession? I shrugged my shoulders and led him to Mom's bedroom. I brewed some coffee, paced back and forth in her tiny apartment, and then decided to go for a walk. When I returned, Father Murphy was leaving her bedroom.

"Do you want some coffee?" I asked him.

"I think you better go in there," he said. "She's ready."

She's ready? I thought. She didn't seem ready before.

"Is there anyone I should contact for you?"

"Yeah, my dead sister." I tried to joke.

"Your mother spoke of a daughter, but she didn't say she was dead."

"I just found out when I went to see my father. He hired a private investigator to find her, but only found out that she had died. This has been a Hell of year."

"Do you want me to stick around?" He sounded sincere.

I almost took him up on it, but then I would have to share my feelings, and I was clutching onto them fearful I would lose those too.

"Your mother asked that I help you with the funeral arrangements. Here's my phone number. Call me when you need to."

When he left, I was almost afraid to see her. I knocked, and she answered, "Come in."

I sat on a chair next to her bed.

"Please hold my hand," she said. I took it, and it felt frail and weak. Life was seeping away.

"Man! This is hard!" Adrien ran his hands through his hair. "I can't go on."

"You must." The giant's voice was gentle.

Mom went on and on about how sorry she was, how terrible she was for not raising Amber and me. Her life was a mess, ruined. She cried and I cried with her, feeling the pain of not having my parents and the crushing reality of death, which had just stolen my father, and now taking her away. It seemed so cruel, so, so cruel and wrong.

"I love you, Adrien," she whispered. The she took her last breath.

That was it. I wanted the priest back in there to tell me what to do next, but he had left. Should I call someone? I did nothing but sit in the chair next to her for the entire night.

I must have fallen asleep because I woke up with the sun in my eyes. Sleep had muddled my thoughts, and I stood up ready to make breakfast for Mom and me. Then I turned toward the bed.

For a long time Adrien stared out into space. We wiped our eyes and waited for him to continue.

It is always painful to say good-bye at death. Dad wanted to meet with each of his kids alone before his passing. Even though I'm dead, the memory of that final visit still brings tears to my eyes. Daddy was always a part of all our lives. He fed and bathed us, held our chubby hands while we took our first steps, taught us to ride a bike, took us to our sporting events, or ballet for me. I could write on and on about my father and how he was always there for us kids.

It was natural for us to assume that that was the way it was for everyone, but I learned in first grade that I was wrong. I met Brandy, a too-skinny, blond girl whose mother drank for a living and had what I called an invisible father.   Brandy once invited me to sleep over. Mom and Dad were not too sure about it, so they invited Brandy's mother over for supper.

"Mom, Dad, really, I'm almost seven years old! I'm not a baby," I remember arguing with them. Now I laugh. Seven years old. I was still just a baby.

The meeting went poorly. "Did you smell the alcohol on her breath?" Mom asked.

"I did. Instead of Catharine going over to Brandy's, why doesn't Brandy sleep over here?" Dad suggested. Mom didn't want anything to do with Brandy, but Dad insisted.

Brandy did sleep over that night and many more to come. She practically moved into the house with us. People often jokingly asked if she was my sister. Sometimes, I would go to ballet, and she would hang around the house. Dad got her interested in basketball. North Carolina later offered Brandy a full scholarship. Brandy's mother also cleaned up her act and found a great husband.

"Do you remember that tall, skinny girl who used to hang around the house?" Dad asked, his breathing labored.

"Brandy? Yes. We practically adopted her. You know she got married and has five kids."

"Yeah, yeah, I forgot.' His mind shifted to another thought. "I am leaving some money for you," he said. "Look under the bed. I have it stashed under there."

"Dad! Really? Mom never found it?"

"I always changed the sheets on our bed, so I didn't have to worry about her finding it."

I am almost too ashamed to write the rest of the conversation, but I must.

"Catharine, Catharine, I want you to follow your dreams. That is why I have been saving here and there for you. I always enjoyed your stories. The rest of the kids made up their own stories, but yours were the best.

"I want you to go to college," he rasped. "There will be money for you to go. I know you're twenty-nine, but I want you to pursue your writing."

Then we argued gently for a bit, but then I promised I'd go back to school. When I started looking online, I had to enroll in classes I didn't really want to take. Why did I need those useless classes? It was going to be a lot of late nights, crummy weekends, and professors who probably wouldn't like my work. Where would it really lead me? Some lame PR job or some tiny newspaper? Since no one knew about the money, I took a cruise and put the rest in the bank.

After our disagreement over school, I hugged and kissed him. I said my goodbyes and waited for the rest of the kids and Mom to come into the room. Dad was always a gentleman. He waited until Mom was sitting right next to him, with his children and grandchildren around him, before expiring. We all cried, sobbed actually. Dad would not have been proud of us at that moment. Stoicism was thrown out the window as we threw ourselves onto the bed and cried. Then, as if we turned off a faucet, we all stopped crying and wiped our eyes. Mom and I covered Dad's face with the blanket.

I looked up at Adrien and began to understand why his life fell apart. When I had read all those rag magazines, I had felt nothing but contempt for him. Now, all I felt was sorrow.

"Adrien," I said. "I'm sorry."

"Sorry for what?"

"For all the bad thoughts I had of you while alive."

"Wait until you hear the rest of my story."

CHAPTER 27

The gentle Adrien had left, with the return of the impassive, cold man. His voice lacked all emotions as he lumbered through the rest of his story.

I covered Mom's face with a blanket. I had her for such a short time, and then she was gone. I was glad she died in peace. I called the parish to speak to Father Murphy. I got his secretary. It was strange trying to explain the situation. Thankfully, she asked no questions.

I had called some of my friends back in L.A., but they were all too busy to show up. That was fine for me. I was actually too busy also, but it would have looked bad if I didn't go through the motions. The only thing I couldn't do was cry. I was finished crying. Now it was time to get back to my life.

I cried a long time after Dad's death. Certain songs, certain phrases, even certain commercials reminded me of Dad. Once, I went to some movie, a comedy, and I sat through it crying. My friend thought I was crazy.

I sat numbly through the funeral. There were prayers, music. I wasn't raised Catholic, so I felt like I was looking through a kaleidoscope with all these crazy images circling around my brain. The parish had a grieving committee. They sat on the right side of the church and pretended to mourn. I turned around and saw some of the vagrants I met in Mom's apartment. Most of them were crying, really crying. Frank even showed up and waved to me.

The drive to the cemetery almost killed me. I asked Father to ride along. Thankfully, he did. We didn't say much. He pointed out various landmarks and buildings. I didn't plan on returning to Chicago, at least to these parts.

Even cemeteries have divisions between the rich and the poor. Of course, money was no object, so Mom's body was laid to rest on the right side of death's train tracks. I ordered a six-foot relief sculpture carved with an acacia tree in full blossom. It wasn't ready for the funeral, so we stood around a pile of dirt. Father prayed more prayers and sprinkled water onto the casket. Then we were back in the limo to the church. I wanted it to take me to the airport, but some strange sense of duty prodded me to continue this farce.

I'm not the biggest fan of boiled ham and salty scalloped potatoes. And, who eats fruit-flavored gelatin? Mom's strange friends were shoveling the food into their mouths as if it was their last meal. Frank was looking for stewed prunes. Mom would have been happy at the turnout. In one of our few conversations, she told me she didn't want to die or be buried alone.

The church basement had seen better years. Broken-down highchairs leaned up against one wall. The wallpaper was more off than on. Pieces of tile were missing from the floor. Mom would want some money to go to the church. I pulled out my checkbook.

Father Murphy stared at the check, probably not sure all the zeros were correct. Then he said, "I didn't do this for the money." He handed the check back.

"I know you didn't do this for the money, but it seems that you could use a little around here." I pushed it back toward him. "You would make Mom happy if you took it."

"You would make your mom happy if you started going to church," he replied.

"No, no, I don't want to hear any of that kind of talk. It's all meaningless. This funeral was for Mom, nothing to do with me," I said. "When I die, just have someone throw me out the back of their truck."

"There are laws against that." Father Murphy laughed.

"It's cheaper than a funeral. All this, for what?"

Father drove me back to the apartment where we said our good-byes. I had to make sure all Mom's drug bags were gone. I must have flushed down a good half million dollars' worth.

I packed my suitcase, booked a flight out that night, and left Chicago forever. I hired a cleaning lady to clean up the place and to sell Mom's bedroom set and other trinkets. A couple of weeks later, I got a check for $500, definitely much less than the value of Mom's items. Someone got a good deal, or the cleaning lady took a hefty cut for herself. I didn't care. It was done, and I could move on with my life.

CHAPTER 28

Adrien went on. A chill crept into his voice.

Strange, I thought all family matters had been settled. Mom, Dad, and Amber were all dead, their ghosts no longer haunting my childish desire for a family. The second private detective found nothing about Amber's death. It was as if she had never lived. My life was a desert of relatives, which was a relief after learning of my own parents' sordid histories. I didn't need more family to complicate my life. Unfortunately, that memo didn't get out to the right sources.

We were shooting *Headstrong* when I started noticing a blond kid, a teenager, hanging around the set. He'd stare at me. I'd return the stare, trying to get him to back down, but he didn't. He stood, watching, not saying anything. That went on for weeks. Every morning, before the rest of the crew showed up, he'd appear.

I was in my trailer one afternoon when he knocked and entered before I answered. I pulled out my Colt 45.

"Hi, Dad," he said.

"I don't have any kids. You must be mistaken." I stood up and leaned outside my trailer to yell for security to get rid of this nut case.

"Miranda Petersen'' he said.

Miranda Petersen was a household name if you spent any time watching television or movies. Love - hate. That's what Miranda Petersen engendered. Variety once wrote, "Miranda Petersen might be considered the world's most beautiful woman if she didn't have such a malodorous personality."

Despite her reputation, women adopted her hairstyle, mode of dress, and even her voice intonations. Posters of Diva Petersen pervaded men's locker rooms, work cubicles, and the hidden boxes in their closets. Magazines had reported the torrid affair of Ms. Petersen and Adrien Inveres. He directed, and she acted in Manhunt, shot exclusively in Venezuela. Adrien suffered numerous attacks, even a broken arm from their altercations. They must have set those differences aside in bed.

I wanted the kid out, but was curious. I vaguely remembered reading about Miranda having a baby. She had had so many men, that no one felt compelled to claim fatherhood. Furthermore, she hadn't requested DNA tests from all her lovers. The tabloids pointed their fingers at me. Unless someone slapped a paternity suit on me, I wasn't going to offer myself up.

"Why now?" I asked the boy.

"I ran away. I wanted to see for myself. I was hoping to leave my hideous existence with Mom to be with my dad."

"She has more money than God," I said to him. "You could have anything."

"She told me you have more money than God," he sighed. "I'm not here for money. I'm here to meet my father."

Sounded familiar to me. What kind of Freudian complex did this kid and I share? Did we have June and Ward Cleaver tattooed on our skulls? Perhaps it was a vitamin deficiency.

"Why didn't she have an abortion?" I asked the blond clone of me.

"I ask her that almost every day, but, she gives me no answer, just her wicked smile."

"What's your name?"

"Geoff."

"What an awful name," I said. "Why Geoff?"

"She knew you hated that name."

"That figures. How old are you?"

"Eighteen."

Eighteen? I couldn't believe my ears. Time flew by. It was a little over eighteen years since we shot *Manhunt.* I was starting to squirm. Nevertheless, there were so many others. Why me? Miranda had put him up to this. I couldn't deny he looked just like an 18-year-old Adrien Inveres. Since there was no DNA to prove my fatherhood, however, I didn't want him around.

"You tell that bitch of a mother that I'm not your father. Go back and tell her that her little ruse didn't work on me."

"She has no idea I'm here. I came on my own. Don't you think we look alike?"

"Yeah, so? You probably look like a lot of the men she slept with. She had a thing for blonds, you know."

"You were the only one." His voice accused.

I looked at my wall clock, 12:35. How do I get this nut case out of here before one?

"Okay, you're eighteen, so you don't really need a father to take care of you anymore. If it's money you need, I can set you up with some. I can even get you a place."

What was I saying? If word got out, I'd have every blond kid in the US trying to siphon my life's savings dry. Despite this mental warning, I continued talking to this wack job.

"Are you going to college?"

"I thought I'd see the world a bit before hitting the books."

"Make sure you don't delay. Once you're away from the books for a while..." I stopped myself. I don't take advice; I don't give it.

"So, listen, what was your name? Oh, yeah, Geoff. I really don't need a kid messing up my life."

"I don't really need money, either," he said. "I was just sort of hoping, maybe, just hoping that, you know, that you and me could kind of hang. You know, like father and son."

What this kid was asking for I could never give. I had no emotional attachment to anyone, and I wasn't about to begin.

"You just pop into my life and expect some kind of relationship? There's no way I'm 'hanging' with anybody. If you want money, fine, but don't expect anything more. I'm a busy man, and having a kid, even an eighteen year old, is bad for business."

What did I just tell this boy? Only a few months earlier I had done precisely what he was doing now. It backfired on me, and it would backfire on him.

"Just give up all notions of a warm, family life, boy. It's just fake Hollywood crap they feed people to make them feel happy. It sells movie tickets, but is not reality."

A shadow crossed his face. Then his face assumed a desperate look, the look of a man about to kill. I was terrified. I exposed my gun.

"Don't worry, I won't hurt your precious body, Dad!" he said. Then he disappeared.

The shoot that day was terrible. We couldn't get one good scene. Everyone screamed at everyone. I was the loudest.

We finished the movie five weeks after that strange meeting. We packed up, headed to the airport, and flew back to our respective homes.

As I pulled up to Hentges House, I couldn't shake the fear that had crept over my soul. Ever since Mom's tale of woe, Hentges House appeared menacing. It was no different today. The staff was all gone. They wouldn't be back until tomorrow. I didn't want to talk with anyone or answer their questions. I did that about five hundred times a day during the shoot.

"Mr. Inveres, what do you think of this costume?"

"Mr. Inveres, look at this shot."

"Mr. Inveres, this. Mr. Inveres that."

I was going to make myself a martini, take a bath, and go to bed. Or, so I thought.

I opened the front door, and there he was, dangling off the chandelier. I gagged on the smell. His skin was decaying. I called the police right away. They appeared about ten minutes later. After what seemed like hours of questioning, I left and stayed at a nearby hotel. I never stepped into Hentges House again after that night.

It became for me more sinister than Poe's House of Usher.

Young Man Found Dead in Movie Mogul's Mansion. The headlines screamed day in and day out. It was ruled a suicide. The body hung for weeks before being discovered by the director when he returned from shooting his latest film. The victim was Geoff Petersen, son of famous model Miranda Petersen. Sources, who wish to remain anonymous, say the young man was also the son of Adrien Inveres.

Adrien let out a loud sigh and continued.

Geoff left a letter, which the police found. It damned me. It damned his mother. Our careers, our lives were ruined. How one little letter had so much power I still don't understand.

I stayed away from the funeral. Miranda was all tears. The tabloids ate it up. It was their steady diet for at least a month or more. Miranda was *Mommy Dearest*; I was the *Grim Reaper*, the one who had taken his life.

I couldn't go anywhere without someone spitting on me or cursing me. Hentges House, which I had listed for sale, bore most of the brunt of the anger toward me. Rocks thrown at windows, cars running into the gates, it soon took on the appearance of a haunted house. The realtor hired security guards, at my expense, of course.

One by one, movie offers were retracted, lunches canceled, dinner parties canceled. My social life canceled.

CHAPTER 29

Adrien Inveres evolved into a fat and slovenly out-of-work movie director. I was standing in the grocery line one afternoon. There, on the front cover of a tabloid, was this corpulent man with thinning hair and slouched posture, flipping the birdie at the camera. There were more stories of drunken Adrien Inveres getting in trouble with the law or spending time at the Betty Ford Clinic than there were of Adrien Inveres shooting a new film or Adrien Inveres winning an award. Those were ancient history.

Hollywood eats up its own. There was no mercy for Adrien Inveres in the town that says anything goes. It was more hypocritical than any old church lady. Here was its adored son, being rejected because he lived his life without restraint, without following the rules.

Adrien interrupted my musings. I grabbed my quill, ready to write.

Twenty or so years just slipped away, but during that time I gained seventy-three and three quarter pounds. Most of those calories came from liquor. There were no women throwing themselves at me except for one.

I was living, so to speak, at the clinic, when one day there was a knock at my door. I had been sober for about a week, but still madder than Hell. I wanted a drink, but I knew it was killing me. I hated myself, but suicide just seemed too easy, a cop-out. I carved this existence for myself so I had to live it.

Genevieve, my favorite nurse, came in. "How the Hell are you?" she said, the odor of smoke from her last cigarette still hanging around her.

"Great," I said. "Just get me some Jack Daniels, and I'll be better.'

"Hah, hah!" she laughed, a rough, coarse laugh. Years of smoking had destroyed her vocal chords. "There's someone here to see you." She tried to comb my hair, but I brushed her away.

"Tell them to get lost. I don't want to see anyone."

"Well, she wants to see you, and I can't really tell this lady no." Genevieve walked back to the door and motioned for the stranger to come in.

Whom was she bringing in? Maybe it was the producer Anna Tripkin. We were emailing back and forth before I checked into Hotel Sober. She probably wanted to discuss the idea I had sent her.

My eyes bulged when it wasn't Anna, but a full-grown Brownie standing at the door. I had only seen these brown chicks in old movies, but right in front of me was a nun in a floor-length brown habit.

"I don't need God, and, don't leave any of those stupid pamphlets behind telling me I'm going to Hell."

"Adrien, I'm Amber, your sister."

"Am I still drunk? Am I hearing things?" I started laughing. "A nun? Really? Get the Hell out of here."

"Do you remember when Dad hired the private detective to find me? He had found me, but I asked him not to reveal my identity. I told him to tell Dad that I had died. Then you sent out a different detective. I told him the same thing.

"I realize now that maybe that wasn't the best thing. Mother Superior told me I must visit you and at least let you know that I exist."

"So you can just leave my life like everyone else?"

"Mother Superior gave me as long as I needed."

"Mother Superior this, Mother Superior that. Do you always do what Mother Superior says?" I mocked. What a wimpy sister I had, not the spirited woman I had expected.

"Obedience is never easy," was her only answer.

"I really don't need this now. Why don't you just go back to your convent? Go on with your life, and I'll go on with mine."

"All right." She turned to go.

"You wanted me to say that, didn't you? It would be so much easier hiding away in your little convent than dealing with your belligerent, asshole brother."

She turned around. "Yes, you're right. Who wants to spend time with a jerk?" That was the extent of her profanity, calling me a jerk. That was okay. I saw the spirit in her blue eyes. She had taken the challenge.

"Take off that habit or will Mother Superior get mad?"

She lifted off the veil to reveal short, amber-colored hair, the hair Mom had described. "Amber," I whispered, amazed.

I'm embarrassed to admit this, but seeing her made me cry. She wept also. She sat on my bed.

"But now they call me Sister Gertrude."

"Gertrude? What a horrible name. Couldn't you have found a better name? Gertrude, ugh."

Amber laughed.

"I bet you this Gertrude chick didn't have the colorful family tree that you do," I said.

"Probably not," Amber veiled herself again. She paused before speaking. "By the way, I did see Mom before she died."

"You did?" That little piece of information tugged at something in my heart. Amber and Mom had their final good-byes.

"It was a bit shocking to find out what Mom did for a living. My adopted parents were very ordinary. Dad worked as a lawyer and Mom stayed home until we were all in school. Then she became the church secretary.

"I have four brothers and five sisters, all of them living very boring lives. They just found out who my biological brother is. They're all praying for you."

"I don't need or want their bloody prayers. Tell them to pray for someone else."

"You tell them." There was that stubborn streak I had seen in Mom.

"Whatever. It's not going to help anyways. So, Sister Gertrude, you play cards?" I didn't expect the response I got. Suddenly she reached under her gown and pulled out a perfectly new deck of cards.

"Sheepshead?" she asked. Amber shuffled like a Vegas card dealer. She dealt out the cards, and we played the entire afternoon. Periodically, some of the residents popped in to witness Adrien Inveres playing cards with a nun. A knock at the door and the "Time to eat," call stopped our last game.

Genevieve came in and asked, "Sister, do you want to join us?" Amber did. It was strange walking alongside this Brownie. People stared openly at us, as if we had some strange disease.

"The food isn't the greatest around here," I apologized.

"Try convent food," she answered as she scooped the mashed potatoes into her mouth. Skinny, very skinny, but she ate very well for a woman. All I could see was Mom. Though they had never lived together, Amber acquired Mom's unique mannerisms, such as brushing against her forehead with her right hand while leaning forward with her left hand cupping her chin. They both had receding chins, giving them the appearance of double chins, though they both were painfully skinny.

"You don't like your chin, do you?" I asked.

She laughed. "Well, it's not my favorite feature. Even nuns can be a little vain, I guess. The wimple helps hide it a bit. My brothers and sisters tease me. They tell me that's the only reason I became a nun!"

Her words stung - brothers and sisters. Jack Daniels, where are you when I need you?

"I'm your brother, your real brother," I said defiantly.

"Yes, little brother. It's strange. I am the baby in my other family, but to you, I'm the big sister." She smiled at me. "I better get going or they'll worry about me at the convent."

"Where are you staying?" I had no idea where convents were hiding in L.A. Ask me where a bar was I'd tell you, but not a convent.

"My order has a house outside of L.A. I'm staying there for as long as you need me."

"I don't need anyone."

"Okay, for as long as I need," she said. "Do you want me to come back, or should I just pack up and head back to Philly?"

"Whatever," I turned away. The resemblance to Mom was painful.

"I love you," she said, plain and simple. Did she mean it, or was it something she learned at the convent?

"Just get out of here."

Adrien had a nun for a sister! I had thought about becoming a nun, but it just didn't seem right. I visited a few convents. The nuns were all very nice, but I felt like I was trying to jam a puzzle piece into the wrong space. I just thought I'd find a man and get married. That never happened, either.

CHAPTER 30

It had been almost two o'clock when Amber strolled in. In my room, all alone, I paced. Not roomy enough for pacing, but back and forth I went like a caged tiger. I had scared her away. She was never coming back. I must admit my personality stunk like limburger cheese, but I wasn't going to accommodate a Brownie, even if she was my sister.

"Excuse me, Señor," Aleric interrupted. "I thought in your country Brownies were little girls who sold cookies."

We all laughed.

"So did I," Ursula said.

"Yeah, why do you call your sister a Brownie? That doesn't seem very respectful." I had to throw in my two cents.

"She was brown all over. Who cares what I call her? It's my bloody story," Adrien pouted. "Just let me finish. Really!"

I skipped breakfast, skipped lunch. Finally the knock came. Brownie walked in all smiles.

"Look what the cat dragged in."

"Were you waiting?"

"Me? Huh. I've been working out another movie idea. In fact, if you want to leave, go right ahead."

"Sure," she turned around.

"On the other hand, why don't you stick around? I need material for my next movie called, *Nefarious Brownies.*"

"Aren't there enough of those already?"

"Nefarious Brownies?"

"Movies about them."

"Speaking of nefarious Brownies..."

"I wish you wouldn't call us that."

I ignored her comment. "Anyhow, speaking of nefarious Brownies, where were you all morning? Torturing little children? Haranguing pre-pubescent girls about the evils of sex?"

"Wow! What novel did you extract that from, little brother? If you really need to know, I've been manning the soup kitchen. Started at four this morning, then took a

155

taxi so I could spend an afternoon of humiliation. Spiritual exercise, you know."

We stared at each other. How many sibling fights would we have had growing up? Me, tugging her pony-tails, stealing her dolls, throwing water balloons at her, messing around in her bedroom, and breaking some precious toy. She, playing the grown-up, mature big sister, throwing her weight around. Would we have become estranged like so many families, or would we have stuck it out, and grown closer as we matured? Neither of us could answer that, the gulf of years filling in all those blanks.

She pulled out the cards. We sat at the table and played again, but not all afternoon. About an hour later, she suggested we go for a walk around the campus.

"No! I don't want people staring at me!"

"Who cares?" she laughed. "People stare at me all the time. I'm used to it."

We meandered through the grounds. Highly manicured flowerbeds catered to the rich, yet pathetic, patrons of this clinic. Near a patch of flowers, Amber fell to her knees.

"Don't start praying here!" I shouted.

She pulled up her sleeves and started weeding.

"What are you doing? They have gardeners for that!" I said to her. I couldn't believe my eyes. What was she trying to do?

"They missed a whole spot here, see? Get down and help me."

"Weed a garden? That's why they hire gardeners." I stood looking down at her.

"Ah, wimpy Adrien. Can't get your precious fingernails dirty." I ducked to avoid a careening clump of dirt.

"Hey, stop that! They're going to throw me out."

Another one, right in my stomach. She had no mercy. Finally, after the sixth clump, I hunkered down and squeezed the dirt between my fingers. Dirt grossed me out, but I wasn't going to let this Brownie get the best of me.

"Hah! Take that!" Right in her face. Touché, back in my face.

"My eyes, it's in my eyes!" I screamed, like a baby, I might add.

"Boo hoo hoo. Baby Adrien got mud in his eyes. Boo hoo hoo."

"Shut up!" I shouted. "It hurts. You try getting dirt in your eyes."

We sounded like ten-and-eleven year olds. I started laughing, laughing so hard I had to take a pee. She laughed too. We looked like morons out there. People passed by, but stayed far enough away.

Adrien looked embarrassed at retelling this story, but when he looked at our smiling faces, he continued.

After we cleaned up, Amber drove, slowly, just like a nun, to the convent for supper.

"So, did you hear about Geoff?" I couldn't call him my son. He was just Geoff, a kid who hung himself in my house, destroying my life while taking his.

She said nothing.

"Did you hear me?" I was afraid of her response.

"You mean my nephew?"

"He was nothing to me."

"Like most.

"How dare you stand in judgment of me! You, who told the PI to get lost so you didn't have to deal with our family."

"You were not the long-lost brother I had hoped for, that's for sure. And, when RJ showed up at my door..."

"Who's RJ?"

"One of the private detectives."

"His name was Robert," I corrected her. I hated that she made a friend of someone that I had hardly noticed.

"Robert James, RJ for short. He told me all about his family. He has a beautiful wife and two cute boys."

"Sounds like you got pretty chummy with him."

"Nope, just spoke with him for about ten minutes. I didn't pretend to come from a normal, happy family. Most adopted kids are not. But...but, let's just say, I was surprised to find what was lurking in my pedigree. I told him immediately I didn't want you to find me.

"But, that didn't mean you were out of my life for good. Mother Superior made you my special prayer project."

"Ah, a lot of good that did!" I interrupted her.

"Maybe not for you, but it softened my heart."

By then we had arrived at the convent. We pulled up to a three-story, pale pink brick mansion. Four long windows, arched at the top, flanked the door on each side. The light and air from the outside followed us as we entered the spacious, yet sparsely furnish living quarters. My nostrils were greeted with savory whiffs. Supper already smelled better than Hotel Sober. A stout Brownie, pushing a cart with a pot on it, entered through the dining room door. She hoisted the heavy kettle onto a sideboard.

"Sister Gertrude, if it weren't for me, we wouldn't be eating supper tonight. You know it was your turn to cook today!"

Amber looked dismayed. An older woman, wearing more fabric than the rest, floated through another door. There were doorways everywhere.

"Sister Felicity, Gertrude is our guest. She doesn't have kitchen duty."

"I'll do the dishes," Amber said.

"You will?' asked Sister Felicity. "Well, that more than makes up for missing supper duty. Wait until you see the mess I left for you!" Everyone laughed, except for me. Dishes? That was for maids, not Adrien Inveres.

I counted sixteen Brownies at the table. They placed me on the opposite end of Mother Superior. The Brownies' heads bowed in prayer. I watched, leaving my hands at my side.

The sisters were intrigued to have a Hollywood type at their table, so I fielded questions between soup, roast beef, rolls, potatoes, and pickled beets. Have you ever had pickled beets? I didn't before then, but after, I made them a regular diet staple.

Finally, Felicity rolled out the dessert. Macadamia nut brownies with caramel topping. How did these nuns stay so thin with food like this? Finally, we finished. The lull was broken by Mother Superior clearing her throat.

"So, Mr. Inveres, you don't pray?" she asked, out of the blue.

"To whom would I pray, since there's no God?" I said.

The sisters, except Mother Superior, chortled at my comment. I stared at the ladies surrounding me. No one ever laughed at Adrien Inveres, especially a bunch of Brownies.

"Sisters," said Mother Superior, "it's rude to laugh at our guest. He is free to believe what he wants to believe, even if he's wrong."

Those were fighting words. I stood up, ready to shout my opinion, when Amber also stood up. "I think Adrien and I will start the dishes." She looked at me. "Grab some dishes and follow me."

Clear the table? This was beneath me.

Sister Felicity was a filthy cook! We were in that kitchen for almost two hours! Amber washed, and I dried. I went through four towels! I had to admit, however, that Felicity could cook. I started imaging Sister Felicity's cooking show. Maybe PBS would carry it or even the Cooking Network. I was sure someone would pick it up. I wondered what kind of ratings we'd get.

"Hello, earth to Adrien," Amber's voice interrupted my musings. "What are you so deep in thought about?"

"I think Felicity should have her own cooking show. I could produce it."

Amber laughed, really laughed. "Felicity has a big enough head! We don't need to encourage it. Besides, you'd have to have a team of a hundred people just to clean up after her!"

Just then Felicity strolled in. "I heard my name. What are you saying about me?"

Amber stared at me, daring."

"You're a messy cook," I answered her. I threw a towel at her. "Why don't you finish up here? The institution for drunks awaits me."

"I was hoping you'd consider me for a cooking show," Felicity replied. "All that work for nothing."

"That's not true," Amber said. "We really enjoyed it! Besides, what would you do with all that fan mail?"

Amber drove in silence. There was something she wasn't telling me. "So, big sister, what's the matter?"

"I need to get back to Philly. My replacement fell ill. I need to get back sooner than I expected."

"Can't you get a job transfer or something?" I pleaded. I tried not to sound too desperate.

"It doesn't work that way when you're a nun."

"Damn the nuns! Quit, leave! Is this really what you wanted?"

"More than anything."

That was more than I could take. I couldn't understand someone giving up her life for such a dreary existence. "What about me?"

"I will visit when I can. You can also hop on a plane and come out to Philly. You can meet all my brothers and sisters. They're not your biggest fans, but they'll be nice to you."

My ego was taking a beating. In my world, everyone loved me or at least pretended to love me. Outside my little world were enemies, and I didn't like it one bit. "Nah, I don't want to meet them."

"Wimp!" Amber said.

"When do you leave?" I asked.

"Day after tomorrow. I'll stay with you all day tomorrow, but then I need to go."

She pulled up to the doors. A guard stood watch. He nodded when I entered. I turned to see Amber waving. Only one more day, then she'd be out of my life. She didn't have to be. I could move to Philly. I could buy an apartment there and visit. It would be up to me.

All night I craved a drink - a lot of drinks. I wanted to get drunk. I wanted to douse the pain. I must have moaned quite loudly because an orderly pushed open my door and asked me what was wrong. "Nothing," I told him.

"Then, be quiet," he replied. "You're keeping the other guests awake."

That's what we were, guests - guests at a treatment center, not patients, not inmates, but guests.

The next day I was ruder, if you can believe that, to Amber than the day before. Bad day. She should have just dropped me at the door and never returned. She put up with it. She didn't reprimand me.

"So, you could never get a man, huh? Didn't want to have sex, huh?" I knew I was hurting her, but I didn't care.

She just smiled, and said, "I was engaged to be married. Six bridesmaids, two flower girls, the country club, a sixteen-piece brass band for the reception, cheesecake for the guests, and a $4,000 wedding dress. Stan, my fiancé, even bought me a one-and-a-half carat diamond engagement ring. He was a wonderful man."

"Who broke it off?" I asked her, thinking it was Stan, but her answer surprised me.

"I did, after my bridal shower. Ever try putting on a pair of shoes that are too small? That's what my impending wedding felt like. Stan was perfect, but not for me. The presents from the shower were still in the back seat of my car when I drove to his house.

"I'll never forget his smile, so big and bright, slowly fading as he looked at my expression. He pleaded. He begged, but I wouldn't budge. I looked out my rearview mirror to see him sprinting behind my car. As I drove away, I watched his figure fade into the distance. When I arrived back at my sister's house, she knew. She had known all along, but never said anything. Mom and Dad were very understanding.

"Gifts were returned, calls were made, deposits returned, my wedding dress sold. In a matter of weeks, the wedding was wiped away as if it never existed. Stan eventually married Samantha, my maid of honor. They were very well suited for one another. I tried entering the convent right away, but I had to wait a year to make sure that it was what I really wanted."

"You dumped the man of your dreams for this? I envy you. I never found Mrs. Right."

"According to the tabloids, you had a Mrs. Right almost every week."

"Ha, ha," I replied.

"I don't expect you to understand, but it would be nice if you respected me."

I continued the rude comments throughout the day. It was like the stomach flu when you can't stop vomiting.

Then it was time for her to leave, to exit my life. Would it be forever, or would I be man enough to visit her? As she pulled open the door to walk out, I said, "Thanks for wasting my time!"

"With pleasure." She kissed my forehead and left.

I scurried to follow her out of the building like a desperate rat. "You'll come and visit, won't you? You'll write, won't you?"

"What am I saying?" I thought to myself. "I groveled for no woman."

What a sad life he led. He seemed like such a loathsome character, yet he was just pathetic. All the world envied him for his talent and money, but who would envy him his loneliness?

Tears spilled from my eyes, freely. I looked and notice Ursula crying, too.

"I am still sorry for being so rude to you," I said, dabbing my eyes. "I guess you don't really know a person."

"Don't get all sappy on me," Adrien responded.

"Adrien, you're getting close to the end. Please finish," the giant said.

Once I left the treatment center, I hung around my house, not doing much, except drinking. What a waste of money and time.

Amber wrote every week. Her letters usually arrived on Tuesday. I sent no replies. It was all one-sided. My friends, Jack and J. Bavet, comforted me Wednesday through Monday.

At Christmas she arrived only to find a drunken, fatter, obnoxious man decaying from the effects of the doctors' prognoses, all six of them - cirrhosis of the liver. You see, I didn't believe doctor number one, two, three, four or five. Once doctor number six said the same thing, I knew I couldn't deny it any longer.

"Do you want to come back with me? Mother Superior hired some remodelers so you could stay with us," Amber asked while we were eating the Christmas dinner that she had prepared for us.

She had wanted me to move to Philly and I asked, "To die there? Is this what you want for me - to go to Philly to die?"

"Either there or in this house, all alone," she said.

Did she mean it? Did she want me to be a part of her life even though I was preparing to die?

I didn't want to sound desperate, so I responded coolly, "I suppose. There's really nothing left here for me," I had told her.

What would I bring to Philly, I wondered. Amber helped me go through the years and years of accumulated furniture, trinkets, and kitchen gadgets. She seemed to know just the right person or institution that would benefit from a dresser, a stove, a mixer. She also contacted Sotheby's for the more valuable items and the movie memorabilia. The auctioned-off items netted a little over two million dollars.

Amber acted like a schoolgirl at the auction. It was all new to her. Strange seeing the world through her eyes, it made everything seem new and joyful. I felt like a ten-year-old kid again, with a sister.

I finally made out a will. Never made one out before then. I didn't think I'd die.

"You're the sole beneficiary of my estate," I told Amber.

"I can't accept anything. I took the vow of poverty."

"Can't you stash a little for yourself?" I was very indignant that she wouldn't take my money.

"It'll go to my religious order. They'll put it to good use."

"Right. Mother Superior will probably buy herself a mink coat or something."

Amber laughed. "Adrien, you're very funny."

Two hours before heading to the airport, we drove around checking out the sights.

"Isn't there anyone you want to visit?" she asked, the question triggering memories of Mom's visits in Chicago before her death.

"No one," I said. "There's only one place I'd like to see."

I wanted to see Hentges House one more time. Would it still hold its menacing power over me? Why was I shaking, I asked myself. What terror awaited me?

I gave the driver the address. As we neared it, I noticed the other estates and the boulevard still decorated with Christmas trees and toy soldiers. Then the driver stopped. There before me was a huge, gaping lot void of any house or building. Hentges House was gone!

"Where did it go?" I asked.

"Why don't we ask one of the neighbors," Amber suggested. Just then, a pickup truck drove up behind us. A man jumped out and walked over to the driver's window.

"Hi, can I help you?" He was very friendly.

"What happened to Hentges House?" I asked. "I used to live there."

"Hey, man, are you Adrien Inveres? Wow! Great to meet you. Anyhow, the house was torn down right before Christmas. It was all over the news. Didn't you see it?"

"No, I don't watch it these days. Why was it torn down?"

"Structural issues. The inspector found serious problems with the foundation. It would have cost way more to fix than to rebuild."

"Do you mind if I just take a look? I'm moving to Philadelphia and I just wanted to see the place before I left."

"Take your time," the man said.

My driver pulled over and parked. Amber and I got out. I walked over to the little family cemetery.

"Are they going to get rid of this?"

"They're moving the graves to a special area at Hillside Memorial. The cemetery agreed to take them," The man from the pickup said.

"Why didn't anyone check with me?" I asked. My family was going to be lumped together in some anonymous cemetery?

"Maybe we could have the bodies flown to Philly," Amber said solemnly. "Could they hold off for a day or two?"

My sister had all the answers. I could take my family with me.

The day was overcast and cool for L.A. We stepped out to see the gaping hole that was once filled with Hentges House. It was gone forever, just like the lives and the history.

The flight to Philadelphia was uneventful, except for one conversation. I told Amber I wasn't ready to become nothing again.

"Nothing? What do you mean?" She was eating her dinner. Amber had never flown first class, and she was enjoying it.

"Nothing, that's what I mean. Once I die, and my body decays, there'll be nothing."

"But there's an afterlife. Heaven or..." She hesitated.

"Hell for me," I answered for her.

"Well, you do have to choose," she said.

"What if I don't choose?" I hated these conversations, but I was the one who started it.

"Everyone chooses through their words and actions."

"I choose Hell," I said.

Amber grabbed my arm. Tears welled up in her eyes. "Please don't hurt me with that kind of talk. Please?"

We finished eating and the rest of the flight in silence.

A large, ugly van met us at the airport. Sister Bridgette jumped out and hugged Amber. She was a good looking woman, if I do say so myself. Gorgeous blue eyes, high cheekbones and full, luscious lips. The Brownie costume couldn't hide her great figure, either.

"Man, what a hottie. She's a nun?" I whispered in Amber's ear.

She answered back, "Behave yourself."

What Bridgette had in looks, she sure lacked in personality. She was not at all impressed with my movie background. In fact, I think she rather despised me.

"Do you know who I am?" I asked her.

"Unfortunately, yes," she answered, not taking her eyes off the road.

"Did you ever see any of my movies?"

"If I didn't fall asleep during them."

"Ouch! Now I know why you're a nun. No man could get close to you!"

"If they were like you, I wouldn't want them coming near me."

"Bridgette! Behave yourself," Amber piped in. "You don't have to like him, but please try to be Christian."

"I'll try," Bridgette answered.

What enthusiasm Bridgette lacked was more than compensated by the rest of the sisters, all waiting outside the convent for our arrival. I laughed. I hadn't seen that many groupies in a long time.

The cold struck me when I stepped out of the car. I shivered.

"I told you you'd need a coat out here. We're not in sunny California."

A Brownie with a blanket stepped forward. She smiled. "May I?" she asked. You'd think she was covering a Michelangelo statue, she was so careful.

"Get the cross out of here," I said when I entered my room, or should I say, cell?

Mother Superior stepped forward. They must clone these ladies, because she looked just like the one in California. Anyhow, she said, "Mr. Inveres, you're our guest, but we have rules. The cross stays."

"Move it, or I'll throw it off the wall!"

"Get a hammer and nail," Mother Superior turned to one of the groupies. "We'll put it in a place you where don't have to look at it."

A nun returned quickly. Mother Superior climbed a chair, removed the cross, then dragged the chair over to my bed. She lifted her arm to strike the nail on the wall.

"Not over my bed! It'll fall and kill me! Just get it out of here."

"Mr. Inveres, do you want to stay here or not? It goes over your head or you go back to California to..." She didn't finish.

They all knew. They all knew I was here to die. That is why they so graciously opened up their convent to me. Were they celebrating that fact? Would they gloat? This egotistical, immoral Hollywood man was getting what he deserved.

"Fine, I'll book the next flight out of here!" Bravado.

"That is your prerogative, Mr. Inveres. Perhaps Amber didn't tell you there were rules here for you to follow. You are welcome to stay under certain conditions."

I lost that battle and many more after that. Had alcohol robbed me of all authority?

Amber spent all her free time with me. When she was busy, I tried to write, but I felt little inspiration. Gradually, life seemed to ebb away. Our walks became less frequent, with naps filling in the gaps. As much as I hated to admit it, death was calling.

CHAPTER 31

Then life pulled me back for just a little while longer. It was April. They expected my death in March.

Amber forced me out of the cell to see the azaleas. Pink bushes flourished everywhere. This would have been a great scene for a movie. My life might have been ebbing away, but everywhere and everything evoked ideas for a scene, a movie - a movie that had to be made.

"Earth to Adrien," Amber's voice called me back. "What are you pondering, little brother?"

"Couldn't you see a horror flick on these grounds?"

"I don't see horror among the flowering trees and bushes," she said. "I think it's a great place for real life to happen, not something on a screen."

Amber bent to inhale the fragrance of some bush.

"I'm going in," I said.

"You're in there all the time. Why don't we stay out a little longer?"

I ignored her and stomped away. She followed me back to the convent.

"What did that comment mean, when we were outside?" I asked.

"You've lived most of your life in some made-up fantasy. It's time you start living in the real world."

"What do you know about the real world, sister? Locked up here, hiding, and escaping!"

"It's not the physical location of where you live. Every conversation gets wrapped up in your mind like a movie. This is real, not pretend. The actors don't come back to life once they're dead."

"Well, that's not true. Your good book talks about the greatest actor who died and came back to life!"

"Why does everything have to go back to religion? Why, Adrien, if you don't believe, do you have to keep bringing it up? Do you secretly believe?"

"Hah! Good one, sister. You wish."

She grew serious. "Adrien, you have to face your mortality. The doctors don't give you much longer. Are you ready to meet your maker?"

"Mr. Sperm and Ms. Egg?" I laughed at my own joke. Amber left, shaking her head.

My stomach started swelling, and my appetite shrank even more. I fell asleep earlier and woke later. Soon, they were whispering, soon. This time, this time he will surely die.

None of my old friends showed up to say good-bye. Maybe they were afraid of the convent. Even the tabloids skipped this news story. It obviously wasn't scandalous enough.

Amber sat with me most of the time. I wanted her to *always* hold my hand when she visited.

"Adrien, I would like you to meet my family." Amber smiled proudly.

"Hell no!" There was no way I wanted to meet the people who had hogged my sister all these years.

"It would make me happy." She persisted.

"So? No! Absolutely not!"

"You don't have to be so ambiguous about it." She tried a joke, but I didn't laugh.

It was okay for the nuns to visit, but not her family.

Mother Superior would come in every afternoon before supper. She didn't say much, just sat.

"Why do you come to bother me?" I asked her one afternoon.

"I'm curious, that's all."

"Curious about what?" I shook my head. Didn't she have a convent to run?

"I'm trying very hard to see..." she couldn't bring herself to say it. I knew what she aiming at.

"He never came. And if he had, I would have chased him out."

"Oh, but we're all made in the image and likeness of..."

"Well, I wasn't. So, did you become a nun at fifteen or something like that?" She smiled! She actually smiled.

"I sang with the New York Metropolitan Opera."

"I don't believe you. Sing!" I commanded.

"My time is up." Mother Superior stood.

"You don't really sing, do you?"

Then she opened her mouth and belted out the best version of Bellini's *Casta Diva* I had ever heard.

"What other operas were you in?" I asked one day.

"Mother Superior played *Carmen*," one of the Brownies piped up. Mother Superior arched her eyebrows.

I stared, trying to picture her with half her clothes on. "No!" I said in disbelief. "You played that lusty woman?" I laughed. "Now you're a nun! That's priceless. I gotta get better so I can make a movie out of this!"

"Let's change the subject, please?" Mother Superior said, giving the Brownie a dirty look.

Sometimes the sisters would fill my room chanting some strange prayer; "Have mercy on us and on the whole world." It was meaningless, but soothing.

My life had been long gone as a movie director. My friends and my career all lost to my drinking. My physical existence was slipping away as well. I hated what my life had become, but I was terrified at the nothingness waiting for me when I departed from this life. Hell would have been better than nothing, or so I thought.

My body would decompose, turn into dust particles, and Adrien Inveres would be no more. True, there'd be a grave marker, the one testimony of my former existence and my past movies, but after a few years, people forget. Maybe some professor would dig up my old movies. Big deal, since nothingness awaited me on the other side of the grave.

Although I slept all day, I feared closing my eyes at night. The Angel of Death, in a chant reminding me of Paul Revere's night ride, haunted my dreams with, *Nothingness is coming, nothingness is coming, nothingness is coming.*

Mother Superior requested a priest visit. Father Enrique showed up.

"I don't know why you're here," I told him.

"When Mother Superior calls, I answer." He smiled, revealing a gold cap on his front left tooth.

"Why do you guys do that?"

"Do what?"

"Use gold for your caps."

"'I don't understand,' he shook his head.

I pointed to his gold tooth.

"Oh, that! Just because," he said, smiling again.

"So, what did you do in your former life? Were you always a priest?"

"Baseball. I was shortstop on a semi-pro team in Puerto Rico. Then I got the call. Baseball was no longer important to me." He grinned again.

"Would you like me to give you Baptism?" he asked me.

"I'm not a baby anymore."

"You're funny, Mr. Inveres."

"So, you watch any of my movies?"

"'Every one of them. Even the bombs."

I winced when he said bomb. "What do you mean, bombs? There were no bombs." I laughed in spite of myself. "What's your favorite?"

"*Basilica.* It was deeply religious."

"I was mocking religion! There was nothing religious about it."

"No, no. You don't get my meaning. It felt like a man reaching out for God, searching, like you."

"You really didn't get the right meaning, Padre." I didn't want to hear his philosophical, religious nonsense.

"Maybe you didn't." He kept smiling. His gold tooth was bothering me. "May I bless you before I leave?" the good padre asked.

"No," I said. Then I turned and faced the wall, hoping he'd leave. He did.

That is how our visits went. Each time he'd try to bless me before checking out. Father Enrique visited me seven times.

"May I bless you?" he asked for the last time.

"If it makes you happy," I didn't feel like fighting anymore.

He made the sign of the cross on my forehead and spoke some prayers in Spanish. I opened my eyes. He was gone.

Nothingness continued haunting my dreams. *Nothingness is coming, nothingness is coming* - it was coming to swallow me up into non-existence. At night, I'd toss and turn searching for some comfort.

On my last night, nothingness disappeared, no longer harassing me with its power. I was still fearful and like a baby, I was trembling. I clutched onto Amber's hand tightly hoping she'd grab me from the clutches of death.

Amber leaned over me, her breath soothing me for a moment, but the agitation returned. I screamed with what little energy I had left. Amber wiped my brow. Suddenly, the room filled with Brownies. They pulled out their beads and began chanting that prayer again. I fell back into my pillow. I heard my last gasp, loud. Then gone from earth, arrival here.

Adrien looked at all of us. He blinked. It was a long story he told.

"Since my death, I've been waiting, probably for you to die." Adrien stared at me.

"Yes, we've all been waiting for Catharine Zimmer to die," the giant replied. "She is the loose ends to all your stories."

CHAPTER 32

The loose ends? What did uncomplicated Catharine Zimmer have to do with these three people? Vengeance ruled Aleric, desperation destroyed Ursula, and loneliness trampled over Adrien. Catharine Zimmer? My life was happy and fulfilling, or was it? Anxiety lived just beneath the surface of my skin, dictating my every thought and action.

Father knew I lived behind the shadow of fear. Catharine Zimmer was afraid of everything – she was afraid to fall, afraid to dream, and afraid to build relationships.

"Catharine, you're so afraid of dying that you're afraid to live," Dad once said to me. He was right. Every walk in the park, every hike up a hill, or every trip to the store meant images floating in my mind of some looming disaster. I went to a therapist for years trying to find out the source of my fear, but we could find none.

Dad began teaching me how to ride a bike when I was seven-years-old. He actually forced me to go outside.

"I don't want to learn," I had protested. "I don't want to fall."

"So what if you fall?" He argued with me.

"It'll hurt!"

"You'll hurt more by not learning. All your friends will be riding, along with your brothers and sisters. Even Mom and I ride a bike, but not Catharine. You can't ride the tandem forever."

"No!" I refused my father. He had given up.

I was eight when I finally got the nerve to try.

"Dad, I need to ride a bike. Mrs. Vista announced today we're having a bike-a-thon to raise money for Mikey's cancer. I can't let the class know I don't know how to ride."

That night I fell ten times, skinned my knees and elbows, but I learned to ride. What freedom, what joy to have the wind blowing in my face, the coasting down the sidewalk, the arduous pedaling up the hill, the panting, but free!

"Time to go to bed," Dad finally said around 9:30 that night. Way past my bedtime, but he couldn't bring himself to stop my joy.

All summer long, I rode my bike everywhere. When we'd visit my grandparents, I'd have Dad mount it on our bike rack. Up and down the long trail back to the pasture, up to the barn, I rode and rode.

The years zipped by and I found myself in high school. I was very popular, but I didn't join anything that I had to try out for.

"I thought you were going out for pom-poms," Dad said. It was Tuesday, and I was *watching television.*

Mom had driven me to practice on Monday. Inside the gym were girls who were coordinated and learned the steps quickly.

"There was no way I would have made the team with all those girls. You should have seen how they could dance."

"So you didn't even try?" The disappointment in Dad's voice crushed me.

"You would have not only made the team, but also have been the team captain." The giant invaded my thoughts again. "Catharine," he said, "we are going to relive a decision you had made. Many opportunities surrounded you, but fear bullied you into non-action. This one opportunity that you had neglected, however, determined the fate of these three people in front of you."

"What?" I asked in shock.

With a wave of his monstrously large hand, we were all back in my parents' tiny bedroom - the night of my father's death. Will I be doomed to relive this night? This once tender moment now became my accuser. An inheritance for me, not for my other siblings. Why? Did writing genius exist? Dad was encouraging a reticent child to take a risk.

There I was, receiving this gift, deceiving my father in front of these four people. The image of the cruise and my empty life followed. Oh, to be sure, there were moments of grace since grace surrounded me in the form of my family, friends, and church. Nevertheless, that one lie, that one deception lived day in and day out, shaped my life, my eternity, and the eternity of these people around me.

"Enough," shouted the giant. "Now let us understand what Catharine's decision meant for all of you!" He led us back to our seats.

"I must admit, I find it very difficult to understand what a young woman in America had to do with me," Aleric interrupted.

"We will start with you," the giant answered.

Again, a large screen, if you would call it that, appeared. A young woman, her red-hair caught in a ponytail, was scrubbing a floor. Next to her was a dark, curly-haired teen scrubbing also. They were laughing. The screen zoomed up.

"That's me!" piped Aleric.

Moreover, I knew the young woman was I, Catharine Zimmer. Ah, the mission trip to San Xavier. I had read about it in the local newspaper. The college, St. Lawrence, hosted this trip every year. Since I decided not to go to that college, any college for that matter, I couldn't participate. Why, then, was I scrubbing the floor next to Aleric?

"You're right. You were not there. You took the money and went on a cruise," the giant answered my thoughts.

Those words, those terrible, terrible words. Would I be doomed to hear them forever?

"You were always passionate as a child for those the less fortunate. Yet, as you continued to live your lie, you became more comfortable and less afflicted for those less comfortable.

"You would have been in your sophomore year at St. Lawrence. Aleric would have been sixteen years old, you, thirty. Your encounter, your words, Catharine, would have set Aleric on a different path."

The giant plunged me into a Frank Capra-esque movie. This is what life would be like if I had chosen a different course.

It was all nice for Hollywood, but deciding the fate of Catharine Zimmer because I took the money was ridiculous.

"Watch, Catharine!"

We both sat down on the floor, laughing. Aleric's smile would have melted any woman's heart. Then his face grew serious.

"I plan to avenge my parents' death. Gutierrez killed them without mercy, and that is what I plan to do with him!"

"Is murder the answer?" young Catharine Zimmer asked. "In my country, we give speeches, pass laws, follow the Constitution. It's not perfect, but it's so much better than killing."

"It is impossible! Gutierrez has his grip on everything and everyone," Aleric spat.

"Do you want to be another Gutierrez?" I was so wise.

My face reddened. I remember thinking thoughts, very profound thoughts that never had a venue, never had an outlet. In bed at night, I'd stand on some imaginary platform proclaiming the truth of freedom and democracy. To whom? No one. No one.

"How can you say that? No one could ever be as bad as Gutierrez!" Aleric scrubbed harder.

The pony-tailed Catharine shrugged her shoulders and replied, "Maybe, but you could end up being worse if you don't change your attitude."

Aleric kicked the pail, and water spilled all over me. He stood up and folded his arms.

"Is that how you deal with problems?" The image of me walked away. Our voices faded out along with our images.

"That went well," Adrien said. "I don't think Catharine's words had much impact."

"Aleric would have rejected her ideas at first, but they would have taken hold," the giant whispered. "Aleric would have led the first bloodless revolution in that country. San Xavier would be a democracy today."

"You expect me to believe that?" Adrien stood up. "Really? The course of history is so precarious that the simple words of a woman from the States could save a country in South America? I just can't buy that!"

"Why is that so unbelievable? You yourself said the course of your life changed with the chance meeting of a movie producer. Why can't the words of one woman alter history's path? It was her destiny, but she neglected to grab it."

Stab me again, I thought. Just keep stabbing me with those words. I will never live them down. Maybe they were my just punishment.

"You're expecting me to believe that all the vengeance in this fiend's heart would have disappeared with the words of Catharine Zimmer?" Adrien laughed in disbelief.

"You forget Catharine had another thing going for her, her physical beauty. Aleric's motivations would not have been very pure at first. He would try to please this beautiful, older woman from America, but, as he learned and cultivated his skills, democracy and freedom would become more beautiful than any woman."

Adrien sighed, loud and heavy. "Right, and what did Catharine Zimmer fail to do in my life? Where was she when I needed her?"

"We'll get to you later. We must now see another chasm made by Catharine's fateful decision."

"Ursula!" His voice boomed. "Catharine and you had two chance meetings. We found that out in your story. Each time she had an opportunity to speak, but she chose silence instead. Had she spoken, Catharine would have imparted confidence, a confidence that would allow you to live your life alone. That was your greatest fear, the fear that pushed you into a marriage that should have never been. Ursula, you would have found the confidence to remain single until you met the right man. You and Harold Simpton never met, and he died without knowing your love."

"Catharine killed Harold? This is good, really good." Adrien shook his head.

They all looked at me accusingly, even Adrien. I was the dictator, the murdering spouse, the drunken movie producer.

All because what I feared most I became - nothing. An empty spot stood in the annals of literary greats. Zimmer. Mediocrity, the criticism of the critics, and the rejection of my books marched in and out, in and out, daily telling me I could never cut it as a writer. I didn't want those evil enemies stalking me throughout life. It was easier to tuck them away in my attic filled with empty dreams than have them mock me.

"I'm not sure your prose stood up to those literary greats," the giant read my mind. He was telling me I was as bland as macaroni and cheese. Finally, I had to face it - no melodrama - I was mediocre.

"Catharine!" His voice boomed. "Your mediocrity arrived along with your fear and laziness. Though you would not be Dickens, your words would inspire, change hearts, and as I said before, change the course of history. Too bad you didn't finish them."

"Finish what?" Adrien asked for me.

"She knows. They're still in their boxes."

CHAPTER 33

"So, we're all free and clear. It's all Catharine's fault, so we can go right into Heaven, right?" Adrien mocked. "I don't need a scapegoat for me. I'll accept the full consequences for my decisions. Catharine, you don't need to go to Hell for me."

"Who said she's going to Hell?" asked the giant.

"She obviously made life a living Hell for everyone, so that should be a fitting place for her. Hey, Catharine, we can burn together!" Adrien said capriciously not fully understanding his words.

"*The Book* will tell us your final destinations."

A golden ladder appeared. It stood about fifty feet high. A table stood on top of this behemoth, and *The Book* rested on the table.

"Aleric, you go first!"

The dictator looked fearfully at us, then began the ascent. He looked like an ant when he reached the top rung.

"It's here!" he shouted. "It's here! Lord, have mercy on me. My name is here."

He floated down to us.

"I guess it's my turn," Ursula said. The golden rungs dwarfed her tiny feet. "My mother, my father. They're in here." She scanned the wide pages. "And, there I am. I'm going to see my parents. There's Tom. He's here, too." Ursula was quiet for a moment. She wiped her eyes.

"Next to my name it says Baby Boy. Who is that?"

"Who do you think?"

Ursula stood thoughtful for a moment.

"He just needs a name," the giant said.

After a few more minutes, Ursula asked, "What about Ty?"

"It is not his time, yet." The giant's voice was somber.

Aleric and Ursula evaporated right before our eyes. Their stories, their lives were gone.

"Are they in Heaven?" I asked.

"A journey awaits them before they reach Paradise." The giant wiped his brow. "Adrien, you're next!"

"I tell you, it's not going to be there." He reached the gilded plateau quickly. His eyes scanned the book. "Yep! I was right. It's not here." He flipped the pages back and forth. "Just do the dirty deed and get it over with!"

"Catharine, help him," the giant ignored Adrien's comments.

"Will it be there?"

"You must find out for yourself."

The climb took hours it seemed. Perspiration dampened my forehead. Thump, thump, thump. Was that my heart really pounding? Finally, my feet touched the final, damning rung. It would decide my fate, or had it been decided so long ago? Adrien stood to my right. There, in gilded calligraphy, were the words Catharine Zimmer-Inveres. Next to it was Adrien Inveres.

"There's your name," I pointed. "Right next to..." I couldn't say it.

"Right next to yours," he smiled. "You? My wife. Catharine Zimmer, the woman that makes prudes look wild?" He guffawed so loud, then stopped suddenly and looked me in the eyes. We gazed at each other for a long time before he spoke again. "Perhaps that explains our strange attraction. Why was Fate so cruel? Why did we never meet?"

The giant interjected. "It wasn't Fate, Adrien, but Catharine's fear and deception. You saw the lost opportunities with Aleric and Ursula, but she also missed her opportunity to meet you."

"Was she to write my story? Interview me? What?" Adrien asked. "How? When? Where?"

"You said it before yourself. A news wire service would have picked up one of her articles. You would have read it, and would have wanted to meet with the writer to discuss movie ideas. As we've seen up here, it probably wouldn't have been love at first sight, but you two were meant to be together."

Adrien held my hands, and his blue eyes penetrated mine. "And we would have lived happily ever after?" Adrien asked.

"Life with Catharine Zimmer would always bring happiness. That was one of her many gifts, but she hoarded it in fear."

I hung my head in shame.

"Of course, Geoff would have shown up. Catharine would have been the mother he craved. Geoff, your son, would have gone on to write books and movies and give you more grandchildren."

"Is his name here?"

"Look for yourself."

"Geoff Inveres. There are my mother, father, and grandparents. There are a bunch of people in here that I had never expect would have made it. There's Tooty! Hah! He must have scraped in by the skin of his teeth."

"We all scrape in by the skin of our teeth. That said, we still must be the ones to choose. No one is forced to go on. So, Adrien, what do you choose?"

"I feel so hypocritical. There has been no God for me. How can I just say yes when I've said no all my life? And yet..." Adrien gazed at me. My heart pounded.

"And, yet, I cannot bear to be away from Catharine for even just a moment. I must spend my eternity with her. Is there room for me, for such a terrible, unbelieving soul who wants to enter only because of love?"

"You have demonstrated that you're capable of love, but are you sorry?"

Without hesitation, Adrien nodded. His sudden humility shocked me, but it also endeared himself to me.

"The name in *The Book* says Catharine Zimmer-Inveres. Since we never married, will I still be in the book?"

"Look again."

I hesitated, and my heart pounded. I found the name, Catharine Zimmer. It looked so sad, but it was there.

"Will Catharine and I be married up here?" Adrien raised his eyebrows.

"In Heaven there is no need for marriage. Nevertheless, you will have an eternity to get to know each other."

"Great! Let's go, Catharine!"

"Not so fast, Adrien. Like Ursula and Aleric, you will embark upon a journey. When you're finished you will enter your heavenly destiny."

"What about Catharine? I want to go with her."

"You will be with her, but not now. Say your good-byes."

It was the most painful parting I had ever experienced. For most of our meeting, I hated this man or hated what I thought I knew of this man. Now I had different eyes. Here was my intended husband. Two shall be one. Adrien knelt on his left knee and kissed my right hand. It was so corny and foolish looking, I laughed. Adrien, proud Adrien, on his knees.

"Good bye, my love." Then he was gone.

"Catharine! For your punishment, you will roam the earth until your appointed time. All mankind's emotions will crush upon your soul. You will feel the depths of despair of those condemned to die. You will seep in sorrow. Your heart will become as parched and withered as a decaying desert. You will taste the bitterness of rejection and loneliness."

"Surely you're condemning me to Hell!"

"No. You must feel the consequences of your life's decisions. My job is finished here. Do you have any more questions?"

"Who are you? And why were you assigned to my life?"

"You will find out in time. Good bye."

"That's it? Nothing more?"

"I assure you, there is more for you to come." He vanished.

An hour must have passed before I realized mud was creeping inside my shoes. Gravestones, some upright, but most of them whispering secrets to the dirt, surrounded me like a macabre game of Ring-Around-the-Rosy. Cold and wet penetrated my thin sweater. My eyes squinted from the stinging raindrops. My body shivered. Already acute loneliness settled into my heart.

There was a block of mausoleums, and I found one with the metal door swinging open. *It has to be warmer inside.* It wasn't, and I began to shiver. Above, old paint peeled itself off from the curved ceiling. There were no glass panes in the large, arched window looking outside.

The tomb belonged to the George and Henrietta Langley family. Below their stone markers were more with the names of Radulf and Jane Langley, Henry and Isabella Langley, and Ferdinand and Joanna Pippitt. All lived and died before the eighteenth century.

My body couldn't control the shivering so I stepped back outside. There I noticed a man shambling toward me. Should I run and hide? I looked back at the tomb, but the man spotted me. I sprinted away, leaving the cemetery behind. He followed. As I was soon to learn in this realm, mountains, buildings, and people appeared and disappeared without warning, and my eyes soon beheld the ocean. Since I didn't swim, I stood there, cowering. I was dead, what was I afraid of? He drew nearer; I closed my eyes hoping it was just an allusion. Then I felt his presence. No allusion.

ACKNOWLEDGEMENTS

SPECIAL THANKS GOES TO GRETCHEN KITZMAN, friend and fellow writer, who marked up her first edition copy of *Stories* to edit and provide improvements to this second edition. Also, thank you for all the kind fans who read and supported the first run of *Stories*. Without you, I might not have continued this writing journey.

ABOUT THE AUTHOR

C. L. PAUR GRADUATED in 1998 with an MA in Communication from Marquette University. She has freelanced for newspapers and magazines Along with novels, she writes screenplays, children's plays, non-fiction, and children's stories. She has also produced and directed children's theatre.

She lives in Wisconsin with her husband and four children.

www.Ingramcontent.com/pod-product-compliance
Lightning Source LLC
Chambersburg PA
CBHW022158240626
47153CB00007B/2714